NICE WEATHER

FOR A

Killing

NICE WEATHER
FOR A
Killing

SEYMOUR CRESSWELL

POOLBEG
CRIMSON

Published 2024 by Poolbeg Crimson,
an imprint of Poolbeg Press Ltd.
123 Grange Hill, Baldoyle,
Dublin 13, Ireland
Email: poolbeg@poolbeg.com

A catalogue record for this book is available from the British Library.

ISBN 978-1-78199-685-0

www.poolbeg.com

Printed by L&C Printing Group, Poland.

ABOUT THE AUTHOR

Seymour Cresswell was born in 1950 in Dalkey, County Dublin. After school, he studied law at Trinity College Dublin, where he started his acting career in DU Players. After college, he tried to become a professional actor and not to become a solicitor but lost both battles and followed a career as a lawyer for many years.

He is an award-winning amateur actor and director. He has written several pantomimes and plays. In 2018 he published a collection of memoir short stories, *A Present of an Orange*, which was very well received.

He no longer works in the law, but divides his time between writing, sailing, gardening, painting and drama. He has three adult children and two grandchildren. He lives in County Wicklow with his wife Clare.

ACKNOWLEDGEMENTS

A very special thanks to: Ferdia MacAnna, through whose creative writing workshops this novel came into being; all members of Ferdia's workshops who gave me encouragement and laughed at my jokes; Sharon Guard and Linda Uhlemann who read the first drafts of each chapter and offered insightful support and advice; Anthony J. Quinn, whose early structural edit gave me immeasurable help in presenting my story; Paula Campbell and Kieran Devlin of Poolbeg Press, for having faith in my writing; Gaye Shortland, Poolbeg Press editor, who helped to tease out the tangles and retained her good humour throughout the editing process; my son Guy, who designed the cover; my wife, Clare, who read and proofread for me with such concentrated dedication and skill, and my daughter Amy and son Hugh, who might otherwise feel left out.

To my beloved Clare

1

I was staring at the image of a partly unravelled man, fearful and red-eyed, with bloodied toilet paper stuck to his face, dressed improbably for a wedding. I was staring at myself in the eccentric mirror of my wardrobe. The wedding was mine, the thought of which frightened the bejesus out of me. That fear had caused me a sleepless night, which accounted for the redness of my eyes. They looked so bloodshot I thought that if I didn't blink I might bleed to death.

I had abandoned my bed at about five in the morning, having failed to sleep for more than twenty minutes at a stretch for the entire interminable night. I went for a run in the rain, had a shower and shaved.

Unwisely, I had chosen a new disposable razor, and the new blade in my shaking hand had caused a cut on my chin. I'd tried to stop the bleeding with some ancient aftershave that lurked in a light jacket of dust on top of the bathroom cabinet. It had stung like hell and made me smell of vinegar, while the bleeding continued unabated. I'd eventually managed to staunch the wound with a piece of toilet paper which I left adhered to my face as I dressed.

I took my suit in its body-bag from my wardrobe and hung it on the wardrobe's wonky door. I had assembled this wardrobe myself from a cheap flat-pack. I had botched the fixing of the door, spoiling the screw-holes, so that the hinges wouldn't hold the door properly. It hung at an aggravating angle, which I couldn't cure and which set me on edge every time I looked in the mirror.

Today, Hilary, my bride-to-be, would march to Mendelssohn. The marquee was on her parents' soggy lawn, guests had been marshalled, wedding presents had been generously bestowed, caterers catered for, flowers bedecked every surface. And I was terrified.

I said a prayer, just in case some random deity or unengaged guardian angel with nothing better to do might lend me a bit of celestial support. I wasn't sure to what religion I belonged. My father was a lapsed and disinterested Protestant. My mother was from a non-practising Jewish family. I had been sent to a Catholic boarding school where I hadn't prospered academically, but had acquired many other life skills, such as drinking, cheating at cards and rolling joints. At university I had advanced my drinking skills and had tried my best to add womanising to my list of achievements, but I had failed to score with sufficient frequency to allow myself to add hanky-panky to my private CV with a clear conscience. Then I had met Hilary in the university drama society, which very much focussed the distribution of my wild oats.

I looked over my speech and practised it aloud, feeling stupid when I came to the bits that read *'pause for laughter'*.

My phone burped. A message from the Gizzard Man. I didn't open it. I turned off the phone and left it on the table.

Unaccustomed as I was to wearing cufflinks, I found that the double cuffs of my rented starched shirt were impenetrable, impervious to all attempts to insert the little links, staunchly defending their virginity. Who had ever thought that these things were a sensible way of fastening the ends of sleeves? Stupid, fiddly little yokes at the best of times, but working with one hand? Cramp crept into my fingers and the tip of my tongue protruded. I even stood on one leg for a while, then hopped with aggravation as the heavy, stiff material refused to submit to the urgent nudging of the link. Eventually I gave in and undid a few buttons of the shirt so that I could take it off by pulling it over my head and deal with the cufflinks with both hands, hoping that I would be able to squeeze my hands through the tethered cuffs. This worked, but the shirt looked a bit battered after I had forcibly entered it.

By a quarter to eight I was in a taxi, knowing that I would be absurdly early, but I told myself that it would be easier to murder some time at the church than to kick my heels in my apartment. I imagined that I could put out the hassocks and iron the cassocks, rub the brasses and polish the pews. There was bound to be lots to do, and I was anxious to show my eagerness, all the organisation of the wedding so far having been undertaken by Hilary and her family. I was also concerned that if I didn't keep myself occupied, I was liable to

3

succumb to the very real temptation of an early-morning drink or two.

By the time I had reached the church, the weather had turned seriously grim, even for a day in early February. A cold and relentless rain spilled from the heavens, accompanied by a nasty northeasterly wind that blew like a condemned soul. I was glad of my overcoat.

The taxi left me at the church gate, and I huddled my way across the gravel to the church, wrestling with my little fold-up umbrella. A sudden, frigid gust attempted to tear it out of my hands. I clung on, but the wind callously turned it inside-out. Manfully, I tried to revert the thing by placing one edge of the now squid-like canopy on the gravel and reaching for the other edge with my spare hand to pull it back towards me. I nearly had it when another gust playfully wrenched the partially restored umbrella from my grasp and sent it fluttering like a shot bird across the puddled church car park. I retrieved it, then stood, defeated, drenched and dithering.

I wondered again whether I was doing the right thing in marrying Hilary. I told myself that I loved her, but I was not at all sure what 'love' was supposed to mean. I admired her beauty, her briskness, her capability, her certainty, her command. She took up the slack in me. She was also earning big-time to complement her family wealth. I had hardly anything to my name. My pay was only a photo-finish ahead of the minimum wage. And now we were about to vow before God and our community of friends and relations to love each other until death. She would endow me with all her worldly

4

goods – these were substantial, and her daddy had promised a wedding gift of a million euro. Hilary would, from this vantage point, swear to love me for richer or poorer. Whatever about richer, I couldn't really get much poorer. I had only my paltry pay, my wonky wardrobe and my awful little car. But I had opened a joint account in our names, lodging all I had into it by way of a symbolic gesture ahead of our vows.

Hilary was so used to having money that she took it for granted, like gravity. I had so little money that I could feel myself floating away on the breeze in-between paydays. We had been a little drunk when I proposed, and she had said yes. In the following sober days, my pride started to nag at me. I needed to pay my way into this wedding somehow, bear some of the weight of the thing, otherwise I would feel totally inadequate.

My bank had refused to lend to me, the Credit Union required a long savings record – I had none, I was too proud to ask friends for help – so I did what I thought, at the time, was the sensible thing and borrowed ten grand from an unlicensed moneylender, whose services I had used before, and knew to be impatient, usurious and brutal in equal measure. He conducted his business from the back room of a pub and was attached to the Quinlan gang. His parting advice to me was to watch my gizzard. A nice, old-fashioned caveat.

I deposited the money into the joint account. I had told Hilary that I had been saving for our wedding for years. She accepted this lie because, I think, she wanted to believe it. I think she believed that everyone had money. Like you believe that everyone has a sore throat when you have one yourself.

On my insistence, the money had been used to pay the florist and the deposit for the caterers. There was nothing left.

My plan was to repay the loan with interest out of the money that Daddy Fenton was going to give us as a wedding present. Even allowing for the strangulating interest rate, the amount would hardly be noticed. Self-delusion is a wonderful thing. I had argued my way into believing that using Hilary's family money in this way wasn't simply drawing attention to my comparative poverty. I had convinced myself that plunging into this shark-infested puddle would somehow peg me up closer to parity with Hilary's wealth.

The porch door was locked. I looked for a bell or a knocker but found neither. I peered through the glass panel of the door. All was dark and gloom inside, but the fact that it was dry and perhaps slightly warmer than it was outside made me long to get in as soon as I could.

I thought about breaking the window, but that sort of vandalism might bring the wrath of the rector down upon me, and Hilary had said that the rector's agreement to the use of the church was a very finely balanced thing. It all hung on Hilary's family's involvement with Kilmurray parish. My heathen status and Hilary's sketchy worshipful practice stacked uneasily against the family's deeper connection.

I was unused to married priests, particularly female married priests. My nervousness on meeting Reverend Karen Quayley for the first time caused me to address her as 'Madam Priestess'. I knew at once that this was embarrassingly wrong by the frozen look on the reverend's face. I ploughed on, speaking of our hopes of fine weather and the deployment of the Infant of Prague under the hedge at Hilary's family home, with a €50 note tucked under the little statue by way of a bribe. This had been met with raised brows, pursed lips and a silence even more profoundly arctic than the frost that had met my ridiculous address of the good rector. I had thought that the €50 was fair enough, considering that I hadn't troubled the inside of a church of any denomination since baptism.

I floundered on, asking if the amount had been too small. Reverend Quayley seemed affronted.

I asked, 'Should I have left more? I didn't know the rules. Is there a price list?'

'You're barking up the wrong faith, I fear,' said Reverend Karen, with a bitter little smile that was given an added twist by her Northern Ireland accent.

Hilary's kick to the shins beneath the table caused me to gasp and slump forward so that my head rested on the table while I tended my bruised leg.

'Is he all right?' the reverend had asked with a frown. Her tone suggested concern over my intellectual capacity rather than my health in general.

So, no breaking and entering then.

I made another assault on the umbrella and was irritated when it righted itself with a pop, without any real effort on my part. One spoke had broken, which gave it a rather louche, degenerate air, but it looked as if it would still serve.

I continued my investigation of the outside of the church, holding the wounded umbrella to one side, towards the wind like a shield, and hanging on to its edge to stop the buffeting gusts from inflicting any further dislocation to its workings. I made my way around to the side of the building, passing a set of mossy steps that led down to the barred doorway of a basement or crypt. No use. I continued until I came to a small porch with another door. Could this be the vestry? The stage door? Like the front door, it was in the gothic style, varnished wood with faux, black-painted hinges of wrought iron. There was an iron ring for a handle. I tried it and, to my delight, it turned. I pushed the door open and entered the church, leaving my ruined umbrella in the little porch. It was very dark inside the church, so much so that I had to grope my way forward. I couldn't find any light switches. I took another step. My foot caught on something and I pitched forward, arms flailing. I came down heavily, hitting my shoulder on the corner of something hard and landing full-length on the industrial-quality carpet that muffled the whole church. *'Fuck!'* I heard myself say on the way down. Then *'Sorry!'* when I remembered where I was.

My shoulder hurt like hell, but I reckoned it wasn't broken. I reached for my phone to use the torch but remembered that I had left it behind on purpose. My eyes were more used to the dark now and I could make out the aisle, stretching away to the back of the church. A faint light showed in the nearest side window, and I blundered towards it. I was rewarded by finding one of the chunky decorative candles placed by the florists, with a box of matches beside it on the sill. I lit the candle and held it high.

What I saw drove all the wind from me. I spilt candle grease onto my hand but ignored the burn. *'Jesus Christ!'* I said, lowering the candle so that I could investigate the sight more closely. I felt a wave of nausea sweep through me and I shuddered.

On the floor, wrapped loosely in a sheet of heavy plastic, lay the body of a man. His mouth was agape in a rictus of horror and his eyes were staring, sightless, wide open. The body was dressed in a tracksuit and runners. Where his forehead should have been was a bloody mess. Splinters of bone, congealed blood, matted hair and desecrated flesh surrounded an awful hole and, as if to confirm to the world that the body was indeed dead, a mess of brains and blood had oozed from the shattered skull onto the plastic sheet.

I sat on the nearest bench and tried to gather myself. My heart was racing and I was panting for air. I thought for a moment that I might pass out, but I drew a deep breath and steadied myself as best I could.

At that moment, I took in the fact that the wedding flowers had already been put in place. They surrounded the corpse like funeral tributes. Jesus, I thought, the murderer had managed to dump the body in the time between the florist's team leaving the church and my arrival. Had the killer been disturbed, or was it their intention to have the body discovered where it lay? I looked at my watch. Eight thirty.

It was beyond doubt a murdered corpse, left in the church by the murderer – perhaps to make a point? I had no phone, so I couldn't react to my first instinct, which was to phone for the police. Having abandoned that idea, I was forced to think of another plan. Run to get help? But where? And what would happen next? The police would arrive with an ambulance, crime-scene investigators, forensics teams, the whole doings. I imagined the wedding guests arriving to find the church sealed off as a crime scene, striped Garda tape stretched across the gate to the little gravelled car park, uniformed Gardaí warding off guests, all decked out in their wedding regalia. Distraught people turning away shocked. The wedding postponed or cancelled.

We had taken out wedding insurance but I was fairly sure that we were not insured for a murdered body in the church. If I called the Guards, the wedding would be called off and everything would go down the toilet. Furthermore, I was afraid that our relationship wouldn't survive a blow like that.

And then there was the Gizzard Man, who had been messaging me that morning. He wasn't going to wait.

I had invested nearly seven years in my relationship with Hilary. Seven years during which I had been more-or-less faithful. We had been together for so long that I couldn't imagine what life without her would be like. We were Arthur-and-Hilary, in alphabetical order, A&H: a team. Who the hell was this guy with the crushed skull in his plastic winding sheet? What right did he have to gatecrash our wedding, to spoil it all? In the heat of the moment, all I wanted was to be rid of the dreadful corpse, brush it under the carpet, pop it in the oubliette, flush it away, hide it, so that the wedding could go ahead. I hadn't killed him; I didn't know who had done it; it was nothing to do with me. I should have walked away and called the Guards, but I didn't. I couldn't bear the thought of Hilary crying in her wedding dress. I was afraid of the consequences of losing the lifeline of her daddy's wedding gift. I acted on impulse; it was a spur-of-the-moment thing.

I gathered up the plastic sheeting at the feet of the corpse and dragged it over the carpet back through the vestry and out the door. The rain had continued unrelentingly, and it pelted down on me as I laboured to drag the corpse to the steps of the basement. Here I paused and had a quick check to make sure that no-one was watching, then dashed back to the vestry to look for the keys to the iron gate that barred the basement doorway. I found a key-rack and silently blessed the thoroughness of the church organisation when the key labelled '*Crypt*' fell to my hand. I ran back to the sunken entrance, descended the four shallow steps, unlocked the gate and swung it open. Its hinges were silent with rain. The door itself was unlocked. I took hold of the plastic-shrouded feet of the dead man and dragged his body down the steps. I inwardly apologised for the unceremonious bashing of his poor ruined head on each of the steps. I didn't bother turning on any lights or checking the state of the basement. I just put him in, slammed the door, locked the gate and ran back through the rain into the church.

I had left my stout little candle burning on the floor where I had found the body. I quickly found the light switches by the front door and turned on all the lights I could find. I checked the time again: twenty to nine. I sat in the front pew, head bowed as I gasped for air, and forced myself to think. Gradually my surroundings made themselves known to me: the long narrow windows with the gothic arches, marble plaques on the walls remembering the dead, the vaulted ceiling like an upturned boat.

The killer must have intended the body to be found when the church was opened up for the wedding that morning. I had scuppered that plan. Was the killer likely to cause a scene because I had moved the body? Would they report the theft to the police? When the Reverend Karen asked the congregation if any person present knew of any reason why Hilary and I should not be wed, was the killer likely to step forward with an objection? No.

There was no longer any doubt in my mind about the wedding. Nothing would stop me from marrying Hilary. She was the only girl for me. I felt exalted.

The murder wasn't my problem. I couldn't have prevented it. I didn't cause it. Eventually the corpse would be found and the murder investigation would kick off. All hell would break loose, but by then me and my bride would be long gone, joined and blessed by the lady priestess, Daddy Fenton's largesse safely in the bag.

2

I heard a noise from the gallery. My skin felt as if a nest of many-legged small creatures had started a migration up my spine. I didn't breathe for a considerable time, straining to hear confirmation of what I thought I had heard. The big brass eagle of the lectern looked aghast, its beak agape in shock, its wings spread in terror, poised for flight, bible and all. In the silence, the constant dripping of the rain in the gutters stepped forward to remind me of the foul weather outside. *Drip, drip, drip*, like the dread tapping of Blind Pew's cane.

Someone was up there, upstairs, aloft in the loft. I tried to tell myself that it wasn't the murderer, but the conclusion was inescapable. It was far too early for the organist or the wedding singer. The noise was too furtive to have been meant as a token to signal the presence of some keen church official, clattering about to register their early arrival. I peered up against the glare of the overhead lights but could see nobody. I didn't want to see anyone. What would I do with a sighting of the killer, other than forget it as fast as I could? If it was the murderer, they were lurking in the shadows for a purpose; it wouldn't make sense as a murderer to hang around your fell handiwork unless you had a definite reason. It took me a little while to work it out. The killer had lugged the body of the victim into the church to make a point: to display their handiwork for someone specific to see, someone who would be at the wedding – whoever would be first in the church. The killer had waited in the gallery so that they could observe the reaction of their target audience when the body was discovered. But there would be no reaction now, because I had spoiled the show by tidying up.

The front door was still locked, so there was now only one way out of the church, and that was through the vestry, which would mean traversing the church, passing right by me and risking identification. The murderer was trapped in the gallery.

Should I let the person in the gallery know that I knew they were there? Would that scare them off? But the murderer wasn't afraid to bash the dead man's brains in, so they were unlikely to be scared of me. I stayed silent and waited for back-up. My best man was due to arrive in fifteen minutes.

During that quarter of an hour, the presence in the gallery and I maintained an uneasy sort of stand-off. I tried to calm myself by doing the yoga breathing I saw on the television. Now, as then, it didn't work. On the screen I had been distracted by the lovely shape of the instructor. Now I was distracted by the ominous presence above me.

Tom Farrington was my best man. He wasn't always very reliable, but neither was I. I should probably have asked Hilary's brother Alan to stand by me. I understood that he was a hedge-fund manager and made pornographic amounts of money. But he was so profoundly boring that I couldn't bring myself to ask him. I guessed now that he might have been a better choice because he would be here by now. I knew this because he had told me once that he believed that if you weren't early, you were late. Right now, I would have put up with the tedium that followed him like a fog, because he was a big lump of a lad, ponderous in thought-process and movement but fit enough to play second row for Wanderers fourths and perhaps to defend me from attack. Too late for that sort of regret, though: I had chosen Tom Farrington, my best pal, a pale and skinny scarecrow of a chap, the sleeves of whose jackets always seemed too long for him. Tom would be useless in a scrap, but otherwise excellent company when he remembered to turn up.

There was another barely audible scuffle from the gallery. I wasn't even sure that I had heard anything. I imagined whoever was there wincing at the indiscretion, holding their breath and trying to be totally silent, still, a shadow. In horrified reciprocity, I held my breath as well. No breathing in the gallery or parterre, while the watcher and the watched sounded each other out. The hush loomed over me with menace. The more silent this watcher was, the more threatening their presence became. As I listened for a corroborating noise, the silence became a sort of negative force, dominating and thickening the air of the church like a gas. The cheerful flowers, so carefully arranged and scattered about the church by the early morning florists, the posies on the ends of the pews, the sprays decorating the windowsills, now looked entirely funereal. The sweet scent of freesias smelled of tainted meat. The stained-glass saints, now faintly showing in the eastern windows, joined the watcher in the gallery to look sadly and solemnly down on the lone and fragile man below them.

My scrambled meditation was disturbed by other, more confident noises from the front door of the church, which made me jump. These noises weren't in any way furtive, they were bold and purposeful noises, made by someone who was unashamed, or perhaps proud of the sound. The church was being opened up for business. It was clear that the locks were being turned and the bolts drawn by a person who enjoyed the power that possession of the keys gave them.

At my school there had been a culture of reverse psychology – if I understand properly what that means. Menial tasks, which would be regarded as a drudgery in the real world, were allotted to certain well-behaved boys as a perk. The job of ringing the bell to signal the end of class, or cleaning the blackboard, or replenishing the shoe-polish tins, these were handed out as privileged functions. It seemed to me that the same mentality applied when those in charge of Protestant churches divvied up the chores. My bet was that some church official was delighted by the obligation that had been placed on them to get up early to open the church, and that they took pride in doing so with a brisk clatter and crash.

I heard voices in the vestibule.

'Hi! I'm here for the wedding?' It was Tom, miraculously or maybe mistakenly early.

16

'Well, you've come to the right place. Dreadful weather, isn't it? Are you for the bride or the groom?' A cheerful hockey-pitch sort of female voice.

'I'm the best man,' said Tom in his wry apologetic way, suggesting that someone must have made a mistake. 'Am I the first?'

I called, '*No, actually, I got here before you!*' I was so relieved to have people around me that were not murderers or corpses that I had almost run to the front door to welcome the new arrivals. I saw the surprise on the face of the owner of the hockey voice and explained, 'I came in through the back door, the vestry? It was open. I got here rather early and switched on all the lights to cheer the place up a bit.'

'I take it that you're the groom?' she said. 'Welcome to Rathmurray Parish church. I'm Jennifer Roundstock, Sexton. I'm sort of in charge of the bricks and other non-spiritual things. The rector was to have been first here, but she was delayed.'

The sexton was a short woman, built like a rounded square. A look of ferocious organization emanated from her, from her short-cropped no-nonsense haircut to her flat, sensible shoes.

I held out my hand and introduced myself. 'Arthur Cummins,' I said.

We shook hands. Tom and I gave each other an untidy hug.

Jennifer Roundstock wrinkled her brow and gave me a sceptical look. 'You've a …' she gestured towards her chin with her hand, fluttering her fingers.

My first thought was a bogey. Not ideal for greeting my bride. I pulled out my handkerchief and did a quick recce of my nose. Jennifer wasn't satisfied.

'No. You've something on your face. Blood, is it?'

Oh, Sweet Jesus, I thought. I've managed to splash myself with the dead man's gore. I felt with my fingers and found the little piece of tissue, now glued to my face with my own congealed blood. I carefully peeled it off.

'Shaving,' I offered in explanation.

Jennifer was still regarding me with something akin to suspicion. 'Are you feeling well? You look like you've seen a ghost.'

This question made me twitch. 'I'm fine, thanks,' I said in as level a voice as I could muster. 'Just a tiny bit hungover and nervous, that's all.'

I was aware that whoever was in the gallery could hear our conversation. I trusted that they had no wish to reveal themselves. All was quiet aloft, but I thought I could feel the nervous anxiety feeding down through the stonework of the church.

Another thought alighted like a carrier pigeon from a distant place: if the rector was supposed to be first in the church, had the body been left for her to find?

'The florists have done a wonderful job, don't you think?' said Jennifer. 'I let them in at about seven this morning.' She had walked up the aisle and was fluffing up one of the big floral arrangements in a business-like way. 'I think they had already been in to the markets. Early risers, florists.'

I thought how the early birds and late workers always liked to sing about it, lest it go unnoticed. Jennifer then excused herself, saying that she wanted to make sure that the vestry was properly set up for the signing of the marriage register.

This reminded me that I was to be married that morning and a groom's gloom rolled over me like a cold weather front. I was to be fixed, fastened, skewered forever like a butterfly in a display-case. No more for me the frenzied flirtations that blossomed into the barely imagined gasping ecstasy of sex with a new partner. I was to commit to one person unto death. Would marriage be like having the same thing for dinner every day – shepherd's pie, for instance? In my over-agitated state, what the sexton said sounded like an executioner telling me that she wanted to make sure that there was sufficient clean straw around the block.

I sat again in one of the pews, whirling with nerves as Tom fixed my button-hole arrangement onto my wedding coat.

'Jesus, man, you're like an electric fence!' he said. 'Are you sure you're OK? Are you sure you want to go ahead with this?'

'*Yes!*' I barked, too loud, too heavily affirmative for credibility. I startled even myself. 'Yes, I do, I mean I am. I'm sure I want to go ahead.'

We heard voices from the vestry. 'Who the hell left that umbrella there?'

I recognised the disapproving tones of Reverend Karen Quayley.

'It may belong to the groom,' said Jennifer. 'He found the vestry door open and let himself in.'

'That shouldn't have happened either. You are supposed to leave all doors locked!' Her voice was scolding, superior.

The rector emerged from the vestry. She was dressed in a blue robe, which flared from the waist and fell to just above her ankles. She wore patent-leather court shoes with a slight heel. The robe suited her well and she wore a diaphanous sort of surplice over it that reminded me of a negligee. I wondered if she had slept in it.

'Good morning, good morning! And how are we on this rather bleak February morn? Your little doll from Prague doesn't seem to have come good for you, I'm afraid. Maybe you should ask for a refund.' This in-joke was delivered with a smirky sort of smile that failed to ignite her eyes.

She was now studying Tom, who was slouched in the pew beside me. I could tell that she longed to tell him to sit up straight and take his hands out of his pockets.

'Oh, Reverend Quayley, this is my best man, Tom Farrington. Tom, this is the rector, Reverend Karen Quayley.'

To be fair to Tom, he stood and shook hands with the reverend.

'Nice to meet you, Reverend.'

I could sense his mind scrabbling for a topic of conversation.

After an awkward crevasse, he said, 'What's it like to be a woman in a man's job?'

My friend could be a trifle gauche at times. I was too wound up to care.

'Do you have an objection to female vicars?' The reverend's voice was remarkably level.

I thought that this must be a question she got all the time.

Tom said, 'No, not at all, ma'am. I guess the altar boys stand a better chance with lady priests.'

'We don't go in for altar boys in this church.'

'What do you have then – girls? I've seen that in some churches and wondered.'

'No. Not girls either. We don't require servants at our altar.'

'Did the aul' union not kick up about that at all? I mean, wasn't there hell to pay when bus conductors were done away with?'

'Not quite the same thing, I think, Mr. Farrington.'

Jennifer the sexton emerged from the vestry. 'I hear cars arriving, Mr. Cummins,' she said, then added a sort of footnote, 'Arthur the groom can greet people at the door. Tom the best man directs the incoming traffic, to the left for the bride and to the right for the groom.' She was gesturing with her hands like an airline cabin attendant.

When we reached the back of the church, she took Tom aside. I heard her ask if he had the rings. A short pantomime ensued while he patted his pockets and removed car keys, handkerchief, hip flask, cigarettes, lighter, packet of chewing gum, packet of condoms, a little tinfoil parcel and a packet of cigarette papers with a torn cover. All the while he was humming 'Chapel of Love' by the Dixie Cups, wildly out of tune. Eventually he found the rings in his waistcoat pocket, wrapped in what looked like toilet paper. He reassembled himself to greet the guests.

I suddenly felt beached and helpless, as the tide of adrenalin from the early morning shock started to recede.

Tom may have been untidy and embarrassing, but he was a good pal. He sidled over to me and proffered his hip flask.

'We've time for a quick spliff if you fancy it,' he murmured in my ear.

I shook my head and accepted the hip flask. 'Here's the first of the day!' I said by way of a toast. I took a good slug from the flask.

He took it back and offered it to Jennifer Roundstock and Rev. Quayley before taking a slurp for himself. 'Let me know, ladies, if you change your minds, or if you'd like a quiet toke out the back before the show kicks off.'

His eloquent eyebrows danced as he made this offer.

'No, thank you, Mr. Farrington,' said the Reverend Karen as she bustled past him to welcome the guests in proper proprietorial manner.

As she was passing through the vestibule, I heard the sudden clatter of shoes descending the wooden stairs from the gallery.

'Geoffrey! I wasn't expecting you here!' said Reverend Karen.

A male voice, edgy with overladen excuse and off-kilter explanation, said, 'Just ah ... checking my ... the *um* ... organ for the wedding organist, darling. I'll see you for lunch later.'

I was just in time to see an overweight, florid man in a jumper and corduroys exiting through the front door.

'See you later, darling,' said the Reverend Karen.

The person from the gallery, the maybe perpetrator of the murder, whose victim I had stashed in the crypt, was on 'darling' terms with the rector. Her husband.

3

I followed Geoffrey Quayley's trajectory out of the church. I saw him letting himself into the large house next door, which I took to be the rectory. I stood for a while in the rather refreshing rain, with my face turned towards the sky. The frigid drops fell on my eyelids and cheeks with a careless impartiality that I found soothing to the tumult of my mind.

I heard a car pull up outside the gate and a man's voice called my name.

'Arthur! Arthur! I need to talk to you!'

It was Alan, Hilary's tedious brother. He wore a big, flapping waxed jacket. He crunched across the gravel in his green wellingtons. He had parked his Range Rover carelessly across the churchyard gate in the entitled way that owners of big expensive cars like to leave their vehicles. He looked bothered.

'Hi, Alan. Nice to see you,' I said and held out my hand in greeting.

He ignored my hand and said, 'Is there somewhere we could talk in private?'

'Yes, I'm sure there is. Come in out of the rain. I think we can go backstage and chat there.'

On our way through the church, we met Tom, who looked quizzical. I thought I'd better introduce him. 'Alan, this is Tom Farrington, my best man. Tom, this is Alan Fenton, Hilary's brother.'

'Pleased to meet you, Alan. You're Alan the accountant, aren't you?' said Tom.

'I'm an actuary actually,' said Alan in a huffy sort of tone, then, as Tom seemed to want to follow us into the vestry, 'and if you don't mind, *er* …' He gestured in the air as if to conjure the name.

'Tom,' my best man supplied without rancour.

'Tim, yes. I need to talk to Arthur alone.'

Tom gave up the chase and took up station again at the back of the church.

In the vestry, Alan took my elbow in an uncomfortably alpha-male grip and looked down at me from his six-foot-four-inch advantage, his face invasively close to mine.

'Arthur, I'm afraid I come with bad news. The wedding's off.'

I was so distracted by the peculiar smell off his breath that I didn't take in what he had just told me. My hyper mind had segued off on a speculation that he had been feasting on roadkill.

He increased his grip on my elbow, causing me to wriggle out of his grasp. He compromised by putting his arm around my shoulders. I had never liked this man and being brought into a sort of embrace with him was not something I enjoyed. Again, I squirmed and pulled away.

He held up his large paws in what he might have thought of as a gesture of peace, but which to me looked like a boxing trainer holding up his mitts for his trainee to hit.

'Did you hear what I said, Arthur? The wedding's off. Hilary says she can't go through with it.'

Alan was not an astute man. He looked seriously puzzled when I burst out laughing. He looked more deeply perplexed when I sank onto a comfortless little hard chair by the door, shaking my head. My laughter, nervous to start with, became bitter and mirthless, tailing off into something more akin to sobbing.

He stared at me for a while in silence, then said something like, 'See you, so,' and left me alone.

Seven years of the see-saw of romantic attachment, gone for nought – all the little acts of affection, the signals of love, the tokens of devotion, dissolved into nothing. Arthur and Hilary, A&H, now reduced to 'ah'. Something that was never meant to be. A match blown out.

A bric-à-brac of emotions crashed down around me. Relief, shock, disappointment, sadness, fear, embarrassment, love. Love? Yes, I wanted to hold her in my arms and tell her how much I loved her. Ridiculous perhaps, but less ridiculous than what now looked like a parade-ring wedding-vow pantomime that we were supposed to have been principals in that morning.

But, as soon as I had processed the notion that the wedding was off and the threat of marriage had gone, the next layer of the onionskin of my stress came to the surface. The dreadful truth of what I had done in the dark of early morning reared up to frighten me. I had covered up a murder so that the wedding could go ahead. But now that there was to be no wedding, a bit like the singer sang of the old lady who swallowed the fly, I had lost the reason why I had hidden the corpse.

It wouldn't matter, now, if guests were turned away by uniformed Gardaí blocking the taped-off gateway to the church. In fact, it occurred to me that the distraction of the crime-scene investigation might be a kind way of deflecting attention away from Hilary's last-minute funk.

So, I was free to run away. No excuse needed. I would be seen as the injured party, the jilted groom, left at the altar. I could walk with a clear conscience. Apart from my deeply problematic contribution, Hilary's parents were paying for the wedding: photographer, videographer, banquet, limousines, the whole doings. But it was Hilary, not me, who had shied at the last fence, so too bad for the Fenton clan.

With the thought of the photographer and videographer, a paralysing question struck me: was there CCTV in this church? The fastidiousness and careful organisation of the rector and the sexton suggested that in all probability there was a camera somewhere, carefully recording everything that happened when no-one was looking. There might be footage of the murderer depositing the cadaver in its plastic gift-wrapping, leaving the body in the body of the church. But what if I also featured in the rushes, in my minor role of body snatcher? What would that look like to the investigating Gardaí?

Was this the time to come clean? How would it look? It was

clear to me that however bad it might appear, it would definitely look worse if I stayed schtum and was called in later.

Tom came into the vestry, looking irritatingly calm. 'What's up?' he said, his eyebrows signalling for the hard of hearing. 'What did Alan the Actuary actually want?'

'The wedding's off, Tom. Sorry about that. Hilary has abandoned ship.' I think I would have wept, were it not for the horror of the monstrous secret that now reared up to displace my sense of loss.

He handed me his flask again and leaned against the wall.

'Fuck me!' was all he said.

After some high-voltage silence, I looked up at him and said, 'Look, Tom, something has happened. I need to talk to the police.'

'*Jaysus!* It's not a crime to cry off at the altar, is it? And, even if it is, is it not a bit shite to grass on your ex like that?'

'No, Tom. It's something else.'

At that moment Rev. Karen swept into the vestry, looking displeased.

'What on earth's happening?' she asked crossly. 'You gentlemen are supposed to be at the vestibule to welcome the guests. What are you doing in here?'

Tom took charge.

'*Ahmmm* ... I think we have a bit of a problem, Mrs. Vicar. The bride's after pulling the plug. We have to stop the clock. The gig's off.'

'Well, really! That's no way to behave. Most inconsiderate, and after all the trouble we've gone to!' said Rev. Karen.

I felt let down by her lack of sympathy. I thought that she might have seen her way to show a tiny bit of compassion for the distraught groom.

'Well, I suppose we'd better take up positions to turn the guests away,' I said, turning towards the aisle.

At that moment I saw a big shadow darken the doorway, and I heard a voice with a nicely turned country accent demand, 'Does one of ye own that twenty-three registration Range Rover halfway across the road? It damned near caused an accident.'

Then Alan's voice from behind the giant shadow said, 'Ah. That'll be my car, officer. Sorry, it was an emergency, I was in a bit of a rush.'

'You'd want to be driving your wife to Holles Street, and she having her contractions, to justify the way you left that yoke! That's not parked, it's abandoned. And if I was going to Holles Street I wouldn't start from here, either. Now shift that monstrosity before I give you a ticket.'

In the tiny gap between the Garda and the door jamb, I watched as Alan found his keys in one of the deep pockets of his waxed jacket and left.

The big Garda was about to leave too when I piped up: 'Excuse me, Guard, I wonder if I could I have a word?'

He stopped where he was.

I could hear Rev. Karen fulminating behind me, so I turned to her and said, 'Look, Reverend Karen, I need to confess.'

She smiled her most condescending Northern Ireland smile and said, 'Again, I'm afraid you're barking up the wrong faith, Arthur. You will find no confessional here.'

'No, I didn't mean that sort of confession. There is something I need to tell the Gardaí. And I'm afraid it involves this church.'

Rev. Karen looked like a hen about to deliver an egg, an expression that sat most peculiarly on her. However, she withdrew discreetly, taking Tom with her, leaving me alone to unburden myself to the giant Civic Guard.

4

I wasn't sure why the Guards wanted me to go to the Garda Station, but they insisted. Tom followed in his car and waited with me until the Detective Sergeant was available to interview me.

After an hour or so of waiting, Tom approached the officer at the desk. 'Excuse me, Guard, but my man here hasn't had any breakfast. Would it be OK if I went out and got him something?'

He returned in due course with a baguette stuffed with sausages, scrambled eggs, rashers, black pudding – the whole builder's smorgasbord in a roll. The Garda provided tea and, all in all, I ate a hearty breakfast.

The DS then introduced himself. 'I'm Detective Sergeant Bowring and this is Garda Bluett.'

Sergeant Bowring was an untidy man in plain clothes, whose shirt kept escaping from the grasp of his trousers, which were in a constant slide down the underside of his large belly. Whenever he had nothing else to do with his hands, he would either hitch up his trousers or tuck in his shirt; sometimes he would perform both manoeuvres together. I wondered if he had put on a lot of weight after he had bought the clothes. Anyway, he ought to have been wearing braces. Occasionally I was treated to a regrettable glimpse of his remarkably hairy lower abdomen.

Detective Bluett, on the other hand, was in uniform, and if ever there was a woman constructed expressly for the purpose of making that outfit look good, Officer Bluett was she.

The combined effect of the Beauty and the Beast had me beaten from the start. No waterboarding, no Pentothal, no electrodes attached to tender parts were necessary to extract my full confession. The problem was that I couldn't bear the sight of the constantly dishevelling Sergeant Bowring, so I simply had to concentrate on the bewitching form of Garda Bluett. When I had finished my account of events, Bowring asked me to wait, and I was left by myself in the interview room. I looked for the one-way mirror, but there didn't seem to be one. There didn't seem to be a camera either. It wasn't at all like the TV. I tried the door, but it was locked. I wondered what had happened to Tom.

It was mid-afternoon before Bowring and his lovely side-kick returned, with an awkwardly phrased but mostly accurate typed-up version of my statement, which I signed.

'Can I go now? I've told you everything I know.'

'We'd rather you remained here, if you don't mind,' said Bowring in a tone that suggested that I was to stay where I was, whether I minded or not.

I didn't really care. My diary had been wiped clear with the cancellation of the wedding, so I had nothing else to do.

'Should I have a solicitor?'

'I don't know what you'd want with a solicitor, Arthur. We've not charged you with anything,' said Garda Bluett.

'Are you going to charge me?'

'We've no plans in that direction at the moment. Tell me, how well do you know William O'Grady?' Garda Bluett had a file in which was a photograph that I couldn't properly see.

'I've never heard of him. Who is he?'

'He's the guy whose body was found in the church. The body that you tampered with,' said Sergeant Bowring heavily.

'Like I said, I've never heard of him.'

'Why did you call off the wedding?' Garda Bluett tossed this question at me like a petrol bomb.

'What? I didn't. Alan Fenton came to the church to tell me that Hilary had backed out. She's his sister.'

'That's not what he said.' Garda Bluett looked at me earnestly.

'What? He says she's not his sister or that it wasn't her who called the wedding off?'

'Don't be smart. You're doing yourself no favours and you're not impressing anyone here.' DS Bowring was turning sour.

I looked to Garda Bluett for solace.

She returned my stare impassively and said, 'Would you mind if I took your fingerprints and a sample of your DNA? It's principally for elimination purposes.'

In my fragile state of mind, I could deny her nothing.

Did Alan Fenton really say that I had called off the wedding? Why would he say that? To save face for his family perhaps. But everyone who was at the church knew that it was Hilary who had cancelled, not me. I'd told them that I had moved the body so that the wedding could go ahead. Why would I then cancel? I concluded that this was merely an interrogation ploy, intended to soften me up to confess to something.

Later that day, while I was still assisting the Gardaí with their investigations, in a state of semi-arrest, I was allowed a visit from Tom.

'What's happening, Tom?'

'I think that Karen and Jennifer may be an item.' Tom was always first with the gossip.

'How do you know this?'

'I overheard them in the church just after you went off with the polis to rummage in the basement. Jennifer said something about how fetching Karen looked in her robes.'

'Actually, I thought she looked rather good myself,' I conceded.

'Well, good luck there,' said Tom. 'As the reverend herself might say, I think you'd be barking up the wrong priest. They were tut-tutting together about desecration of the church and all of a sudden it got dead lovey-dovey. Quite moving, really.'

'And how does that affect anything, I wonder?'

'Oh, and the forensic lads took away one of the big brass candlesticks for a closer look. It would make an ace mace, to be fair.'

'You mean they think it might have been used as the murder weapon?'

'*Mmm.* A big, heavy candlestick. All the better for putting your lights out!'

'They tell me that the dead man's name is William O'Grady. But that's about all they've told me. Do you think I should lawyer-up, Tom?'

Tom ignored my question but fished out his phone and started massaging it with his thumbs. 'Says here that William O'Grady is a self-employed tax consultant. He works from home. He lives quite close to the church. He's a keen hill-runner. You can't beat the old social media, you know! I could tell you things about yourself that'd set your hair on fire.'

'All very interesting, but there's nothing in what you've just told me that would suggest a motive for killing him. Even though I'm not all that fond of accountants, myself.'

'Or actuaries, actually,' added Tom. He was still thumb-dancing on his phone and now he started scrolling. 'Hang on, here's something. He's an active gay rights campaigner. Very open about his own preferences, fair play to him. Also active in trying to persuade gay people in high places to come out.'

'I wonder could this be a homophobic killing? I mean did someone kill the poor chap because he liked men? That's a bit prehistoric, isn't it?'

Tom looked thoughtful, his eyebrows brooding. Then they twitched. 'But why go to the trouble of leaving the body in the church?'

I couldn't think of anyone I knew who was sufficiently homophobic to kill for their phobia. I dismissed the idea. But Tom's question about the reasoning behind the placement of the corpse remained as an active itch in my mind.

'Did I tell you that I was certain that there was someone hiding in the gallery when I found the body?'

Tom nodded.

'But did I tell you who it was?'

Tom's eyebrows begged me to say.

'It was Rev. Quayley's husband, Geoffrey. He came galloping down the stairs just after you arrived. She didn't seem surprised that he had been there. He said something about checking his organ and scooted over to the rectory.'

'I'll never understand Protestants,' said Tom.

My shoulder, which I had hurt when I fell in the dark of the church that morning was now beginning to give me serious gyp. I was massaging it, double-checking for broken bones and trying to ease the pain. I was concentrating on a particularly painful spot and, as I did so, I remembered that whatever I had hit had moved under me. I also remembered something else I had seen when I held the candle aloft. There had been a low four-wheeled trolley in the church. It was this that I had collided with when I tripped in the dark. But it wasn't there when I came out of the vestry having confessed to the big Guard. Someone had moved it.

Tom continued to knead his phone, occasionally making grunts of frustration and every now and again little cries of satisfaction.

'*Aha!*' he said, waving the phone in the air. 'Geoffrey Quayley is the organist at Rathmurray Parish church. It says so on the parish website.' He looked up at me as if coming up for air, then dived again into the virtual world of his phone. 'And!' He held up a finger for additional emphasis. '*And!* This is good: William O'Grady was the parish treasurer.'

That *was* good. Might offer a clue to the murder.

Geoffrey Quayley's position as church organist offered an

explanation for his presence in the loft that morning. It tallied with his explanation to Rev. Karen. I guessed that he would have his own key to the church, so that he could practise whenever he wanted and could tend to the needs of his organ. I knew nothing about church organs, but maybe they needed to be turned on and primed for visiting organists, who might not know where all the switches were. But what had he seen? He would have had a grandstand view of what went on in the church while he was tweaking the stops and flexing the bellows above.

It was early evening when Garda Bluett popped in to let me know that I was free to go home, but that I should let the Gardaí know if I intended to leave the country. I knew that I had committed some sort of minor crime by moving the body but, in the context of a murder, such an innocent (if that is the word) act should surely not bring much weight down on me – the Probation Act, or a fine or a suspended sentence at worst, coupled with an admonition from the judge not to tamper with any other murdered corpses that I might stumble upon. The venial nature of my offence was why I had not called in a solicitor and had freely and willingly given and signed my statement. But now I was worried that the Guards suspected me of a deeper involvement in the murder. I also suspected that Sergeant Bowring might be lazy. I was sure, also, that he was old school. Having discovered that the dead man was gay, he might develop a casual attitude towards the investigation and carelessly allow innocents such as myself to become entangled in the net of the criminal justice system. I knew enough about the clumsiness of that system to fear the consequences.

'But am I a suspect in this, Garda Bluett? And I'd like it if I could call you by your first name?'

'Why would you want to know my first name?'

'Well, it's only fair. You've been calling me Arthur all day. A bit of reciprocity would be nice.'

She stared at me for a moment, then said, 'I'm Francine. They call me Frankie.'

'Which do you prefer?' Someone had told me once that most of the Maggies and Kates of this world preferred Margaret and Katherine. It was a good guess.

'Well, I prefer Francine. It sounds more feminine, I guess.' She gave me a shy smile. It was like watching a sunrise.

'Listen, Francine, I've got some bits of information that you may already know, but I thought I'd tell you anyway. It might save time.' And I told her about William O'Grady's business, his position as parish treasurer and the fact that he was openly gay. I told her about Geoffrey Quayley being the church organist and I told her about the disappearing four-wheel trolley. I didn't tell her about Tom's suspicions about Karen and Jennifer because I had no proof, and I wasn't sure that it was anyone's business.

Judging by the detailed notes Francine was taking, much of my information was new to the police. Was there a police bias against the internet?

When I had given her all the additional information I had, I asked her for her card with her phone number.

'What do you want that for?' She gave me a suspicious look.

'Just in case I come up with anything else relevant to your enquiries,' I said. 'That's what they do on the telly.'

She didn't have a card, so she wrote her number on a page from her notebook, writing '*Francine*' underneath.

Tom drove me home. Never has a best man been better. He dropped me off outside my apartment block. It was still raining as I sloshed my way to the hall door and let myself into the lobby. My apartment was on the first floor, and I prided myself on always taking the stairs. Two flights weren't a huge climb but it was a matter of principle.

When I reached my floor and pulled open the spring-loaded door, I was startled to see Hilary sitting on the floor outside the door to my apartment. She must have forgotten her key.

Hilary, my dear friend Hilary. My bride-not-to-be? There she was, looking absurd in jeans and an anorak, her hair still tortured up into a fanciful coif with wilting flowers entwined in the tight braiding, her face barely recognisable under a mask of foundation, blusher, bronzer, lip-gloss and mascara. She had been crying. Her tears had eroded the make-up under her eyes like the delta of a dried-up river. Her lip was quivering.

'Oh, Arthur!' she said, barely looking at me, her hands plunged deep into the pockets of her jacket. 'I'm sorry, Arthur, love.' She was fighting to keep her voice under control. I wanted to hug her, but I wasn't sure that it would lead to anything useful.

Tears and salty kisses were the stuff of lust, and lust was the last thing I needed.

I carefully opened my door and let us in. There was a peaceful reassurance about my untidy flat. It smelled just the same as it had when I had left it that morning, bound for matrimony. The sweet-sour tang of sheets that should have been changed, questionable runners and washing-up that had been left undone. I lit a scented candle that Hilary had given me for my birthday, perhaps because of my slack domestic hygiene.

I found that I was very glad to see her. I made tea and, as we drank it, I told her all that had happened. I was keen to get her take on events. She was always practical and direct, where I was usually serpentine and convoluted.

Straight away she asked, 'Why didn't you just call the Guards when you found the body?'

I knew that that is exactly what she would have done. It was the proper thing to do. I explained that I didn't want to let the body upset the wedding. Obviously, with hindsight, the course of action I had taken was all for nothing.

Hilary had realised the same thing and started to cry again. 'Look, Arthur, it's not that I don't love you. It's just that I don't want to marry you.'

'Well, I was in the deep heebie-jeebies myself anyway. I shouldn't have proposed in the first place. I think I should be apologising to you.' I wasn't sure how true this was, but I thought that a light whitewash of untruth might do no harm.

'I came round here because my mother was having catatonic conniptions, my brother was being a dick and my father wants to shoot someone. Also, I wanted to talk to you. To tell you face to face. It's not your fault at all. I should never have said yes. Anyway,' she said with a shuddering sigh, 'as Bertie Aherne used to say, we are where we are.'

5

I reunited with my mobile phone and ordered a takeaway while Hilary attacked the washing-up. I keyed Garda Bluett's number into my contacts.

'This place is a disgrace, Arthur. A pigsty.'

'Sorry about that,' I said, moving my overripe runners from the sitting-room to the bedroom and shutting the door again smartly as if to prevent their escape.

'If you can't be bothered to keep the place tidy, then you should get a cleaner.' Hilary was standing at the sink wearing a pair of pink Marigolds that she had found in a cupboard – I must have bought them as part of a failed spring-cleaning jag. They were absurdly big on her. 'I really can't understand how you can live in such squalor. You need to get a grip on your life, Arthur. Man-up and organise yourself better. It seems to me that your life is in the same state as your apartment: a chaotic mess.' Her voice had taken on a hectoring tone.

I said, 'But, Hil, hang on there a minute. You've bowed out. You've left the stage. You've surrendered your rights. Thanks for doing the dishes, but let's not start telling each other how to live our lives, *eh?*'

She was silent for a while, standing with her back to me, her ears pink, energetically scouring one of my saucepans with a green scratchy thing attached to a sponge. I began to feel sorry for the poor pot that was on the receiving end of such a walloping.

I retreated to the sitting-room and moved some of the clutter around a bit to give the impression of tidying. The door-buzzer sounded and I went down to collect the takeaway. When I returned, Hilary was perched on the settee, still in an overload of emotions, but slightly calmer. The stint at the sink seemed to have exorcised some minor demons.

'Is that the end of us, then?' she asked bleakly, as I unpacked the food.

'I'll give this lot a quick nuke,' I said, loading the lukewarm takeaway cartons into the microwave and avoiding eye contact.

'Are we over, Arthur?' She sounded on the point of tears again. 'And by the way, who's Francine?'

I had left the torn page of Garda Bluett's notebook on the coffee table beside my phone. I felt myself colouring as I replied, 'She's one of the investigating Gardaí. She gave me her number in case I thought of anything further that might be of use.' Although this was wholly true, it felt like a guilty lie as I told it to Hilary. Then I told myself that Hilary had surrendered all rights to my faithfulness; she had left me at the altar and I owed her nothing. But that's not really how I felt. I still didn't want to hurt her, even if that meant avoiding the truth. I wanted to continue to have an affectionate place in Hilary's heart, to be loved by her, even after she had stiffed me in the most public way. My desire to be loved and, I suppose, my desire to love, was so strong that I couldn't bring myself to admit that we were no longer lovers and that, in truth, our friendship had been stretched beyond breaking point.

I reached out for the scrap of paper as casually as I could and put it in my pocket, where it smouldered while we ate the over-spiced chicken in silence and pretended that it was tolerable.

When we were finished, Hilary stood up.

'I should go, Arthur.'

My lips were fizzing from the hot jalfrezi sauce, and my mouth felt violated in the way that it always did with spicy food. But there is something rather nice about the feeling of the tide of spice receding. It distracted me completely from the reality of the scene that was being played out.

'Yeah, I suppose it's getting late,' I said, knowing that it sounded lame.

I stood too and made my way to the door to let her out. I realised that I bore her no ill will or malice. We had stood together at the edge of a vast mistake, and she had blinked first. She was always stronger than me. But any love I might have had for her was exhausted and had been replaced by gratitude.

She stopped by the open door and turned, I thought as if to kiss me. In my weakness, I nearly surrendered.

Then an unworthy part of me felt cheated when, instead of leaning in for the kiss, she said, 'Are you not in trouble with the Guards for moving the body, Arthur?'

'Yes, I'm afraid I am. But I think that the cops believe that I'm more deeply involved, somehow.'

'You know he was the parish treasurer. God rest him, but he wasn't a popular man.'

'Oh, really?'

'It's only parish gossip, and I only have it second-hand from my parents, but it seems he had taken on a sort of mission to 'out' everyone in the parish who had unconventional sexual preferences. It seems a strange thing for a gay man to do, except, I suppose, that he felt that hiding one's sexuality in the closet encouraged hypocrisy and allowed room for discrimination. He didn't make many friends over that. Not that any of that would justify killing the wretched man.' She paused, irresolute, on the threshold, then reached out with one hand and stroked my arm and said, 'Well. Goodbye then, Arthur,' and left.

There was a missed call on my phone from Tom. I called him back.

'Hilary's been here,' I said.

'And?'

'Well, it's over, I guess.'

'You were always quick on the uptake, buddy. Listen, how deep is the pile of shite you're in?'

'You mean with the police? Deep enough, and I think they'd like to prove that it's deeper.'

'Look, Arthur, I think we need to man the shovels. We need to find out what happened. If we wait for Plod to do it, your life will be completely fucked. I mean, would you want to lease an aircraft from a murder suspect?'

Tom Farrington had only the slenderest grasp of what I did for a living, but he was absolutely right in thinking that my employer wouldn't waste any time in firing me if I was caught in a line-up.

———

I slept badly that night, my head caught in a loop of conjecture and tangled flashbacks. I was up early and after a breakfast of Aldi's best crunchy granola, I took my rented wedding suit back to the hire place.

The man there inspected the suit for damage. 'Good day, was it?'

'Yeah! Great, thanks.' I may not have sounded very convincing but I couldn't begin to tell him what had really happened and I was sure he didn't care.

I rang Tom and he came around to my place. We started to scribble down some ideas about the crime. I really felt the absence of one of those glass screens you see in the operations centre of TV crime-drama investigations. I wondered if they used special markers for those, or if whiteboard markers would work. A flipchart would have come in handy too (different markers for that, though). And photographs of all the people so that we could draw lines attaching them. We only had an A4 pad and a scrawny little biro that looked as if it had been liberated from a bookies shop.

We wrote down all the names in a circle: Arthur, Tom, Hilary, Alan, Karen, Jennifer, Geoffrey, with the victim, William O'Grady, in the centre.

'I'm glad that you think I'm a suspect,' said Tom.

His voice gave no hint of sarcasm. I think that the idea of being under suspicion rather appealed to him. Rather meanly, I crossed his name off the circular list.

'OK,' I said, 'and we know that I didn't do it, so maybe we should take my name off too.'

'How do we know that you didn't do it?' Tom's eyebrows reached for his hairline. 'I mean, I'm sure you didn't, and you're sure you didn't but how do we convince Sergeant Bullring that you didn't do it?'

'It's *Bow*ring,' I corrected.

'Yeah, it is a bit tedious all right, but we can't have you going down for something you didn't do.'

I was unhappy with the way this was going, but I could see Tom's point.

He went on, 'Let's look at what they have on you. If there's CCTV, you're probably featuring on the recording, dragging the body out of the church. Unless they have footage of whoever it was that brought the body *into* the church, they may assume that it was you too. Your fingerprints are going to be all over the gaff and they may even have your DNA on the plastic sheeting. If I was the cops, you'd be my number one suspect.'

'Thanks for that, Tom. You're a real pal.'

'You're welcome, buddy.'

It was hard to guess if he had read my sarcasm.

We sat in silence for a moment, staring at the names on the page. I could think of only one way forward.

'I think we need to talk to some of the people on the list,

to see if we can find a motive for the killing of William O'Grady. There has to be a hint in the fact that the body was deliberately left in the church. Was it a message? And if it was a message, who was it meant for?'

'I guess the message was "You're next". It's like the old horse's head in the bed thing, isn't it?'

'No, Tom, it's not in the least like anything from *The Godfather*.'

'How do you know it wasn't gangland-related?'

'Oh, come on, Tom, this has none of the signs of an organised-crime hit.'

'And you'd know that, would you? Is that your BA in Social Sciences talking or have you become a detective all of a sudden?' The eyebrows gave a sceptical twist.

I paused. I didn't want to fall out with Tom; he was all I had at that moment.

'Sorry, Tom. Didn't mean to diss your suggestion, it's just that everyone on the list looks unlikely to be involved in organised crime.'

The eyebrows untwisted. Their owner and trainer said, 'So, it's a disorganised crime, so.'

Like so much of what came out of Tom, this remark was better left alone.

'Any danger of a cup of coffee around here?' he asked.

Tom and I drank our instant coffee at the kitchen table and considered some possibilities and more impossibilities. We stared at the piece of paper with the list of names all gathered around the name of the dead man like Scouts at a campfire.

Was the body a message for the florist? We dismissed this

as being too far-fetched. Anyway, the body wasn't in the church when the florist was placing posies on the pews. The timing of the delivery of the cadaver was very precise, aimed at a slot when nobody should have been in the church.

Was the body a message for me? It certainly frightened the bejesus out of me. But the killer couldn't have known that I would be arriving so absurdly early. And I didn't know the dead man. The message couldn't have been meant for me.

This brought us to the conclusion that the body was intended as a message for someone who had a key to the church, who would be likely to arrive between the flowers and the wedding. So, we needed to find out who had keys. Then I remembered that the vestry door was left open, so we put a question mark against that.

A horrible thought occurred to me: if the timing was so precise and I was not expected, had I actually disturbed the unsub as they placed the body? After I had written 'Unsub disturbed?' sideways in the margin of the page, I explained to Tom that 'unsub' is American police drama language for 'unknown subject'. I was really warming to this investigation.

We assumed that there was an alarm system. The alarm hadn't gone off when I arrived, so someone must have turned it off before my arrival. The killer? So, who knew the passcode for the alarm system? Certainly Karen Quayley and Jennifer Roundstock. Oh and Geoffrey Quayley, of course. But who else?

The single sheet of A4 paper was getting very crowded with scribbles. We attached a fresh sheet with Fabric Elastoplast because I couldn't find any Sellotape. We badly needed that glass panel.

If Rev. Karen Quayley and Jennifer Roundstock were an item, was it possible that the dead man knew about it? Was he pushing them to come out and declare their affections to the parish? What was the Church of Ireland attitude towards gay rectors? How would the Select Vestry react to the news of the liaison if it were to be made public? But would Rev. Karen have the strength to deliver sufficient blunt-force trauma to kill the victim with what seemed like a single blow to the head? Not only that, would she be strong enough to move the body from wherever the deed had been done (and that was another question – we needed another sheet of paper now) and lug the dead body into the church for me to trip over in the dark? Unless, of course, she had killed him right there. If the big brass candlestick was the weapon, there might be fingerprints on it.

And what about Geoffrey Quayley, above in the loft, tinkling on the virginals?

Tom sat back and surveyed the scribblings. The eyebrows were pulled down and together, suggesting deep thought. After a beat, he said, 'You're not going to like this, but I think we should get Hilary onto the team.'

I remained silent as I thought this suggestion through.

'But, Tom, it'd be weird. I mean yesterday she abandoned me at the altar and today I'm asking for her help. Why? We'd need to be desperate.'

Despite my reticence to recruit my ex, my head told me that I was deeply desperate. I recalled the words of the Gizzard Man as he handed me two envelopes containing bundles of filthy fifties. '*Pay up punctual, pal, or I'll bleedin' burst you, right?*

Watch your gizzard.' The line was delivered with a grim smile and a pat on my knee, both of which increased the menace of the promise. I was deeply in debt to people who would do me serious physical damage if I didn't pay. It occurred to me that making strange with Hilary would not improve my ability to satisfy the Gizzard Man.

Partly reading my thoughts, Tom said, 'We *are* desperate. Look, Arthur, her family is part of the Rathmurray parish. They know the people. Hilary knows everyone on our list. She'd be useful.'

But the idea was beyond my depleted levels of courage.

'Would you ask her, Tom? It might be better coming from you.'

'You've some fuckin' nerve for a jilted chicken. But I'll do it. Maybe you've enough on your plate without having to dance the reconciliation tango.'

6

Tom stepped out onto the balcony of the apartment to call Hilary. I couldn't hear what he was saying, which I found annoying. A primitive bit of my brain felt that he had no right to be talking to her privately. I felt trespassed upon, even though I had asked him to phone her. I watched his body language, which was irritatingly casual and relaxed. Occasionally he would turn, in mid-conversation, and look at me through the window, as if something intimate between Hilary and me was being discussed. The eyebrows flicked a 'howaya?' at me and he grinned as if he had just been let in on some particularly lurid and unflattering personal detail. Eventually he slid back the door and stepped into the sitting room, his phone still at his ear.

'OK, OK. Yeah. Yup. OK, bye, bye, bye, b-bye, bye.' He took his phone away from his head and disconnected, shoving the phone back into his trouser pocket. He threw himself down onto the sofa, hands behind his head. After a pause, during which it became clear to me that nothing was going to be disclosed without a struggle, I gave in.

'For the love of God, Tom, what did she say?'

'Hilary?' He sounded surprised that I wanted to know. 'She's coming round, now. Might be better to take her off the suspects list.'

I made a list of the questions I thought Hilary might be able to answer, and Elastoplasted it to the bottom of our very dog-eared piece of paper. Tom, meanwhile, had made himself comfortable on the sofa and it looked as if he was having a nap.

On the front-door intercom, Hilary's voice asked for a hand with something. I buzzed her in and roused Tom from the sofa. At my insistence he went down to the hall to help Hilary. A few moments later the pair pushed open the unlocked door to the apartment carrying a flipchart, complete with what looked like an A1 block of paper, and a plastic wallet containing a set of dry-markers.

'Thanks for agreeing to come,' I said to Hilary.

We were so shy of each other after yesterday that we almost shook hands.

Tom struggled to erect the easel. The paper kept wanting to flop forward and overbalance the tripod and each of the legs had developed an independent life.

'I think you're supposed to take the paper off before you put it up,' I suggested.

Tom was having none of that. 'No, no, I have this. It's just a little awkward, that's all. Just let me adjust the length of this ...' He was on his knees in front of the thing, trying to keep it vertical while fiddling with one of the legs. Before he could

51

secure it, the leg telescoped shut, causing the tripod and the heavy block of paper to fall over, pinching his hand. He jumped backwards, '*Fuck ya! Ya stupid fuckin yoke!*' He levelled a kick at the capsized easel while grasping his injured hand.

Hilary intervened like a referee at a TV wrestling tournament, '*Woah!* Steady there! I borrowed that from my office. Here, let me do it, for God's sake!' Her tone was accusatory. She stepped forward to take over. She did a quick inspection of the thing to make sure nothing was bent or broken, then, with the appalling deftness I knew her to be capable of, she laid it on its back, collapsed all its legs, righted it and systematically extended each leg in turn until the tripod was standing as it should. Then she turned and disarmed me with, 'Actually, you're right – it's easier without the paper.'

Tom and Hilary sat on the sofa, I sat opposite them on the footstool, and we went over the notes that Tom and I had put together. Then Hilary stood beside the opened flipchart with a felt-tip pen in one hand and our A4 sheet held between two fingers of her other hand as if she was afraid she might catch something from it. I thought she was going to transcribe our notes, but no, she had her own take on things. I had never seen her do this before, but she had the ability to write on the chart and at the same time talk about something else. I was so mesmerised by this display of extreme multi-tasking that I failed to notice that none of our careful notes and schematics made it onto the chart. Finally, she crumpled our morning's work into a ball and tossed it fastidiously into the wastebasket. I allowed a small whimper of protest to escape unnoticed. She sat again on the sofa to survey what she had written. The only survivor from our old notes was the list of possible suspects, but now their names were written in a row. The name of William O'Grady now appeared top centre in a neat box. I was surprised she hadn't placed a cross over it.

'Now, you said you had some things to ask me?'

I was a bit overwhelmed by her briskness and couldn't remember anything. I was on the point of rescuing our notes from the wastebasket when Tom stepped in.

'OK. Do you know if there's CCTV in the church?'

'Yes, of course. Alan gave a large donation to fund it. You can even follow Sunday service online.'

'It's just that it might have caught the murder in full murder mode,' said Tom. 'Also, our man Arthur here may feature in the footage.'

'I'm sure the Gardaí will have thought of that already. Anything else?' she said briskly, seemingly with no concern for my defence.

Tom brooded for a minute, then asked, his brows dead straight and neutral, 'What do the Protestants make of gay priests?'

'I think the jury may still be out on that one, Tom.'

'Wasn't there a thing about a Presbyterian guy in Sandymount last year only?'

'Yes, but Rathmurray is Church of Ireland. Not quite so fundamentalist.'

'But not liberal either?' I asked.

There was a silence, as if Tom and Hilary had forgotten that I was in the room. I decided to press on regardless.

'I guess it wouldn't be useful for the progression of a vicar's career if it were to be discovered that they were gay.'

Hilary didn't respond. I suppose she felt that her family's religious tradition was under attack by a non-believer.

I decided to add, 'No disrespect. I mean, the Catholics are completely homophobic.'

Tom said, 'I think that Catholic priests should be allowed to marry. I mean, if they really love each other, why not?'

This provoked a groan from me and Hilary and, for the first time that day, I felt that we were on the same wavelength.

I decided to be brave. 'Is it known in the parish that Reverend Karen and Jennifer Roundstock are an item?' I asked tentatively.

'Oh, God, yes. That's been the chatter of the Parish Council for ages. I think most parishioners rather enjoy the idea. It does no harm and makes them feel liberal. It's impossible to keep anything secret in the parish. It's like a big dysfunctional family.'

I remembered that Tom and I had, in our original notes, reduced the possibility of a secret liaison between the vicar and her sexton to a love heart with Karen/Jennifer written inside it. Hilary had not migrated the notion to the new notes. Now I knew why. I was annoyed that Hilary was a step ahead of us.

'Right,' she said, 'we need to talk to these people, find out more about the background.' As she was saying this, she was writing the names Tom, Arthur and Hilary on the chart. Then under each name she wrote a list of people each of us should talk to. 'I'll take Karen Quayley. I have some apologising to do there, which will give me an in. Tom, you have a chat with

Jennifer Roundstock. Just find out a bit more about the lie of the land regarding the dead man. And for God's sake be discreet.'

Tom's eyebrows made a figure of innocence as if discretion was their by-word.

Hilary continued, 'Arthur, you see if you can get Geoffrey Quayley to chat. Use the apology thing to get in there and see what happens.'

'OK, and I guess I'll talk to Alan as well? You're too close, Hil.'

'Fine,' she said briskly as if she was dismissing a class. She put the felt-tipped pen down on the ledge of the tripod, zipped up her little briefcase.

'OK, I'll see you later. What time?' I asked as I put on my coat.

'Five, sharp. Here,' was her crisp reply.

I realised that I had allowed Hilary to take over as leader of the investigation. I didn't really mind, because if you picked Hilary to play on your team, she always assumed captaincy. Going along with it saved a lot of silly pointless argument.

———

The rain had stopped at last, but a catabatic wind from the northeast was threatening to freeze-dry anything that strayed out of doors. I dashed to my car and started up. Everything fogged up immediately, making it impossible to drive. The ancient machine had a rainwater leak somewhere and, when it rained heavily, as it had the previous day, the carpet in the footwells became sodden. Successive garages had charged me good money but had been unable to trace the leak. The last man had suggested drilling a hole in the floor, so that at least the water wouldn't gather. Hilary had dismissed this as a poor idea because, she said, the water could just as easily come in the hole as drain out of it. Now, after yesterday's torrents, there was so much water in the car that, when I cornered, the water sloshed about like a tiny tsunami. I resolved that, as my first gesture of freedom, I would get my garage to drill several holes in the floor of the car.

Hilary had sent me Geoffrey Quayley's phone number. As I sat in the car waiting for the heater to improve visibility, I called the number.

'*Haaahlo?*' The voice was tentative, as if taken by surprise by the technology of the mobile phone.

'Is that Geofrey Quayley? The organist?'

'This is he. May I ask who is calling?' His delivery was precise, his Northern accent curled with gentility.

'I'm Arthur Cummins. I was supposed to be the bridegroom yesterday. Look, Mr. Quayley, I'm in a difficulty and I would really like to have a chat with you about what happened. Where can we meet? This morning if possible.'

We arranged to meet in Cabinteely Park, beside Agnes Conway's enigmatic two-sided concave/convex face sculptures.

He was there ahead of me. He wore a big tweed overcoat, silk scarf knotted around his throat and a wide-brimmed hat. Heavy brown brogues and corduroys. Stylish, in a British sort of way. Rather red in the face and stout.

I introduced myself again.

'How can I help, Mr. Cummins?'

'Well, I know you were in the church early yesterday, around the same time as me, and I wondered what you might have seen?'

Geoffrey Quayley looked affronted. His jowls quivered. I wondered if the affronted look and quivering jowls were a permanent feature of his appearance.

'But I've told all this to the police already. Why should I have to go over it all again with you?'

'Because the police seem to think that I'm involved in the murder, and I'm not. I had nothing to do with it. But proving a negative is very hard without some support.'

I suggested that we sit for a while. We walked slowly to a nearby bench. Quayley had the waddling gait of a swan on land.

'The dead man was parish treasurer, wasn't he? He was an accountant. Was he a good treasurer?'

'Being married to the rector is a strange position – you're part of the parish but not part of the parish. I know things that I shouldn't really know. But I don't think I'd be telling tales out of school if I were to tell you that there's a huge hole in the parish finances. Sure, it's been all over the press about the murder anyway. Everyone's speculating that Willie was after stealing the money.'

I said nothing, waiting for Geoffrey Quayley to spill more beans. I watched a seagull float above us, observing our every move in case we had food with us. 'It's been a major stress for Karen to deal with.'

'I'm sure. Can I ask you, Mr. Quayley – did you see me coming into the church yesterday morning?'

'It was very dark. I'd gone there early to set up the organ. It needs to be switched on a bit before it can be played. Temperamental old thing, really. The florists were in with Jennifer Roundstock just before me. I don't think she knew I was there. When they had finished, Jennifer must have turned off the electricity at the mains because all the lights went out, and of course the organ pump wouldn't work. We have an auxiliary arrangement, but it's tricky. I was trying to engage it in the dark. I'd no torch with me, you see. Then I heard something. I got such a fright I sort of hid. I'm not a very courageous person, Mr. Cummins. Then I heard other movements and sometime after I heard a crash and someone cursing and apologising. Odd.'

'That would have been me, I'm afraid, Mr. Quayley.'

'Please call me Geoff. Karen always uses the full Geoffrey, but it rather reminds me of my mother scolding me. I prefer Geoff.'

'And I'm Arthur. Art, if you're short of time. You didn't see who brought William O'Grady's body into the church, then?'

'No, like I told the police, I could hardly see anything in the dark, and I was startled by the sudden noise from the church and hid.'

'You see, Geoff, I was hoping you would be able to clear me with the Gardaí. I mean, if you'd seen who brought the body in and could say that it wasn't me.'

'I'm sorry, Arthur, I can't help you there. And I'm sorry that you had such a difficult day yesterday.'

I was wondering if he was being entirely forthright. He might have witnessed the murder itself from his grandstand position. And, if so, why was he holding back? Was he the murderer? But I wasn't in a position to cross-examine him, and there was something disarmingly endearing in his gentle demeanour, which softened my need to press him further.

'Well, I guess Hilary and I weren't meant to be married. I think she was very brave and did the right thing to call it off.'

'Sometimes it's better to get the hurting over with at the beginning.' Geoff had his hands in the pockets of his once-expensive overcoat, the collar turned up around his face, so that I couldn't see his expression.

I decided to ask one more question. 'You don't have to answer this,' I said, 'and I'm only asking because of my unusual position as one freshly jilted ... but how are you about Karen and Jennifer?'

This prompted a long silence during which I cursed myself for blundering in where I had no business. It was the sort of question Tom might have asked if left off the lead for too long.

I decided to abandon further efforts at questioning and was about to stand up to take my leave when Geoff suddenly said, 'It's both of us, you know. Karen and me. We're both facing in the opposite direction, if you catch my meaning. We should never have married. But we were both from the Protestant North, where same-sex attraction is regarded as a sinful disease and a sure way to hell. There had been a bit of nastiness up there, which is why we came south. We married because we were friends and loved each other as such. Still do, I suppose. Marriage was the best cover for both of us. Willie O'Grady sniffed it out, of course. He is … was gay, of course, and had an overdeveloped … I think they call it "gaydar"? An intuition for gay people. It's useful if you're gay yourself – saves you from approaching the wrong person, but otherwise it can be destructive and dangerous. Luckily, we have a very liberal church council. Karen and Jennifer came out to the council, with my blessing, and the council supported them more or less unanimously.'

'Geoff, you have been very kind and open with me. I'm very grateful to you. I'll keep all the personal stuff to myself, if you want.'

'I love these sculptures. Don't you?' he said. 'They change completely depending on where you stand. Depending on your point of view. Like people, I think. How little we understand each other. There's nothing secret about anything I've told you. If it helps get you off the hook for something you didn't do, then use it all, if you have to.'

We sat in silence together for a while on the bench, contemplating the arc of seven identical sculpted faces which appeared to move and flicker with the changing light.

Then, with a shy smile, he asked, 'I wonder if you could possibly give me a lift back to the rectory? Karen has the car and it's a bit of a hike from the bus.'

I couldn't imagine Geoff Quayley as a murderer, but I was sure he was holding back about something. Was that just the habitual caution of gay people, or something more? I decided to give him a lift. He might say more in the intimacy of a car.

We walked up through the park to where I had left my car. I apologised for the state of the inside of the car and explained my problem with the penetrating damp.

As I drove, Geoff said, as if he had been reading my thoughts, 'Even nowadays, gay men have to be careful and secretive. You daren't be open about it. People have been murdered, you know?'

'Do you think William O'Grady's death was a homophobic attack?'

'I don't know what to think, Arthur.'

'How well did you know him?'

There was a long silence, from which I gathered that he might have known the dead man well. I left him at the rectory, standing in the gateway looking lost.

7

Back at the apartment, which now had an unnatural tidiness to it, I made myself a cup of tea and sat down to ponder. Hilary's rethinking of our notes made no sense to me, no matter how long I spent staring at the flipchart. Too much had been lost in translation. Whatever her thought processes were, they didn't coincide with mine. I thought I might resurrect our old Elastoplast notes. I found them filed in the wastebasket, much wrinkled, but still sensible to my eye.

In what I told myself was a paradigm shift, I picked up the black marker from the ledge of the flipchart and started to write on the windowpane. I wrote the list of names of those people we wanted to talk to, intending to cross Geoff Quayley off in a symbolic exoneration. However, the marker didn't work like it did on the telly. It only left an illegible faint grey smudge on the glass, which I wiped off with the side of my hand, leaving me with an indelible black stain that stubbornly refused to shift, even after I attacked it over the sink with the green scratchy thing. Wrong sort of markers, I supposed.

My phone rang. It was Francine Bluett.

'Arthur?'

'Yes, Francine, how can I help you?' I put a smile in my voice and tried to exude as much charm as could conceivably be transmitted over the mobile network.

She wondered if I could call to the Garda station at nine the following morning? I wondered if I shouldn't be a little cautious.

'Tomorrow isn't good for me, I'm afraid, Francine. I've a lot to do. You know, tidying up after the cancellation of the wedding and so on.'

'Actually, Arthur, that wasn't an invitation. If you won't come voluntarily, we'll send a marked car round to pick you up.' There was ice in her tone.

I backtracked. 'Nine o'clock tomorrow morning? It's on the calendar. See you then, so, Francine.'

The line went dead.

Hilary had called for a regroup at 5 o'clock. My phone told me it was three thirty. I decided to check in with Tom. I called him.

'How are you getting on?' I asked.

'Do you fancy a pint?' he said obliquely.

We met in the Harbour Bar, down beside the harbour in Bray. The tide was out, baring the muddy Dargle estuary. Little birds flirted with the water's edge, scuttling up the mud as each successive wave pushed into the harbour. The wind set up a fine din of Chinese gongs as halyards flogged against the masts of the cradled boats in the fenced yard of the sailing club.

In the Harbour Bar there was a fire burning in the grate of

the snug and a quiet buzz of conversation among the early drinkers in the main bar. We ordered pints and sat by the fire.

'I had a chat with Jennifer Roundstock,' Tom said. 'She had very little to say about the murder. Except that she didn't like the dead man at all.'

'Did you take any notes?'

'No, I thought that would look a bit ... you know. I mean, I was supposed to be there to have a chat, not to interrogate her.'

The pints arrived. I stared at my pint, annoyed and disappointed, my interest in it depleted. Tom took a long pull on his pint and brought his lower lip up over his top lip to remove the Guinness moustache in a practised gesture.

'But I did record our chat on my phone,' he said, replacing his glass on the table and producing his phone from his pocket. 'She didn't know I was recording. Is that some sort of crime?'

'Probably, but you're some genius, Tom, you know that? Can we listen?' I had my earbuds and we plugged into his phone, sharing the buds. He played the recording.

Tom: *Hi, Jennifer, thanks for agreeing to meet . . .*
[unidentifiable noise]
Jennifer: [more noise] *. . . your friend's wedding being cancelled.*
Tom: *To be honest, I think the humour had gone off him anyway. He wasn't all that keen.*
Jennifer: *Well, that's good anyway. Would you like a coffee?*
Tom: *That'd be great, thanks.*
[Long passage of muted sounds possibly of a conversation

continuing in another room – much laughter but nothing discernible – ending with a loud crash as, possibly, a mug of coffee was placed beside the phone on the table]

Jennifer: . . . *and then the Gardaí arrived and discovered the body in the crypt. I think you know the rest.*

Tom: *I suppose you knew the dead man?*

Jennifer: *Poor Willie O'Grady? Oh, yes. He was parish treasurer, you know. Horrible man. He was such a nuisance. He liked to pry and spy and generally poke his nose in where it wasn't wanted. He was a busybody, I'm afraid.*

Tom: *And now he's just a body.*

[Silence, as the impropriety of Tom's witticism settled]

Tom: [Impervious] *Any idea who might want to kill him?*

Jennifer: *That's what the Guards wanted to know. Sergeant Bull–something and his rather charming assistant.*

Tom: *And?*

Jennifer: *Well, he had made a complete hash of the parish finances. A large unaccounted deficit in the funds. That had made a lot of people very angry, but it's hardly a reason for killing him, is it?*

Tom: *And what had he done with the money?*

Jennifer: *Nobody really knows, but it's thought that he gambled it on the stock exchange* [unidentified percussive noise, then silence.]

I pulled the earbud from my ear and nursed my pint for a moment. My faith in Tom's sleuthing abilities had crashed again. He seemed to be very pleased with his interview with the sexton.

'What the hell were you two laughing about when she went to make the coffee?'

'Oh, that! Sorry, I should have said. I followed her to the kitchen and asked her if she had noticed anything strange or out of place when she was in the church that morning. She said, "You mean other than you and your friend Arthur?" I wasn't expecting a sense of humour. It made me laugh. We both laughed. Then she told me that she had tidied away the trolley from the apse when we went out to greet the guests – it would have been dreadfully in the way for the wedding. She said she wondered what it was doing there. By the way, isn't an apse some sort of snake that Cleopatra did a thing with?'

I thought that Tom's question was best left alone. Anyway, this extra bit of information explained the laughter, and the vanishing trolley. I had to concede that it wasn't Tom's fault if she had no information that might have brought us closer to the killer.

'What's that on your hand?' Tom asked me.

I glanced at the black stain on the side of my left hand. I'd forgotten about the failed marker experiment.

'It's just marker,' I said.

Tom's curiosity seemed satisfied with my answer. He took a generous pull on his pint and said, 'Have I ever told you about my theory of irresistibility?'

'No, Tom, you haven't.' I sampled my pint and waited for Tom to elucidate his theory.

'I've found, over the years, that the more I have to drink, the more irresistible I become to women. Seriously, though.'

'Really?'

'Yeah, honest. Thing is, I've never been able to prove the theory, because just when I reach the point of irresistibility, I either pass out or can't remember what happens next. But I'm fairly sure that my theory works.'

'And how's that?'

'Well, if the woman I'm chatting to is drinking too, after a while she becomes more amenable, or less hostile anyway. I remember once with my last girlfriend, we had been drinking quite a lot one evening and eventually she said, "Oh all right! All right! For fuck's sake, let's do it then! Just shut up, will you, in the name of Jesus?" I wasn't sure what she meant, and by the time I came back from the bar with more drinks, she seemed to have gone.'

'Tom, that's nonsense – you know that, don't you?'

'Oh, yeah,' he said, and the eyebrows rose to an inverted V-shape as he focussed again on his pint.

———

We were back at the apartment in time for our rendezvous with Hilary. We were there ahead of her, and I congratulated myself on my self-discipline in only stopping for the one pint.

I decided to use the time to call Alan Fenton's office to make an appointment to see him next day after my re-grilling by the Gardaí. I rang the number Hilary had given me for Alan's office.

A very brisk female voice answered all in a single singsong breath, without pause or punctuation, '*GoodafternoonMinataur MazeSolutionsmynameisDaphnehowmayIhelpyou?*'

'My name is Arthur Cummins, I'd like to make an appointment to see Alan Fenton tomorrow afternoon.'

'Mr. Fenton is not available tomorrow. Is there anything else I can help you with, sir?'

I wondered if I should pull rank by telling her that I was to have been Alan Fenton's brother-in-law but the damned wedding got called off. I decided against it.

'Please let him know that I called and that it's urgent.' I gave her my number.

'I'd be happy to leave that message with his PA. Is there anything else I might assist you with this afternoon?'

'Could I possibly speak to Mr. Fenton's PA?'

'I'm sorry but she's all tied up at the moment. Perhaps if you called later, she might be free? Is there anything else?'

I battled to clear my mind of an image of a woman in a business suit trussed with duct tape to a revolving office chair. 'If you don't mind my mentioning, it's extremely rude to ask a client to phone again, even if you are tied up, Daphne,' I said, still struggling to erase the soft-porn bondage image.

After a short pause of incomprehension she said, '*Minataur MazeSolutionsaregladtohavebeenofservicetodaygoodbye.*'

I felt as if I had been slapped, limply, several times in the face. I thought about reporting all of this to Hilary, and there might have been a time when I would have done so but, although Hilary and I were still playing for the same side, in view of our rather strained circumstances, whinging to her about her brother's business etiquette was not something I wanted to try.

After I had ended the call, Tom and I stared for a time with mutual incomprehension at the flipchart, unwilling to make any additions to it without its mistress.

Then the hall-door buzzer went, making me jump. It always does that – it's too loud, but there seems to be nothing I can do to tame it or soften its shrillness. I've tried stuffing newspaper into the machine, but for some reason that only made it worse, forcing the tone into a high castrato, which persisted even after the newspaper wadding had been removed. Now it tended to scream, rather than buzz, to announce visitors.

A stale feeling swept over me when I heard Hilary's voice on the intercom. It was like breathing in the air from a balloon that I'd just inflated. I buzzed her in and struggled with my guilt about the stale feeling until she arrived at the apartment door.

'Hi, there,' I said, and felt myself blush.

I asked myself privately why I was so awkward with her. Could so much have changed so quickly between us that I was now embarrassed to have her in my flat? She seemed unaware of any social awkwardness or indeed any stagnancy and sailed past me at the door, dumping her handbag, car keys and a stiff red paper bag from Avoca on the coffee table with a proprietorial crash.

She took up station at the flipchart, popped the lid of the black marker and started to write while talking to us over her shoulder. I found that I couldn't concentrate on what she was saying and what she was writing at the same time. I wondered if there was something wrong with my brain.

Beside Karen Quayley, she wrote, '*Alibi: Geoffrey Quayley. No motive.*' When she stopped writing and the marker had stopped its squawky progress over the chart, I was able to take in what she was saying. She told us that her chat with Karen had gone well. She had seemed glad to talk, she was very shocked by the discovery of the body in the crypt. Nothing had suggested that she might have any knowledge of the killer or be in any way involved herself.

I relayed the gist of my conversation with Geoffrey Quayley and Tom played the recording of his conversation with Jennifer Roundstock, while Hilary wrote seemingly disconnected things on the chart.

'The Guards aren't finished with me yet,' I said. 'I got a call from Garda Bluett. They want to interview me again tomorrow morning. I'd like to have something to offer her.'

'The flowers in Lidl are good value.' Tom was deadpan.

I didn't rise to the bait. 'I meant by way of information, or suggestions. I'm afraid they're going to charge me with something. If I can arrive at the Garda station with information that might distract them from me, they might lay off a bit.'

Hilary said, 'Let's look at what we have.' She again took command of the easel.

Had she been this dominant in our relationship, I wondered, or was this a new development of her character, brought on by her cancellation of the wedding?

She went on, 'Right. We seem to have ruled out Karen, Jennifer and Geoffrey. We've discovered that Karen and Jennifer's relationship was out and widely accepted, so blackmail is not a likely motive. We've discovered that there's money missing from the parish accounts but we don't know how much or where it's gone.'

There was a silence.

'Not much to cover your ass, buddy,' Tom offered.

'I think I'll call Francine,' I said. 'Make a pre-emptive move.'

This time it was me who stepped onto the balcony for the sake of privacy. I'm not sure why I did this, but something in me was enjoying the truant thrill of my attraction to my fair cop, especially in my state of quasi-grass-widowerhood, and I had a desire to keep our conversation private. I tapped my touchpad and she picked up on the second ring.

'Who is this?'

I was disappointed that she hadn't yet added me to her contacts.

'Hello, Francine, this is Arthur Cummins.'

'And how can I help you, Mr. Cummins?'

'You may not be able to tell me, but has anyone looked into the hole in the parish funds?'

'Looked into the hole? Are you making a joke?'

'No, no, no, no, no. It's just that the missing money seems to be at the centre of this case. I can't think why poor William O'Grady would end up dead because of it, but there's a lot that I don't understand here.'

'Yes, I can see that. One of the things you don't seem to understand is that in a Garda investigation, information is gathered by the Gardaí, not given out. I can't tell you anything about the investigation, Arthur.'

Well, at least we were back to first names.

'OK, Francine, I understand. But anyway, I'd like to know if forensics have confirmed that the candlestick was the murder weapon. I'd also like to know what's on the CCTV recording, if any fingerprints of interest were found in the church, and do the victim's bank accounts show anything that might tell what happened to the missing money? Any help you can give me would be very much appreciated. OK?'

'I thought I was clear about this, Arthur? You're trying to drive the wrong way up a one-way street. I can't give you any of that information. All right?'

'OK. What are you doing next Thursday evening? Or is that under the shroud of Garda confidentiality too?' I decided that I might as well strike boldly.

There was a silence, which my flirting antennae suggested bore encouraging pheromones.

'Francine? Are you still there?'

'Sorry, Arthur, the line was scrambled for a moment, there.' There was a laugh in her voice. 'Look, I can't give you information and I can't give you a date either. Goodbye. Oh, don't forget that we have an appointment in the morning. Bye.'

'That's a date,' I said, ever the pedantic optimist. But the line was dead.

Flushed with the tiniest glimmerings of success, I re-entered the apartment. Tom and Hilary were in the kitchen examining the contents of my fridge with archaeological focus. Cartons and jars were being interrogated for 'best by' dates, lids were being removed and noses applied. A process of triage was being carried out on my refrigerated groceries. Two groups were being formed on the counter: the largest consisted of things that were clearly off and a much smaller group of things that were still edible. I thought Tom and Hilary were being unduly fussy and told them so. Hilary reared away from one particular jar of Tesco Finest Red Pesto of uncertain age.

'Jesus, Arthur! There's nothing but green fur in this.' She thrust it from her in disgust, as if it had proposed something indecent. 'Bin it, for God's sake!'

'You'll catch ptomaine poisoning, man!' said Tom, whom I knew kept a particularly bio-diverse fridge himself.

'Actually, there's no such thing as ptomaine poisoning,' said Hilary. 'It's been disproven since the beginning of the twentieth century.'

'Well, then what's the problem with this stuff?' I asked, looking sorrowfully at the ranks of condemned food lined up on the counter.

No answer was forthcoming from my ex, as she swept the putrid groceries into a black bag. There's a saying about an ill wind, which I never fully understood, but I thought that there was a possibility that the apartment might smell slightly less rank after this ancient stuff had been disposed of.

'Is there anything edible here at all?' Hilary demanded.

I opened a cupboard and showed her my stash of pot noodles. This caused her to bridle, I thought, rather more violently than was absolutely necessary.

'I said *edible*, Arthur.'

Tom's contribution of 'I rather like pot noodles,' was delivered with such diffidence that it slid away unnoticed.

We went out and bought takeaway fish and chips and a bottle of rather sour wine. We ate from the cartons and wrappers on the dining table and drank the wine in coffee mugs. Tom declined the wine because he had his car with him. He ate lightly, then said that he had an early start and left Hilary and me to finish. I guess we were way past the need for a chaperone.

Hilary dipped each chip into a pool of ketchup before devouring it, and sprinkled more salt and vinegar onto her battered fish before tearing it apart and consuming it with the eager relish of a cannibal starved of human company. Although she was clearly enjoying the indulgence of the takeaway, dispatching her portion with greedy speed, she complained continuously about the quantity of batter on the fish (too much), the quantity of fish within the batter (too little) and the amount of saturated fat in each mouthful (far too much). She also drank most of the wine, which I reckoned was OK because she had paid for the bottle.

'Do you have any lemons, Arthur?' she asked, holding her glistening fingers splayed, clear of her clothes. She knew full well that the answer would be no, but nevertheless made a face when this was confirmed.

'Pity. Lemons are best thing for fingerbowls.' She licked her fingers with the fastidious delicacy of a Persian cat, before making her way daintily to the kitchen sink to wash her hands in washing-up liquid. Then she picked up a tea towel and sniffed suspiciously at it before drying her hands.

Yes, I told myself, yes, I had once loved this woman, but I couldn't explain why. I understood the attraction of her shape and her very pretty face, but what else held me in her spotlight? Was it her extraordinary competence at so many things? Computers, filling in forms, understanding tax, dealing with waiters, changing a wheel, wielding a hammer – all were grist to her mill. She was so deft that she made the rest of the world look dyspraxic. Was it her ferocious business acumen – her talent for organisation and her eye for a good deal? Or was it her unassailable confidence?

And I really can't say what attracted her to me. I still hold a hammer just below its head and can always be guaranteed to bend the nail or miss it completely. I have been known to drive for miles on a flat tyre rather than attempt a roadside wheel-change, waiters ignore me, tax baffles me, I always fill in forms with a bottle of Tippex beside me, and computers make me feel like a goat staring at lightning.

And yet Hilary and I had been a couple since our college days, together forever, or until our wedding day anyway. She made me feel safe – she'd always have an answer to anything unanswered. She was sure when I was confounded. Confident when I was unsure.

I suppose I offered her an opportunity to be masterful. I didn't pose a threat to her and was as placid as she was temperamental. I'm not saying that I was a pushover to her control-freakishness, but I was happy enough to allow her to take control, to apply the plaster she would have in her handbag if I cut my hand trying to change a light bulb. I guess I was 'yin' to her 'yang' or was it the other way around?

Her father was a self-made millionaire, I think. We never talked about money. My dad had suffered major losses in the 2008 crash. We never talked about that either. I guess we came from the same social background. But she came from newly arrived money and I came from recently departed money.

I could have told her about the very expensive loan from

the man in the pub at this moment, but I decided not to. Secrecy becomes a habit.

'Arthur,' she said, 'I'm tipsy. Can you please drive me home? I'm sure I shouldn't drive after all that wine.'

I wondered if this was a seduction ploy, although I couldn't work out why she would want to seduce me, having so publicly spat me out at the altar. I picked up my car keys and she gathered up her handbag and her bright-red Avoca shopping bag with the red ribbon handles.

I drove in the dark and the rain to her parents' house and parked on the sweeping gravelled driveway. Hidden lights lit specimen trees on the vast and immaculate sward of the lawn. The rain showed as drops of gold in the floodlights. A separate light showed a sculpture of a scantily draped figure from antiquity nestled in a niche in the freshly barbered hedging. I wondered if it was entirely fair that this stone person, who clearly wanted to hide their nakedness in the hedge, should be picked out so mercilessly by the spotlight, like an escaping prisoner spotted from a guard tower. People had clearly been engaged to keep the place in showroom condition, if 'showroom' can be applied to a garden. I couldn't imagine Hilary's father lugging a wheelbarrow. The house itself was dark except for the enticing glow of lights from the hallway, offering a promise of opulent, carefully manicured living to match the impeccable garden.

Hilary got out, shouldering her bag. She reached into the back of the car and grabbed the red Avoca bag, which promptly burst, spewing its contents into the stygian wetness of the interior of my car. She had left the bag on the floor behind the passenger seat, which was, of course, a morass. The bottom of the bag had become soggy, and it gave way when she lifted it.

'*What the hell? For fuck's sake, Arthur!*' She was scrabbling on the oozing floor, gathering together the contents of what had been a stiff, glossy paper bag, but which was now a useless red tube with ribbon handles.

I passed her the plastic Lidl shopping bag that I used for sitting on to keep the worst of the damp from seeping up from the car seat. She angrily dumped her bits and pieces into it, but she continued to search in the car for something she couldn't find. It was dark and wet and the interior light in my car glowed an ineffectual orange. She was getting very agitated.

'Jesus, this bloody car. It's a hopeless wreck, Arthur, just like you. It needs to be scrapped. Useless heap of crap.'

I wondered at the extended simile and whether it was meant fully to refer to me, equally with my car. It certainly didn't make me feel good.

'What are you looking for, Hil?' I asked diffidently. 'Unless you need it right now, we can search for it properly tomorrow in the daylight.'

'Use the torch on your phone, Arthur. Stop standing there lollygagging. A little help here, please!'

I fumbled for my phone and couldn't find the torch function, never having used it before.

Hilary yanked the seat forward on its runners and sprang back, cursing in the rain, holding her hand. She uttered a stream of vulgarities with the fluency of a nun lisping a litany. '*Oh, shit, fuck, bugger, son-of-a-bitch, cunt!*'

'Are you OK?' Yes, it was a stupid question.

'Of course, I'm not OK, you fuckwit! I caught my hand in your fucking seat. Have you a first aid kit?'

'*Ummm.* Not really. No.'

'Oh, Christ almighty, Arthur, you are the most useless fucking idiot! Can you do nothing right?'

I made the mistake of reaching for her injured hand in the way a parent might offer to kiss a child's bruise better.

'Fuck off and leave me alone, would you?' She warded me off with her uninjured hand. 'This thing hurts like hell. I need to wash it and disinfect it. Jesus alone knows what I might catch from your dung-heap of a car. I should have a tetanus injection. Just leave me here and go home. OK?'

I made a very badly mistimed joke. 'I suppose a ride is out of the question?'

Hilary had exhausted her reserves of foul epithets. She straightened, still clutching her injured hand and stamped her foot in fury. '*Just fuck off to hell, Arthur Cummins!*' She was crying, but I couldn't tell if it was from pain or anger. She kicked the passenger door of my car shut with such force that it rebounded without closing properly, earning itself another farewell kick, which left a dent in the panel.

I climbed, chastened and subdued, into the driver's seat and drove away, leaving the girl who so nearly had been my wife standing on the gravel of her parents' house in the pitiless February rain, clutching a second-hand Lidl bag and her injured hand. The porch light came on as she turned, keys in hand, to open the front door.

8

The heavy fat from the deep-fried food gave me indigestion that kept me awake for large portions of the night, the rest of which was spent on a nightmare steeplechase of speculation about the murder, my abandoned wedding, the police and the Gizzard Man.

Obedient to my imperative invitation, and keen to progress my interest in the lovely Garda Bluett, I showed up at the Garda station at five to nine. The Garda at the reception greeted me by name – a level of notoriety that I had never particularly aspired to.

'Ah, Arthur. Good morning. How are you today? Detective Sergeant Bowring is expecting you. Please take a seat through here.'

How is it that Gardaí assuming first-name familiarity has a flesh-creeping, cloying feel to it that is so revolting? I am willing to allow only one exception to this, and I had an appointment to meet her, albeit chaperoned by Sergeant Bowring. I was ushered into the interview room, that bleak place where I had spent most of my wedding day, or what would have been my wedding day. The room smelled of guilty perspiration. I can't describe it better than that because I have never smelt that particular odour anywhere else. I attribute it to the fact that innocent people had no need to perspire there, but guilty folks probably sweated a good deal while being interviewed. In years gone by, both cops and robbers would have smoked, and the reek of tobacco smoke would have disguised the peculiar smell of guilt, in the same way that it tended to hide the smell from the gents' toilets in pubs.

My musings were interrupted by the arrival of Garda Bluett, who was in plain clothes today: jeans and a blouse. Her blonde hair was nicely drawn up into a high ponytail that I thought particularly fetching.

'Nice to see you, Francine,' I ventured, standing gallantly.

'Please sit down,' she replied without a flicker.

Francine hit a switch on a box-like machine that was sitting on the battle-scarred table. She told the machine the date and time of day, then introduced us both by name. My TV crime drama experience told me that this was a sign that anything I might say was being recorded and possibly used against me in court.

'Hey, Francine,' I said, my panic surfacing like a drowning swimmer, 'I think I need a solicitor if you're going to charge me.'

'We just want a further little chat – Arthur.'

I noticed that she paused for a millisecond before saying my name, just like Bart Simpson does when he calls his father 'Homer' – it offered a tiny disrespect, detectable only to the thin-skinned. I wondered if it was part of her training and whether I had been fantasising about any glimmer of interest that she might have shown the day before.

Then Sergeant Bowring swept in in a cloud of armpits, Brut and self-importance. He sat at the table opposite me. I wondered if the odour of guilt had come from him. Garda Bluett told the recording machine that Detective Sergeant Bowring had joined the meeting and noted the time.

'Well, Arthur, do you have anything else to say to us?' Bowring said in the tone of the captain of a firing squad offering the blindfold prisoner a cigarette.

'I think it's all in my statement and what I have told Garda Bluett.'

'OK,' he said, opening the file that he had brought with him. 'Let's go over it all again.'

He proceeded to read my written statement paragraph by paragraph, plus Francine's additional notes, pausing occasionally to ask if what he had just read was correct and if there was anything further I'd like to say. I had nothing to add.

'We've got the results of the forensic examination. You need to know that your fingerprints were found on the plastic sheet that the deceased was wrapped in, and in the church. You also need to know that the CCTV shows you moving the body. This makes you our number one suspect for the murder, Arthur.' He looked up from the file to watch my reaction.

I put on my best poker face and asked, 'Was there anything else on the security tape?'

I saw a look being exchanged between the two Gardaí.

Then Garda Bluett stepped in with, 'No. The rest of the tape was wiped clean.'

'Was that normal for the set-up in Rathmurray parish?' I asked.

'No. The tape only gets wiped once a month.'

'Thank you, Garda Bluett, that will be all,' I said with a grin. I immediately regretted it, both the jest and the grin, neither of which went down well. This was not the place for little jokes.

Sergeant Bowring, whose face looked as if he had been holding his breath for longer than was usually healthy, said in a low voice, 'I have an answer for you if you want to play the jester, Mr. Cummins. You can, if you wish, spend the night in the cells – there's plenty of room for jokers there.'

'Sorry, Sergeant. I'm very nervous. It makes me foolish, sometimes. I meant no harm.'

'Indeed!'

'Are you really going to charge me with the murder? It's just that, if you are, I'll need to get a solicitor, won't I?' I directed my stare at Francine Bluett who remained impassive as a lovely waxwork. 'I mean, I think you know I'm innocent of the murder. I didn't do it.'

Bowring wasn't to be deflected. 'Tell us about your relationship with the dead man. He was the parish treasurer, wasn't he?'

'I believe he was the treasurer, yes, but I never met him before our sad encounter yesterday.'

'What do you mean by 'sad encounter'?'

'Only that he was already dead when I tripped over him in the dark. That's not a happy way to meet anyone.' Dead horse and flogging came to mind, but I kept the thought to myself, having decided that figures of speech disagreed with Bowring and only served to encourage apoplexy.

'Is that a bruise on the side of your hand?' Bowring was craning to get a better look. 'Karate chop gone wrong?'

'It's marker ink. I can't get it off,' I said, blushing at the thought of being found out graffitiing the windowpane of my apartment.

Bowring looked at me with suspicion, or I think that's what his look was supposed to mean.

'Are you a rich man, Arthur?' This came from lovely Francine.

'Not by any means.'

'How much do you earn in a year?'

'I think that's my business, don't you? And I don't see what bearing it has on anything. Let's say that I just about cover my rent and my groceries.'

'And your employer – it's a multibillion multinational aircraft-leasing company, isn't it?'

'Again, I don't see how that can have anything to do with the murder. I'm a very lowly employee.'

'Not a highflier then?' Corrosive sarcasm oozed from Bowring's enlarged pores.

If there's one thing I can't stand, it's a bully. I'd had enough of the sergeant's overbearing attitude.

'Oh, I see. You can make jokes, but not me. I'm to remain serious, with a threat of imprisonment dangling over me if I so much as smile, but you can wisecrack to your heart's content? I'm not happy for this interview to continue without a lawyer. Please put that on the record. And I'd like to leave now, please.'

Bowring looked discomfited. And I thought I saw a hint of admiration in Francine's very fine blue eyes. I stood up and waited for the door to be opened. I'm not very good at this sort of confrontation and I found that I was shaking.

Bowring stood, shoving his chair noisily out behind him as he gathered his papers and stomped from the room.

'Nice one, Arthur,' breathed Francine, making my already over-extended heart dance a little tarantella.

I left the Garda station none the wiser as to what Bowring wanted from me. Maybe he thought I might break down and confess? But I had already owned up to the totality of my involvement. I had no more to offer. However, I still felt the sergeant's breath on my neck, and my natural state of latent guilt made my hair stiffen. Didn't Kafka write a book about this?

9

I was having lunch in the Purty Kitchen, that ancient establishment which boasts Captain Bligh among its former patrons — a quite decent bowl of seafood chowder for a price that bordered on piracy, but food everywhere in our little neutral country seems to come with that tag. The ambience was pleasantly muted, which suited my mood after my meeting with the Gardaí. I had come away with one piece of information and had given nothing. The information I had scored was that the security camera tape had been unseasonably wiped before I arrived. This suggested that whoever had delivered William O'Grady's body to the church the day before yesterday knew where the recording equipment was closeted and how to operate it to wipe it clean. They also knew how to operate the alarm system, which had been turned off before I had blundered in. Only a small group of people could be so expertly intimate with the security systems of the church and some of those wouldn't qualify for the final line-up. I felt that our digging was at last producing something.

I was lunching in that particular corner of Dun Laoghaire because it was close to Alan Fenton's office, MinotaurMaze Solutions. Although it was predictable, I found myself disappointed that I hadn't received a call from Alan's PA. Nobody, not even brisk Daphne, had returned my call. I had no appointment. But I decided to goad the bull in his lair, so to speak, and arrive unannounced. I strolled up Old Dunleary Road towards the glass box that housed Alan's empire and entered the lobby, with its soaring atrium complete with its own private rain forest. Glass and marble everywhere and, through hidden loudspeakers, what might have been André Rieu smoothing out the wrinkles, if any were to be found. A pharaoh would have been happy to have been mummified here (but perhaps without Mijnheer Rieu soothing his sarcophagus).

I approached the reception desk and announced myself as William O'Grady. I said I had an appointment with Alan Fenton. The uniformed security man with a shaven head and a tattoo of a swallow (but it might have been a fly) on his hand, asked me to wait, indicating a huddle of matching armchairs around a low table with today's newspapers and a vase of fresh flowers.

I hadn't had the presence of mind to bring a book and I don't knit, so I whiled away the waiting time with my mobile phone. I opened Facebook and keyed in Alan Fenton. Mark Zuckerberg's gossip site confirmed to me that Alan Fenton managed a hedge fund – MinotarMaze Solutions. I had to look up what a hedge fund was. It seems that my never-to-be-brother-in-law was in charge of a large and actively managed portfolio of non-standard investments and derivatives (I looked up that too), funded by investors who had appetite for risk and greed for profit in more or less equal degrees. The page told me that Alan the Actuary was skilled at spreading the risk of the more white-knuckle investments against more solid flutters. According to his profile, which looked to be entirely autobiographical, he was particularly skilled at risk-spreading. He invited investors to invest and promised returns of up to 80% within five years. I found it spooky and uncomfortable to read this too-good-to-be-true hype in the vestibule of the man's own office. I wouldn't have trusted him with my Communion money.

There was a certain amount of chatter on his page, mostly in the form of luscious testimonials lauding Alan's prowess in managing the fund and in bringing great rewards to the happy investors. The language of these had the same rattle to them as the wording of his profile. I wondered if they had also been written by Alan.

'Mr. O'Grady?'

It took me a moment to recognise my alias. I looked up from my screen. An impeccable young woman stood demurely by me. She was dressed in what looked like a sort of livery. I don't think she would have chosen the clothes herself. 'Please follow me.' She held out her right arm in the direction of the all-glass lift that was gaping at the back of the atrium. I pocketed my phone and followed her to the lift, wondering at my sense of trepidation and likening myself to a latter-day human offering being led into the labyrinth.

The lift ascended five floors of vertiginous cliff-face and

stopped to yawn again, this time offering exit into the building's top floor. I was shown into what looked like a boardroom, with an oversized oval table of richly veined dark wood, with stainless-steel and cream leather chairs of Scandinavian severity gathered around it. A huge window offered a dizzying view over the Coal Harbour, the West Pier, Dublin Bay, Howth Head and a hazy beyond. A sideboard bore bottles of water and a bowl of mints.

My guide left me. I sampled a mint and admired the view, standing at a respectful distance from the edge of the abyss.

'*Arthur!*'

I jumped at the sound of my name arriving seemingly amplified into the room without anyone having entered to announce it. I whipped round, startled, to see that the wall-sized plasma screen opposite the window had activated, offering me a twice-life-size image of Alan Fenton's face, looming over me.

'That was a strange sort of prank to pull, there,' it said. 'Using a dead man's name. Could you not have picked up a phone and called me?'

'I tried that, but I was asked to call again. I thought I'd save time by coming to you in person. But can we not meet in the flesh?'

'No can do, old man. I've politicians to lobby and deals to do. Post Davos stuff. I'm in a business hub at Schiphol on my way to Boston. This is a way of being two places at once. Now, what can I do for you? Oh, by the way,' he interrupted me before I had even started, 'I'm expecting a call here and I may have to excuse myself – it'll be from the Tánaiste's office.'

I was impressed by the high-level naivety that drove Alan's desire to impress. I wondered if anyone could possibly be taken in by this Wizard of Oz technique.

'Can I ask you, Alan, if I had gambled money on the stock exchange, would it be possible to trace the money back to me?'

'Are you suggesting that MinotaurMaze Solutions is some sort of gambling den?'

His hackles were roused rather easily, it seemed. 'Not at all. I'm just asking you, as an expert on the stock exchange and the wider market, if money invested and lost could be traced back to the original investor.'

He liked the compliment offered in the sub-text. 'Yes, but you'd have to know the entry point. Regulated entities are required to carry out identification checks for anti-money laundering purposes.'

'Is MinotaurMaze Solutions a regulated entity?'

'We are supervised by the Central Bank for some of our activities, yes. We pride ourselves as being super-compliant. I liken it to a sheet on a bed – it should be wide enough to tuck in.'

I didn't like the idea of being in bed with this genius. 'Can I ask you what your investment entry level is?'

'Like the Rolls Royce, Arthur,' he was purring now, like the car he alluded to, 'if Sir has to ask that question, Sir can't afford it.'

'Have you a problem with the question, Alan?'

'Not at all, Arthur. I just thought that we'd be a bit grown-up for you, old man. Entry levels vary, but at the moment our minimum is five-hundred thousand euro.'

'Was William O'Grady a client of yours?'

'Look, Arthur. I know that you and my sister are doing a sort of Famous Five thing, but you should stay out of business that doesn't concern you. I know you don't have the sort of money it takes to enter the big-boys' game. Just leave that to those of us who understand the markets.'

'We'd be the Famous Three.' I wondered at his maths, this master of the markets. He looked nonplussed. I explained, 'Hilary, Tom and me. We'd be the Famous Three. And you haven't answered my question about William O'Grady. His name seemed to get me access here. Was he a client?'

'Do the Guards know that you're fannying around annoying people like this? I've a good mind to report you. Look, I've got to go. Goodbye.' The screen went black. I helped myself to a handful of mints from the bowl on the sideboard, unwrapped one and popped it into my mouth. The rest I shoved into my pocket. As I sucked the sweet, I did a quick mental assessment of the strange meeting with Fenton. His evasion about whether there was an account in the name of William O'Grady, coupled with the fact that the dead man's name was sufficient to get me access to Fenton, suggested very strongly that there was, in fact, such an account, and that it must have had a substantial chunk of money in it.

I took the train back to Bray. A man in a garage down by the Maltings was drilling some holes in the bottom of my car.

10

The man in the garage had changed the channel on my car radio and had thoughtfully left a large piece of paper, with the outline of two feet printed on it, in the driver's footwell. I guessed that the paper was intended to protect the car from oily feet. It had become water-logged from the swamp that was the floor of my car, and turned into papier-mâché, so that it was almost impossible to remove except in single, soggy handfuls. Of course, I didn't notice this until I got to the car park of my apartment and my feet had nicely churned up the protective paper. I wasn't convinced that the new holes were working.

I should, by rights, have a space in the underground car park, where the car would be sheltered from the rain and the rainwater leak would be less aggravating, but someone else's car is always parked in my space. I had tried leaving notes on the windscreen of this trespasser, starting with polite requests to park elsewhere and working towards threats. But nothing had worked, so my ancient jalopy had to brave the elements above ground.

I hoped that the colander effect might improve things, but I noticed that there was mould forming on the faux-leather covering on the steering wheel. Maybe it was time, I thought, when I was out of earshot of the car, to think about taking it to the big car park in the sky.

———

I boiled the kettle and activated a carton of Jerk Chicken Pot Noodles. I was allowing the contents to stand for the recommended minute when my phone rang. I use a rather outré ringtone of what might be a flock of barnacle geese assembling for a migratory stopover.

It was Tom announcing that he was in the vicinity and suggesting a rendezvous at mine.

On arrival, he declined to join me in some noodles.

'I've a pal who paddles in the markets,' he said. 'He's up on all the gossip and has even given me the odd tip.'

'Don't you mean 'dabbles' rather than 'paddles'?'

'Ducks dabble,' said Tom, 'My pal paddles.'

I thought I'd leave it there.

'Anyhow,' said Tom, 'I asked him if he knew anything about MinotaurMaze Solutions. I told him that I had half a rock that was looking for somewhere safe. He told me to be careful. The word on the ground is that Alan Fenton's business is in serious difficulties. He said that some counterparties had closed on their positions, leaving Fenton with big losses on a couple of undisclosed naked shorts that he had taken in breach of the regulations. He might even be using new investors' money to settle deals, instead of investing it like he should. Looks like he's a bit of a Ponzi.'

There was a great deal to take in here, starting with the idea that Tom might have a pal who invested in the markets, moving on to the proposition that his pal might believe that Tom had half a million in need of a roost, and ending with what might or might not be a questionable joke. My quasi-best man never ceased to amaze me.

I made no comment and continued to fork my noodles. I don't know what Jerk Chicken tastes like, never having jerked a chicken, but I'm fairly sure that it doesn't even faintly resemble the flavour of these noodles. But they were tasty in their own humble way.

'I'm not sure what "closing a position" means,' I confessed.

'Is it not like what happened Clearys? Didn't they close their position on O'Connell Street?' The eyebrows were all innocence. 'Do you remember that song, you know, after they'd finished putting up the Spike?' He sang, making percussive noises by slapping his chest, a regrettable sound: *"I can see Cleary's now, the crane has gone – I can see all bicycles in my way ..."*

His grasp of the melody of the Jimmy Cliff classic was slippery. Happily, he didn't know any more of the lyrics, one way or the other. It was a thing with Tom – he knew, or thought he knew, the first two lines of every song ever written.

I stood to dispose of my now-empty pot of noodles in the kitchen trash. When I came back into the sitting room, Tom had written in red on the flipchart beside Alan's Fenton's name:

'EXPOSED IN NAKED SHORTS.' I again regretted the absence of the glass screen, from which this could so easily have been redacted. I quietly marvelled at my grasp of terminology.

'Tom, I'm certain that William O'Grady was a client of Alan's. He more or less admitted it to me today. If Alan Fenton's having difficulties delivering on his deals, he may not have been able to pay O'Grady what he owed him.'

Tom was on the scent like a ferret. 'And if poor Willie had "borrowed" parish funds to play financial craps with, he would have been very cross if Alan couldn't pay him back, wouldn't he?'

Now I was following the line myself. 'And O'Grady wasn't above a bit of blackmail, was he? He could have threatened to report Alan to the Central Bank.'

Tom finished the hypothesis. 'Which would have made Fenton very angry. And very desperate if he couldn't pay up.'

'You know,' I said, 'I think that the chart tells us more by what's not written on it than what is. I mean, how much money is missing? And why was the loss not reported to the Gardaí? Alan said that the entry level for his fund is half a million euros. Did the parish have that sort of money?'

'I'll get Hilary to ask Karen Quayley,' said Tom, pulling out his phone like a gunslinger might whip out his revolver. 'Five hundred large seems a lot. But Fenton might have wanted to suck up to the parish treasurer. He might have been prepared to bend his own rules to let him into the magic circle at a discount.'

I wondered if Karen would like to hear her Select Vestry likened to a cut-price coven.

'Listen, Tom,' I said, 'not a word to Hil about our suspicion

that Alan is in the financial manure. She might tell him.'
Having said this, I fell silent, stunned at my lack of trust in
the woman who I had been about to vow to have and to hold
until separated by death.

'You never told me how you got on with your new girlfriend
this morning,' Tom asked, having written 'HOW MUCH?'
beside William O'Grady's box at the head of the chart.

'I'm not really sure what the Guards hoped to achieve by
interviewing me again. I think Bowring just wanted to frighten
me. But I did find out that the only CCTV record is of me
moving the body. The rest of the tape had been wiped.'

'Interesting.'

Tom tried Hilary's number but she didn't pick up. He texted
to ask her to phone him.

'I've got to go, Arthur. Some of us have to work, you know.'
He stood, pocketing his phone. The gunslinger holstering his
piece.

'You know that I'm on honeymoon, don't you?'

'Oh, yeah. How's that going?' The brows were ironic.

'Goodbye, Tom.'

'Yeah, see you.' And he was gone.

———

That evening, just when I was settling down to watch *Pointless*
on the TV, the front-door buzzer screeched at me. I wasn't
expecting anyone, so I asked who was there on the intercom.
A male voice told me that I had a large delivery from Argos. I

thought it was probably a wedding present and went down to open the door. Two big men were standing there. One of them looked vaguely familiar.

'You Arthur Cummins?' said the bigger of the two.

'Yes,' I answered warily.

'We're here to deliver this!'

What happened next lay buried in my subconscious for some days afterwards. Details of it drifted back at intervals in no particular order. I have pieced it together now, as I remember it.

I wasn't expecting the head-butt. It came from the guy with the non-speaking part. It caught me just on the bridge of my nose, sending little lightning bolts of pain across my face and making my eyes water. I put my hand to my nose. I was bleeding. I crumpled to the floor of the entrance porch.

'*Watch your gizzard. Do you understand?*

'*Do you understand?*' the big one said, slightly louder.

'Yes. For fuck's sake!' I barely recognised my own strangled voice.

I have never been good with my own blood, which was now leaking in some profusion onto the concrete floor. My assailant availed of the opportunity to kick me very hard in the ribs.

I guess I had received a bursting.

I don't know how long I lay there after they left, but *Pointless* was over by the time I made it back to the apartment.

11

Imust have dripped blood all over the entrance hall, into the lift (principles are fine, but I had just been assaulted), along my corridor and into my flat. The sort of trail that bloodhounds find especially easy to follow. My first thought was that this was a matter for the police. My next thought was of Francine. They were not quite the same. I keyed in her number.

My recollection of what happened next is a bit confused. I remember an ambulance and trying to make a joke about something or other. I can't remember if anyone laughed, but it's unlikely. I remember lying in a hospital bed in Tallaght, with Garda Francine Bluett sitting in a chair beside me.

'Arthur? How are you doing there? You're in hospital. You passed out in your apartment and I called an ambulance. You took quite a bang.' She looked lovely when she was concerned. She pressed the button to summon the nurse.

I tried to tell Francine what had happened, but for some reason my tongue wouldn't do what it was told and I couldn't make her understand what I was saying.

The nurse arrived, closely followed by a doctor, or at least a person wearing a stethoscope draped around her neck like a scarf. The nurse (male) and the doctor (female) were very kind. They said that I'd had a CAT scan and there didn't seem to be any serious injury. But it seemed pretty bloody serious to me. They shone a little torch into my eyes, saying things like, 'Look at my ear' and 'Follow the light with your eyes'. My nose had swollen so much that I couldn't really follow much with my eyes because the swelling kept getting in the way. My face hurt like hell. Then the doctor said that I would be kept in for observation overnight.

I tried to tell them that my face hurt and that I had a bad headache, but they didn't understand what I was saying. They asked Francine, 'Are you his wife?' and she laughed and said she was a Detective Garda and that I was connected to a case she was investigating. But I fancied that she stayed for longer than seemed professionally necessary.

I didn't sleep at all that night. At least I don't think I did. Every time I nodded off, a nurse would wake me to take my blood pressure, asking me for my name and date of birth and checking, I suppose, my vital signs. Anyway, I retained my vitality through the night and was able to eat some porridge for breakfast. This was suggested by the new nurse – they change shift at six – because the X-ray had shown possible cracks in my upper palate and I should avoid attempting to eat anything solid for a day or so. My nose was well and truly broken, my left ribs well and truly cracked. I was visited by a different (male) doctor, whom I hoped had been talking to the previous (female) doctor from last night. The new man said I could leave whenever I was ready, but that I should make an appointment to come back to have my nose reset when the swelling had gone down. I mumbled my thanks and was pleased to note that I seemed to be making sense again.

I went to the bathroom and examined my face in the mirror for the first time. What I saw made me laugh, which hurt. My reflection looked like something you might see in a funfair arcade in a distorting mirror. Both eyes were a spectacular shade of purple and my nose was so swollen that I was virtually unrecognisable.

Hilary came to collect me. This was a kindness, but I found myself growing increasingly distant from her. She had become more and more a stranger to me since the day of our aborted wedding. Her sense of order, her desire to be in control, her constant stream of advice as to what others should do, especially me. Everything she did had been thought through, snags identified, problems dealt with. She always read the terms and conditions of everything. She read the instructions. She remembered to tax her car. She filed things away in neat order. In my mind I saw her sitting calmly, feet crossed neatly at the ankles, as she observed the world as a place that she had tamed.

All this organization was alien to me. I fluffed along in what I thought of as a good-humoured way. I assumed that nobody of my acquaintance would take it badly if I forgot their birthday or if I overlooked sending a Get Well card for a hospital visit. As far as I was concerned, printed instructions were to be ignored until something went wrong. Terms and conditions bored me. I hadn't the patience for pages and pages of small print. Jesus, life was too short. My slovenly soul must have been attracted to Hilary's neat and collected aura. Maybe, on a subliminal level, I desired her to impose her order on me. A sort of benign domination. Sexy, in an abstract and painless way. But now that Hilary had cut the mooring rope and had cast me adrift in the world again, I observed with horrid fascination all her characteristics that repelled me. I was like a fridge magnet turned the wrong way round; I wanted to push away.

All the same, it was decent of her to pick me up from hospital, and she was looking lovely in her tight white jeans. I told myself to get a grip.

Back at the apartment and still on our 'honeymoon', so work didn't interfere with our lives for another while, Hilary made omelettes, cracking each egg with a business-like stroke of a table knife, splitting the shell and emptying the raw eggs into a bowl for beating. As each egg cracked, I winced.

I had no appetite for Hilary's omelettes. I felt tired and lay down on the couch to sleep.

As I dozed, tiny fragments of memory, like bits of shell in the omelette mix, started to come back to me. The first was that there had been two men. I couldn't see their faces. They may have been masked. Why was one of them vaguely familiar to me? I remembered that one of them had spoken, but I couldn't remember what he had said. I slept.

When I surfaced, it was evening. Hilary had gone, but Tom was there. He had brought a shoulder of vodka. The thought of alcohol made me nauseous. I told him so.

'Don't worry about that,' he said. 'This is for me.' He poured a generous slosh into a cup. 'I couldn't find any glasses.'

'There's ice in the …'

'I'm ahead of you, buddy.' He rattled the ice in the cup by way of demonstration and cautiously sniffed a carton of orange juice that he had found in the fridge. He decided it was potable and poured some into the cup. 'Cheers, Big Ears!' He surveyed me for a while in silence. 'Your ex was a bit snippy about something. I don't think she likes anyone interfering with her flipchart.'

We sat in silence, trying again to make sense of the slogans on the chart.

'D'you think those were Fenton's goons? Hilary told me that you were assaulted by two big lads, one of whom gave you the Ringsend kiss.'

'Look, I don't know, Tom. They might have been Fenton's heavies. I really don't know. I have a vague idea that one of them was familiar to me, and I can't for the life of me think why.'

My subconscious told me that the boys came from the shadowy man who had lent me money that I now couldn't repay. I was ashamed of my stupidity for borrowing in this way. I decided not to tell Tom about it. The effort to put it out of my mind caused my head to hurt. I massaged my temples, avoiding the bruises.

Tom's eyebrows did their quizzical configuration and he said, 'Well, if they weren't Fenton's, it's a bit of a coincidence that they'd arrive around here and give you a smack on the nose just after you had been asking him about his connection with the late Willie O'Grady. No?'

As we were talking, a memory floated by me like dandelion down. It was a man's voice saying, '*Watch your gizzard!*' But the voice didn't sound like Gizzard Man's. The memory came with a visual memory of a swallow. In February? I dismissed it.

The eyebrows gave a lurch, signifying a minor brainwave in the inner workings of their owner. 'I think I know why nobody has blown the whistle on Fenton.'

Tom poured himself another vodka, added ice and more orange juice, finishing the carton. He swallowed back a thoughtful gulp of his drink and said, 'It's like a chain letter.'

'Ah Jesus, Tom, you can do better than that. What the hell are you on about – "chain letter"?'

'Would you care to step out onto the balcony? I feel the need for a calming toke of resin. Here's one I made earlier.' He held aloft a readymade spliff, rolled in liquorice paper and looking like a long slender cigarette – which reminded me of cigarettes a girlfriend of mine liked to smoke – they were made of menthol-flavoured tobacco and revelled in the incredibly politically incorrect name of 'More'. I remember that they made you feel as if someone had left a door open in the back of your head and there was a draught blowing through.

We stood on the balcony. Tom lit up. I declined his offer. I was still woozy from my head-to-head the previous night.

'What I mean by a chain letter is that, if you are the last man caught, you will have sent out fivers to everyone on the circulated list, but you'll get nothing back. It's like dominoes. In Fenton's case, everyone is afraid to bring down the house of cards in case the whole thing falls on them. As long as he's still afloat, there remains a chance that his ship might come in and he might be able to pay.'

'Tom, you know you've mixed up at least five metaphors, there. What the fuck are you smoking?'

'Speaking of dominoes, are you hungry? I could eat a farmer's arse through a gorse-bush.' He pulled his phone out, dialled and ordered a large pepperoni pizza with extra sausage and a side of sweet potato chips.

I decided to stick to my noodles; they promised a gentler treatment of my possibly cracked palate.

12

I received another call from Francine. I was expecting, perhaps, another summons to the Garda Station, but there was a different tone to her this time.

'Can you meet me for a coffee, Arthur?'

A thrill ran through me that made my broken nose throb.

She suggested the café in Cabinteely Park. We met at eleven. She was in plain clothes with a down-filled jacket. She wore her sunglasses on top of her head.

'Jesus, Arthur, you look worse than you did in hospital!' was her opening comment. 'You have two beautiful black eyes!'

I tried to think of a gallant riposte, but I was still suffering a bit from brain-fuzz and decided to keep my trap shut. We collected our coffees and went upstairs to sit at a table that overlooked a bit of the front courtyard. I knew that this wasn't a social meeting, but I allowed myself the self-deluded thrill that I was on a date with the lovely law officer.

'I thought I'd break a few rules and meet you unofficially, Arthur. I'm relying on you to keep this discreet. D'you think you can do that?' She enchanted me with her clear blue eyes, lowering her head slightly to look directly into my own bloodshot and bruised peepers. Her tone was that of a junior-school teacher exhorting her students to behave themselves.

'Of course, Francine,' I mumbled.

'OK. Well, here's the thing: Sergeant Bowring has a fixation that you killed William O'Grady. I can't shake him. He's convinced. He doesn't trust you. He says that a spoilt bridegroom has a mark on him like a seminarian who's jumped the wall. Then, he quotes the following reasoning: one, you were in the church around the time of the murder; two, you hid the body in the crypt; three, your prints were on the plastic shroud; four, Q.E.D.'

'But what about motive? I had never met the dead man.'

'He says that degenerates like you are capable of random acts of violence. No motive necessary.'

'Me? Degenerate? Where did that come from?'

'Well, he doesn't like the way you make jokes. And the lady rector says that your friend Tom Farrington offered her cannabis. The sergeant is convinced that you are a pot-smoking hippie type. He doesn't like them.' She sat back and took a sip of her coffee, watching me.

'But surely you don't believe that I did it?' There was a bewildering pause. 'Do you, Francine?'

'That doesn't matter. He's on the point of sending your file to the DPP for a decision as to whether you should be charged with the murder.'

'Look, can we talk off the record here? You're not recording this, are you? Will what I say be used against me?'

'Relax, Arthur. I've told you that I'm breaking the rules by meeting with you like this. My career depends on this never getting out. Do you understand me?'

'Do you know that William O'Grady was a client of Alan Fenton's?'

Francine Bluett would have been a formidable opponent at the poker table. I couldn't tell whether she already knew. I decided to press ahead anyway.

'It seems that the word on the dealing floor is that Fenton's business is in difficulties. I think that O'Grady might have "borrowed" some parish funds to invest in one of Fenton's gambles that went to buggery in a biscuit tin.'

'That's a colourful expression, Arthur,' said my coffee companion.

I was watching the way the early spring sunlight managed to find its way into the loft-like upstairs space of this little coffee shop. You would almost be persuaded that there was warmth to the sunlight, but in reality it was as cold as a courtesan's smile. I shuddered and pulled my jacket closer around me. It was probably the after-effects of my concussion.

The sunshine was lighting up Francine's face now, sneaking in, low, through the skylights. She flipped down her sunglasses to shield her eyes.

'I know about your sleuthing efforts – you, Miss Fenton and Mr. Farrington. Just take care that you don't end up interfering in a Garda investigation. My sergeant wouldn't take kindly to that.'

'We'll be very careful, don't worry.'

'Yeah, sure. Careful enough to earn you a loaf in the face?'

I offered her what was meant to be a rueful smile.

I asked, 'Have you made any progress identifying the boys who attacked me yesterday?'

'I'm breaking the rules again here, Arthur,' she said, shifting in her chair. 'But there's CCTV footage of two lads approaching your apartment building around the time of your assault. They're both wearing ski-masks. Their faces aren't visible. We've nothing to go on, unless you can remember something.'

The tattoo of a swallow floated up on a weak thermal of memory. I decided not to dismiss it, but it was as vague as an unremembered dream so I chose not to share it with Francine.

'Can you tell me anything about the coroner's report on the dead man?' I asked by way of a diversion.

'He died of a blow to the head with a heavy object. You probably guessed that from the state of him when you stumbled on his body.'

'Do you know where he was killed? It can't have been where I found him or there would have been blood all over the shop.'

'You know well there's a limit on what I can tell you, and I can't tell you that, Arthur.'

'Do you have a weapon? Did forensics find anything on the candlestick?'

'No. Nothing at all. Sergeant Bowring insisted that forensics examine it, but there was nothing, it was clean.'

'Clean, clean? You mean not even the fingerprints of the usual vestry team?'

'Nothing at all.'

'Isn't that a bit odd?' My bruised brain stirred to investigate this unusual state of affairs. I thought I was on to something interesting.

'Not really, Arthur. You see, the candlesticks get a rub with Brasso once a week, and the cleaner always wears rubber gloves. The ammonia in the Brasso kills any DNA and the cleaning removes all fingerprints. So, the candlestick was as clean as a whistle.'

'So, we seem to be going around in circles, don't we, Francine?'

'Just back off with your private investigations, OK? Whoever it is that doesn't want you snooping around may not stop at a head-butt if you stir them up again. Leave this to the professionals.'

I made my way back to my mouldy car and sat for an impatient five minutes while the fog cleared from the inside of the windscreen.

I realised I was very frightened. Terrified. Now that Daddy Fenton's dowry had vanished, short of selling an organ I saw no way of paying the Gizzard Man. I would, I thought, probably be directed to the same pub where I had met the man if I did decide to exchange a kidney or a slice of my liver for cash.

13

It was on the news. A dawn raid by the Fraud Squad and Criminal Assets Bureau and some representatives of the Financial Regulator. A biggish posse of uniformed Gardaí and a squad of plainclothes officers with tabards proclaiming their police status. Someone must have alerted the press, because the cameras arrived at the same time as the cars and vans with flashing blue lights. Viewers were warned that the footage contained some flashing images. I got a glimpse of Francine Bluett looking lovely in her uniform, her peaked hat pulled down over her eyes to shield them from the lights. She looked like a pop star in uniform. The TV reporter told the cameras that the Gardaí had raided the Dun Laoghaire offices of MinotaurMaze Solutions, the business run by financier Alan Fenton, and had seized documents and laptops relating to the business. In a formal statement to the press, a Garda spokesperson said that the raid was part of an ongoing investigation into certain allegations of fraud and money-laundering. An arrest had been made.

The screen showed a man being led away in handcuffs with an overcoat draped over his head. He was stuffed into a Garda car and driven away.

So, Alan Fenton's business had gone down the toilet in a slurry of publicity.

At the very end of the report was a short mention of murder victim William O'Grady, whose funeral was to be held the following Friday, being among the defrauded clientele.

—•—

I thought that Hilary would just stay away, but I was wrong. She stormed into my apartment in a state of thermonuclear fury.

'What the fuck do you think you're at, Arthur? Telling fucking slanderous lies to the police about Alan's business? How dare you? How fucking dare you?'

'*Woah there*, Hilary. Hang on a moment. I didn't tell the police anything about Alan's business. How could I? I don't even understand what he does.'

'Well then, who wrote that on the flipchart?' She was shouting and pointing a finger in the direction of the chart where '**EXPOSED IN NAKED SHORTS**', still took up a place of prominence by Alan's name. 'How could you fucking do this to my family? And just because I didn't go through with the stupid wedding. I can't believe that you could be so childishly vengeful. You're a dirty bastard, Arthur Cummins, and I'm glad I didn't marry you!'

She grabbed the flipchart's tripod and dragged it towards the door. It overturned and the heavy ream of paper swung forward. The three legs of the stand splayed, each in a different direction, resisting all efforts to remove it from the apartment. It reminded me of a cat at the vet's resisting eviction from a cardboard box. Hilary eventually lost patience with the thing and swung a kick at it, missing completely and stubbing her toe against the coffee table.

It was probably not the best moment for Tom to choose to arrive at the apartment, but my old friend was not known for his timing. His arrival was heralded by a shriek from the buzzer and his voice squawking on the intercom: *'Jaysus, Arthur! Did you see they've busted that fucker Fenton, the actual actuary?'*

I glanced at Hilary who was now sitting on the floor, nursing her wounded toe and muttering tearfully incoherent imprecations at me, *'Bastard! Fuck! Bollox! Buggering motherfucker!'*

'*Em* ... Tom, Hilary's here. Will I buzz you up to join us?'

'Hi there, Hilary!' came the voice on the squawk-box. *'Sorry about your brother getting caught!'*

She staggered to her feet, limping badly, and hauled the semi-erect tripod towards to door in an effort to escape before Tom arrived. She was in a fully frothed fury now, red-eyed, tears and snot streaming, all of a tremble, uttering little whimpers of rage as she fought the flipchart. Cautiously, I navigated around her to let Tom in, and he and I watched in silence as Hilary sought to impose her will on the uncooperative metal stand. She shook it, she twisted its telescopic legs, she banged it on the floor, she cursed it with explosive expletives, but it remained obdurate. Short of biting it, it was hard to see what else she could do to persuade the thing to fold up. Eventually, showing admirable improvisational skills, she opened the window and threw the easel out. The wind took it, causing its A1 pages to flutter like a giant white bird as it fell to the ground. For a moment I thought that she, herself, might jump out after it, but instead she chose to storm out the door, limping and swearing, slamming it behind her with a vehemence that was bound to cause complaints to the management company.

I walked to the window and closed it, giving a glance below to catch Hilary hauling the flipchart across the grass verge towards her car, ploughing a neat furrow through the lawn. I was tempted to linger to see how she was going to stow it, but I thought that it might seem intrusive in the circumstances.

'So, I guess it's off again, then,' said Tom, his eyebrows maintaining a perfectly straight line. As if to underline the permanence of our parting, when I next tried to use our joint account, I found that Hilary had blocked it, rather spitefully shutting away what little money I had.

<hr />

The headlines the next day were rather wonderful: 'MINOTAUR ALL BULL' proclaimed one, displaying a remarkable degree of classical literacy, 'MILLIONS LOST IN A MAZE' yelled another. There were photographs of the figure being led away under a tent of waxed cotton coat. This was the Irish equivalent of the USA walk of shame. I wondered if it was going to be possible to give this villainous fraudster a fair trial. It seemed that the Financial Regulator had been alerted to irregularities but hadn't managed to stir from its torpor to regulate – until now, when it was too late to recover the lost millions. Officiously checking security on the stable door long after the horse had departed.

'Did you hear they're burying your friend William O'Grady on Friday?' said Tom.

'I guess I should go to that. Do you want to come? It feels sort of appropriate.'

'Yeah, time to touch base with our friends in the parish. And your other friend, Garda Bluett, will be there as well. Don't the investigating police always attend the funeral of the victim in case a suspect does something damning? You'd better watch your Ps and Qs, buddy.' The eyebrows gave a sceptical tilt.

14

The filthy weather, that had made a misery of what was to have been my wedding day and most of the following week, lifted its soggy veils for a moment and allowed the sun to shine on the funeral service for the body I had found in the church. Tom and I travelled together and arrived at the church early.

Reverend Karen, looking comely in her robe, like a Shakespearean boy player, took the service. The undertaker, a tall appropriately cadaverous man, stood just inside the porch, showing mourners where to sign the book of condolences. I wrote, '*Sorry*' beside my signature. I still felt bad about the unceremonious way in which I had manhandled the dead man's body into the crypt. Reciprocally, it crossed my mind that he might have thought, were he not dead, to apologise to me for hijacking my wedding, but insofar as he had done me a favour in that respect, I didn't hold his silence against him. My eyes met the eyes of the undertaker as he handed me my copy of the order of service. He wore his professional air of mourning around him like a shroud. I wondered how many murder victims he had buried.

Tom followed me into the church, and we sidled into a pew towards the back. It was as if my wedding day had been a very catastrophic dress rehearsal for this day. There were the flowers, the candles, the church officers and the dead body. Only this time he was properly boxed, whereas he had been less salubriously parcelled when last I had encountered him.

The organist was doodling a sort of generic sacred tune which seemed to have no beginning, no middle and no end. *Amen.* I was surprised to see Geoffrey Quayley in the congregation. I would have expected him to be up in the loft, serenading the mourners. He looked unwell. Maybe that was why another organist was laying down the chords on the organ that morning.

Hilary and her parents were absent. Bearing everything in mind, this wasn't surprising. But I thought it was slightly cowardly in a way. Face the music and all that.

Tom nudged me in the ribs, which caused me to grunt with pain. 'There's the gorgeous girlie Garda.' He tilted his head and the eyebrows pointed in the direction of Francine Bluett and her sergeant who had taken up a discreet position at the back just opposite from where Tom and I were seated. I smiled at her and was rewarded with a guarded sideways glance and a slight nod.

Tom said, 'Jesus, you're well away there, bud.'

There were two men standing in the side aisle wearing navy-blue Crombie overcoats that looked as if they had been put on them for purposes of restraint. One had his hands in the pockets of his coat, the other had his hands joined in front of him, holding a bowler hat. He had a shaven head and a tattoo on his hand. A swallow, or was it a fly? He was staring straight at me.

'Don't look now, Tom, but do you see the two big lads over to the left by the baptismal font?'

'What's a baptismal font?'

I wasn't sure if he was winding me up. 'Ah, Tom, don't make me point' – my whisper was slightly exasperated – 'they're over to the left, standing. D'you see them?'

'What about them?'

'I think they're the boys that did me over the other night.'

Before I could stop him, Tom had taken out his phone and had taken a photo of the two men under the pretence of switching it off. They seemed to have been taken in by this pretence – at least they didn't react. I felt my phone burp in my pocket. Tom had sent me the picture. 'Send it to your sweetheart,' he muttered.

There was a strange feeling of home about the Kilmurray parish church although I was not of that parish and only a very sketchy Christian. But I had been through a lot within the walls of that little disestablished place of worship, albeit in a very short space of time. I also felt a strange sort of bond with the dead man.

Listening to the eulogy, delivered by a fellow gay activist and civil rights campaigner, I was impressed by William O'Grady's unrelenting passion and crusade for parity. A gay friend had once described me as being straight to the point of

116

tedium. I wondered if it was very un-woke of me to think that a person might be tediously gay. The murder victim, in his whole-life battle against prejudice had, it seems, become very bitter. Although his eulogist did what he could to paint a rosy picture, from what I could gather from the sub-text, the late Mr. O'Grady hadn't been very loveable.

After the service, the coffin was carried out by six pallbearers. Two of them were the burly guys in the overcoats. The organist played a processional piece. I thought I recognised it as Bach. It was full of the complicated curlicues and mathematical convolutions symptomatic of the great composer. As we shuffled towards the door, I saw the visiting organist coming down the stairs from the gallery. He was a youngish man about my own age and was carrying an old-fashioned music case, a satchel with a metal bar. We were both caught in the congregational congestion for a moment.

'Lovely music, thank you,' I offered. 'Did you have any difficulty cranking up the organ? I believe it's a bit temperamental first thing in the morning.'

He laughed. 'Thank you. No. It's simple. All electric. You just switch it on and play. No problems.'

I had only asked about the organ by way of conversation as we shuffled our way out of the church behind the mourners. This casually delivered slice of information now cast doubt on Geoff Quayley's explanation for his presence in the organ loft on the morning of the cancelled wedding. I couldn't immediately work out how this affected the whole sequence of events, but it seemed now to confirm that he was hiding something. Hadn't Reverend Karen offered Geoff as her alibi? Was that her lie to cover both of them? Could gentle Geoff have bludgeoned his former lover to death?

Tom and I slid away as soon as we decently could. I didn't want to tangle with Sergeant Bowring or anyone else connected with the murder, although I did pause to forward Tom's photo of the two men in overcoats to Francine, with a message to the effect that I thought they might have been my visitors.

I dropped Tom off at the DART and went home. By way of habit, I tried the underground car park. It was like scratching a patch of eczema. And of course there was another car in my space, some behemoth SUV, a Range Rover or something. Resigned, with a sprinkling of reflexive anger, I parked my car under the open sky and made my way to my apartment.

As soon as I opened my door, I felt that there was someone else in the flat. It's not a big space and it doesn't take enormous perception to feel the presence of another in the normally inert ambience of my home. Hilary still had a key, I couldn't bring myself to reclaim it, bearing in mind her tempestuous state of mind at the end of our last meeting, but I quickly discounted her as a possible visitor. And nobody else had a key.

I froze with my mouth open, like a howler monkey freshly darted with curare. My intruder was standing still too, evidently making every effort to be invisible, but I could hear his breathing.

'*Hello?*' I tried. '*Who's there?*' I was ashamed of the wobble in my voice.

My intruder stepped out of the kitchen, a big man carrying a shotgun.

Oh, sweet Jesus, I thought, this is the Gizzard Man come for his pound of flesh.

I felt my bowels loosen, and in a frantic bid to maintain some self-respect, with no thought for my safety I made a dive for the bathroom, making it just in time to save myself and my undergarments from disgrace. As I sat there with my trousers around my ankles, I heard a voice coming through the door.

'Hi, Arthur. You had me worried there! I might have shot you – you shouldn't have made that sudden move.'

I recognised the voice. Alan Fenton. He must have got the key from Hilary. It was his car wedged into my parking space. His preposterous hubris oozed under the door of the bathroom. Did it not occur to him that he had no business lurking in my apartment with a shotgun and that I was entitled to move however I liked in my own house? But there was no point in making any effort to deflate his idiot ego, so I let it go.

As I emerged, unexpectedly purged but with my dignity intact, I found myself facing him in the sitting room.

'Alan, what in the name of Christ are you doing here? I thought you were in gaol. I saw them leading you away with your coat over you.'

'Not me, old man. That was my money-laundering reporting officer. Decent skin called Flaherty, I think. No point me being there in person for the shit-storm. He'll have to take the heat for the moment.'

'Would you mind putting the gun down, Alan. It might go off.'

He looked down at the gun as if it had been thrust into his hands unexpectedly. He had been pointing it at the ceiling, now he brought it down, bringing me suddenly into range and causing my hands to rise in a reflex of protest and possible surrender. For a green wellie type, Alan Fenton was horrifyingly casual with a shotgun.

'What are you doing in my flat, Alan? If you don't mind my asking. And why are you waving that bloody gun around?' By this time, he had opened the gun and had ejected the cartridges. I felt my heartbeat return to something like normal.

'Need somewhere to lie low, old boy. Couldn't go to the old dears' house. Inappropriate and obvious. Thought no one would think I'd be here, so here I am.'

'On the run from the law?'

'*Au contraire*, old chap. Dodging the bad boys. I'd been doing some business for the Quinlan group, and they're a bit upset that their investment has gone west.'

'Are you kidding? Money-laundering for organised gangsters?'

'I wouldn't put it quite like that, Arthur, old chum. Just putting a better face on the origins of some funds.' He looked like he believed that he was totally innocent of any wrongdoing. 'They said they could tolerate a shrinkage of up to 20%. Problem is that the markets turned against me, and the shrinkage was, like, total.' He put the opened gun on the coffee table and the cartridges in his pocket.

He was wearing what I took to be some sort of shooting

jacket. It looked as if he had dressed for the occasion. It had several pouch-pockets that bulged.

'What happened your face, by the way? Been in the ring?' he asked.

'Don't pretend you don't know. Your two heavies gave me a broken nose. Put me in hospital.'

'Not my men, old boy. Not my style. Sounds more like my clients. The Quinlans made me take on two of their lads when I took on their investment. Wanted them to keep an eye on me. Nice lads, actually, but I didn't set them on you, I swear.'

It was as if someone had let most of the air out of him. All the strut and bumptiousness was gone. His ego had shrunk more or less to the size of that of a normal human. He needed a shave, and he could have done with a shower. But even in his depleted state, cornered and caught, I could feel no sympathy for the man.

'Well, I can't sleep on the sofa. It's too small for me. I'll have the bed and you can sleep on the couch.'

'Hang on there, Alan. You're not invited for a sleepover. I need you out of here.'

He was standing in the doorway of the bedroom, showing no signs of wanting to leave. He was behaving as if I was the guest and he was the host, relaxed and in charge. He reminded me of his sister, without any of her redeeming sexiness.

My house-guest was a big man, a good six foot four in his socks, which, by the way were smelling powerfully, he having taken his shoes off for the sake of quiet. I couldn't think of any way of getting him out of there. He had taken up residence like a hermit crab.

'Sorry, old man, can't leave you, I'm afraid. Not till I can find appropriate alternative accommodation. Probably abroad. I'm thinking of Malaga. Where do you keep your laptop?'

He wasn't asking if he could use my computer, he was asserting his self-appointed right to use it.

'What do you want it for?' I was thinking that the police might add harbouring a known criminal and aiding and abetting to the list of my crimes. Sergeant Bowring would be ecstatic.

'Stop faffing around and just give it to me, OK?' He was so used to asserting his dominance that he expected me to roll over.

I did.

'What's the password?' He was now seated at the dining table making everything around him look small. His giant fingers looked outsized and uncomfortable on the keyboard. I hesitated. My password was something I would never ordinarily share with anyone, not even my best friend. Besides, it was personal, and I certainly didn't want to disclose it to this troglodyte bully.

'Come on, I'm waiting!' He held up his hand, palm upwards and wiggled his sausage fingers by way of a hurry-up.

'Alan, just back up there a bit, will you? You've more or less broken into my flat, you've waved a gun at me, you've told me that you're taking over my bedroom, and now you want me to give me the passcode for my laptop! There's a limit, you know?'

'And your point is?' His face was a perfect blank. He really didn't see anything wrong in any part of this catalogue of social crimes. 'Just tell me your bloody password. You can change it afterwards. Stop being a such a silly fucking virgin, for God's sake!' He was standing now, menacing me by his sheer presence.

I suppose I could have held out. I could have refused. But there was nothing on my laptop that was worth risking another beating, and I strongly believed that Fenton would beat the password out of me if I demurred. I decided to swallow my pride.

'It's Francine (capital F), hashtag, one (figure), exclamation mark.'

He sat again but was still staring at me blankly, his early-hominid-like brow furrowed. 'Key it in.' This came as a command rather than a request.

I bent over the computer and tapped in 'Francine#1!'

To my surprise he didn't seem to take in this point of weakness, this jeer-worthy personal detail, this hostage that could be used as a bullying tool. He just dived into the internet to browse his social media to check, I assume, what was being said about him. I stayed aloof, having no desire to become privy to his world except in a broad sense. He reacted with oaths and shouts of outrage to what he found. It was clear that his empire of 'fungible intangibles' (his expression – I had to look it up) had crumbled completely and everyone had turned against him. It was also clear that he was surprised by this and in complete denial as to any wrongdoing. Possibly, he felt the same way about the killing of William O'Grady.

'Listen,' he said, straight-faced and unblushing, 'why don't you slip out to the supermarket and buy me something to eat? Steak would be good. I like mine blue. Just wipe the cow's arse and walk it through a warm kitchen, eh?' He ground out this ancient saw as if he expected a guffaw and a round of applause for his original wit. 'Do you need money for the shopping?' He pulled a fat roll of notes from one of the pockets of his jacket and stuffed three fifties into the breast pocket of my shirt.

I felt like a hooker being paid in advance for some brutal and demeaning act.

'That should cover it. By the way, calling the cops wouldn't be a good idea. Remember I've got my old pal Purdey with me.' He slapped the stock of his huge side-by-side beside him. 'Oh, and leave your phone with me, all right?'

I left the apartment feeling violated. I drove to my nearest supermarket and bought two steaks, a bag of frozen oven chips and a bottle of red. I stopped short of buying flowers. Then I drove to the Garda station and asked for Garda Bluett.

'Can we talk?'

'Yes, but it'll be on the record, OK?'

'Doesn't matter. Alan Fenton's holed up in my apartment. He has this huge great shotgun with him.' I explained how Fenton had been in the flat when I arrived home.

'What does he want?'

'A rare steak and some red wine,' I said, showing her the Supervalu bag containing the necessary groceries.

'I'll have to stop you there, Arthur.'

'Why, Francine, what's the matter?'

'Nothing, Arthur. I just have to stop you.' There was a pause while she gathered herself to formulate her next question. 'What's Alan Fenton doing in your apartment?'

She was speaking with the same slow-but-firm tone that might be used when speaking to a mentally impaired person or someone who doesn't speak English. I sensed that the next level upward would be shouting.

'I don't really know, Francine, but he's afraid of the Quinlans and reckons they won't look for him at my apartment.'

'How come he let you go? Did he not think you might tell us?'

'I'm not sure he's thinking at all. He wouldn't be great at that. He's taken my phone as a hostage. He seems to believe that the Minotaur train wreck had nothing to do with him. He thinks he was entitled to steal all the money entrusted to him. I'm not sure he's all there, to be honest.'

The Garda Armed Response Unit must have already been on their toes because they were mobilised within fifteen minutes of Francine's alert. Bray being Bray, I suppose it's possible that they have a team on permanent standby like a Lifeboat crew waiting for the maroon to go up. Perhaps I underestimated the combined effect of a murder, a huge fraud and a gangland assault on a member of the public (me) to ginger up the agents of law enforcement. It was nice to know that my case was being taken seriously. It was a pity that my Garda-of-choice didn't seem disposed to take me with corresponding seriousness on a personal level.

By arrangement, I was to approach the apartment block first, with the armed Gardaí as back-up, all squashed into an unmarked white Ford Transit in the open-air car park.

I parked my car, leaving all the windows open a crack to see if that would stop or at least slow up the propagation of mushrooms on the floormats. Francine had given me a Garda cell phone which had been set up as a one-way walkie-talkie, so that the Guards could hear what was happening in the vicinity of the phone without anyone else necessarily knowing about it.

After all the frenetic gathering of the troops and the sight of the terrifying array of deadly hardware in the hands of the Response Unit, I found myself very nervous on approaching the front door of the apartment block, armed only with the makings of a steak dinner for two. I let myself into the building and climbed the stairs. All seemed alarmingly normal in my corridor. I was the only one that was out of the ordinary – unarmed ahead of an armed police raid.

I knocked on my own door, feeling self-conscious. There was no response. I knocked louder. Still nothing.

'*Alan?*' I called, close to the door. I knocked a third time, this time quite loudly. There were strict management company rules about causing any disturbance on the premises, so I approached the shouting thing with my foot on the soft pedal. Still no response. I called his name louder. Nothing.

I pulled out the Garda phone and put it to my lips. 'There's no answer. I'm going in,' I said as I put my key in the lock, thinking I sounded like a phoney version of a hero in a TV police drama.

Alan Fenton was lying full length on his back on the bathroom floor. Actually, his feet overflowed into the hallway, in his enormous brown brogues. There was blood and other matter all over the tiles and the walls and a splattering on the ceiling for good measure. The shotgun was lying beside him, the muzzle facing what had been his head. The air was thick with the stench of violent death.

I dashed to the kitchen and evicted the contents of my stomach into the sink.

Then I put on my rubber gloves and did a quick rummage in the still-warm pouch pockets of Fenton's jacket. The rolls of notes were mainly five-hundreds. A lot of them.

'Francine?' I called into the phone, 'Oh, sweet Jesus, Francine. The poor bugger's dead!'

15

My immediate problem was that I had nowhere to stay that night. My apartment had been declared off limits. It had been cordoned off with Garda tape, and a uniformed member of the force was stationed at the door to prevent, I guess, me from entering. It didn't matter – I didn't want to go back in there anyway. The shotgun blast had turned my bathroom into a chamber of horrors.

I wondered if, when the tape was taken down, I would be expected to clean up the carnage with the bucket and sponge from under my sink, on my hands and knees washing away the congealed mess of blood, bone and brains? Or was there a clean-up unit in the Gardaí? Or did they employ a special bloody bucket-and-mop contractor? I tried to remember if there was anything in my lease which prohibited permitting guests to blow their heads to pieces on the premises. Then I began to wonder if I wasn't going just a little mad.

I dragged my punch-drunk concentration back to the problem in hand. Where was I going to stay, now that I was homeless? And I had no access to money since Hilary had blocked our joint account. So, now I had no means of paying for a hotel. I wasn't taking into account the bundles of notes I had looted from Alan Fenton's body. I couldn't pay for a hotel room with a five-hundred euro note; it would have drawn attention.

Before everything went pear-shaped with Hilary, I would have been able to stay at her parents' house, but now that I was probably being held responsible for fouling the wedding, causing the collapse of Alan's business, bringing odium to his family and, ultimately, for his death, I guessed that I would be persona-non-whatever in that household. I made a mental note to message Hilary with my condolences in the morning, knowing that in my distracted state I was very likely to forget. My hands were shaking uncontrollably.

I did a quick audit of my current state of trauma. In the space of what was supposed to be part of my honeymoon, my bride-to-be had bolted, I had come upon two massacred corpses and I'd had my nose gratuitously broken by two strangers. No wonder, I told myself, I was a bit jittery. When I tried to focus my concentration on my homeless predicament, my mind would offer me a rerun of the state of the man on the floor of the church, interspersed with vivid hallucinations of Fenton's brains on the ceiling of my bathroom. My heart-rate would suddenly kick into panic mode, leaving me gulping for air like a newly landed salmon – though I suppose a fish would be gulping for water?

With considerable effort, I swatted away the intrusive visions of bloody mayhem (and fish) and pondered on my immediate difficulties. If Hilary's was out of the question, then what about Tom's? I had seen Tom's place, in behind the pizza place by Bray railway station. Fond as I am of Tom, his gaff wasn't suitable. I'm not at all picky about where I billet but trust me when I say that it just wasn't suitable. For anything. It would have seemed churlish to mention my predicament to Tom and then to spurn his malodourous slightly sticky couch. So, it looked as if my car was going to be my boudoir, for this night at any rate. I sat in the driver's seat and contemplated spending the night in it. It was like sitting in a Petrie dish with fungal cultures spawning all around me. It was going to be a long and miserable night. I had no sleeping bag nor anything else to keep out the cold. I had less than a quarter of a tank of fuel. I couldn't keep the engine running to work the heater. Anyway, wasn't that supposed to kill you with carbon monoxide?

Maybe I was being a little naïve when I texted Francine from my mouldy car: 'I don't suppose I could crash at your place tonight?'

I sat for a further hour in the car in the rain with the windows so misted that droplets were running down the inside, keeping pace with the droplets running down the outside. I was listening to the radio and dozing when the migratory geese in my phone kicked off, causing me to jump. My screen said it was Francine. My heart jumped again.

I picked up.

'Arthur, don't be a gobshite, there's a good man. Of course you can't stay at my place. And if you want to avoid a world of misery, I suggest that you come to the station right away.

OK? You'll be comfortable enough here for the night and you'll get a cooked breakfast.'

'You're pulling me in again, aren't you? What for, in the name of God?'

'The suspected murder of Alan Fenton.'

It was like being kicked again in my cracked ribs. Resisting the impulse to say 'What?', I paused while I took in what she had just said.

'Is this Sergeant Bowring's idea?'

'Afraid so. You were the last person to see Fenton alive. The sergeant reckons you overpowered Fenton and blew his head off. You didn't need a motive for killing William O'Grady, and you don't need a motive for this murder either. End of.'

'What if I don't come in?'

'Like I said, you'll find yourself in a world of nastiness. Evading arrest, obstructing a Garda enquiry, not co-operating with the Gardaí in the course of their enquiries, harbouring a known criminal, illegal possession of a firearm ... I could go on. Just come in and we'll give you a nice cup of tea. You've had a bad shock.'

Francine's tone had ranged from harsh rebuff of my accommodation suggestion, to frustration at her sergeant's obstinacy, to formal robotic litany of my possible offences and finally to something approaching warmth. I was in bad need of some sort of reassurance that the world hadn't gone completely mad. I grasped the wisp of kindness with both metaphorical hands.

'OK. I'm coming in,' I said, the melodrama of the words ringing in my ears.

'Good – and, by the way, the two lads in the photo you sent me from William O'Grady's funeral are freelance enforcers that the Quinlans use. What the hell are you doing with the Quinlans?'

'You know as much as I do, Francine,' I lied.

What were those guys doing as pallbearers at Willie O'Grady's funeral? Was that a further threat to me? Or a reminder of some sort?

The Garda at the desk greeted me like an old friend. 'How's it goin' there, Arthur? You'll be after Detective Garda Bluett, yes? Just take a seat in the interview room and she'll be with you shortly.'

'I wonder if I could have a cup of tea, please, Guard?'

He stared at me as if I had just run over his cat. There was a pause that was like the silence after a bag of cement is dropped into a stairwell and all ears on all floors strain to hear the consequent thump when it hits the bottom. This spell was broken by the shrill ring of the desk telephone. The Garda picked it up.

'Bray Garda Station, how can I help you? [*Yammering on the phone*] Yes, ma'am, that's illegal all right. [*More yammering*] No, ma'am, I can't send out a car to arrest the man. [*Yammer*] Because it may be against the law, but it's not something we can arrest someone for. [*The yammering went up a pitch*] Because if we went around arresting everyone for that sort of thing, all the jails would be full. [*Yammer, yammer, yammer*] Well, you go ahead and write to the Minister for Justice, ma'am, and be sure to give her my very best. Goodnight to you, now, ma'am.'

He carefully put the receiver down and regarded me blankly, as if trying to place me, having returned from a land far away. The fog of incomprehension cleared and he said, 'I'll let Garda Bluett know that you're here, Arthur. Just take a seat in the interview room, please. You know your way around, don't you?' There was no reference to the cup of tea.

I wandered into the interview room with its harsh fluorescent lighting and indestructible furniture. I sat on the now familiar chair at the battered and scarred table. It wasn't hard to imagine the generations of people who had taken a turn at helping the Gardaí with their enquiries in this room, at this table, on this chair. There were cigarette burns on the edges of the table and various initials inscribed in the woodwork. I wondered who would be so keen to make their mark that they would carve it on police furniture. Someone desperate, I supposed. I began to shiver. Not because I was cold, not because I had a fever, but because the accumulated shock was playing havoc with my nervous system.

When Francine Bluett came into the room, I realised that I was sobbing uncontrollably.

'Arthur? Are you OK?'

What the hell did she think? I snuffled back the stream of mucus and wiped my nose on my sleeve in a complete abandonment of dignity and lied, 'Yeah, Francine. I'm just fine, thanks for asking.' I blew my nose. My handkerchief fluttered in my trembling hand like a flag of surrender.

I stood impulsively and saw her draw back in anticipation of violence. But I had no violent intent, I simply needed to make a physical movement to short out some of the appalling nervous energy that was coursing through me.

'Sorry. Didn't mean to startle you, there. I just …' Then I saw that she had brought a paper cup of tea and had placed it on the table. 'Thanks for the tea … kind.' I tried to pick it up, but my hands were shaking too much. After two attempts to lift the cup off the table, with my hands flapping like birds around a feeder, I gave up.

'Do you need a doctor, Arthur?'

'To be honest, I don't know what I need, Francine,' I said, surveying the pool of milky tea that now surrounded the paper cup.

'As it happens, he's in right now, taking blood from a drunk driver. I'll get him to have a look at you. He might be able to give you something.'

The doctor looked like a retired butcher, big red face and hands like hams. Francine withdrew on his arrival.

'Had a bit of a shock, have we, *eh*?' he asked 'us', while rooting in his bag for something. He pulled out a succession of little tubs of tablets, examined the labels through the glasses he kept perched on the end of his potato-like nose, rejecting them in sequence, storing them in the pockets of his tweed jacket and searching again in the depths of his bag. All the while he was humming the opening riff of Eric Clapton's 'Cocaine'. Finally, with a flourish, he produced a little white phial of pills and shook it like a maraca, while singing, '*Cocaine! Da-Da-Da-Da-Da – da-Daa! Da-Da-Da-Da-Da – da-da-Daa! Do-Ba-Die-Do-Ba-Die-Do-Ba-Die – Cocaine! Da-*

Da-Da-Da–' He must have seen my askance stare, because he broke off in mid-riff. 'Not entirely appropriate, I know.' He shrugged. 'Well, if you don't like my singing, sue me.' He sat opposite me at the table and scanned me with his rather bloodshot eyes. 'You're suffering from post-traumatic stress, young man.' He held up his hand indicating that I should stop, even though I hadn't started. 'Please don't tell me what it was that upset you, because then I'll have to go around with your visions in my head, which is no use to anyone, is it? I'm going to give you some Valium, which will dull the edge of your jitters, OK? One in the evenings before food. If you're still jumpy after a few days, check with your GP – you may need therapy.'

He paused and ran his hand over his face. I could hear the abrasion of bristle on his hand.

'The cops and the other first responders get this a lot,' he went on. 'It's a bastard, and we medics don't have all the answers, I'm afraid. Exercise is good. If you get very uptight, talk to someone; eat well; go easy on the drink and drugs; be patient. A patient patient. That's about it. Goodnight.' And he was gone, leaving me with the phial of pills.

I swallowed two, just to be on the safe side, washing them down with the now cold tea, holding the cup in both hands. I had reasoned that the tremor in my hands was unlikely to be the same in both of them, so if one hand is twitching in one direction, the other might be convulsing in the opposite direction and the two spasms might cancel each other out. It sort of worked.

By the time Francine returned, the Valium was beginning to kick in and I was enjoying the calming effect. But she brought Sergeant Bowring with her, which wrecked my buzz.

'Mr. Cummins! We meet again!' He plonked a file on the table and dragged a chair over, the legs giving out a screeching protest.

It was clear that he hadn't found time to wash since our last interview. There was a familiar pervasive bang of armpits and aftershave about him that infected his vicinity and caused me to flinch.

'So, you've found another dead body, I see,' he said, opening the file and examining the photographs of William O'Grady and the more recent ones of Alan Fenton. 'Do you intend to make a habit of this, Mr. Cummins?'

I reckoned that he didn't require an answer.

'What was Alan Fenton doing in your apartment, Arthur?' asked Garda Bluett, now seated beside Bowring.

'He was hiding.'

'Some sort of degenerate game, was it? A boys' romp? Slap and tickle in the bathroom?' Bowring was snarling at me. Flecks of white spittle gathered in the corners of his mouth. His breath smelled of ancient cigarette smoke and malfunctioning septic tank.

'Hiding from the Quinlans,' I expanded.

'And where did you get the shotgun, Mr. Cummins? You have no licence.'

'He had it with him. It must be his.'

'So, you were sheltering an armed, wanted criminal. That's a criminal offence, you know.'

'I think, for it to be a crime, I'd have to have at least invited him in. He was uninvited and unwanted.'

'And now we're some sort of barrack-room lawyer, is that it? I think you lured the poor eejit to your flat and blew his brains out. We know you paid a visit to his office just before we raided it. Why were you there?'

'If you are going to charge me, you should say so. I think I should be cautioned and I should be allowed to have a solicitor with me when I'm interviewed.'

'Are you telling me how to do my job now? You're a jumped-up pup, so you are, Cummins. *Scum.* You've nothing to offer except cleverality and smart-aleckry. Well, I'm having none of it! You're not fooling anyone except yourself with your lies and nonsense. You've killed two people already, and I'm going to see to it that you're locked up before you do any more damage.'

'How do you think I could have killed Alan Fenton, Sergeant?'

'Don't be acting the fool with me, Cummins. You know well you shot him point-blank with the shotgun.'

'But Fenton's a very big man. I'm not.'

'*You shot him, then came here to spin a fairy story to Garda Bluett and call out the Armed Response Unit on a wild goose chase!*' Bowring was shouting now and his colour was darkening.

The Valium was helping me to stay very calm. 'Look, Sergeant, the gun was Fenton's. He arrived with it. I'll bet you anything you like that he has a licence for it. To shoot him I'd have had to overpower him and take it from him. Can I ask you if there was any sign of a struggle in the apartment?'

Bowring seemed to concentrate on the file for a moment, saying nothing.

'If the answer isn't in your file, Sergeant, I can fill you in. There was no fight, no struggle, because it was his gun, I didn't take it off him and I didn't shoot him. Now if you're not going to charge me, I'd like to be left in peace, if you don't mind.'

My relationship with Sergeant Bowring was never going to be friendly. He stood, his paunch thrust out manfully before him and his hands reflexively attempting to recapture his shirt in its act of escaping from his trousers. He looked as if he was literally pulling himself together. He was very angry.

He wagged a stubby finger at me. 'Think you're smart, do you? Mr. Know-It-All Cummins. Well, you're in for a queer shock, my man, when I catch up to you. I can tell you that!' And abandoning his file, he stumped from the room, leaving the door wide open.

In my seething state of shock, overlayered with a sort of icing of tranquiliser, my crush on Francine was almost too much to bear. I could feel the tears tingling on my eyelids and my breath tightening again into a sob.

Francine stood up. 'Come on, I'll show you where you're sleeping tonight.'

She led me to the cells and showed me into the first of four tiny rooms on a narrow corridor. There was a bed with a plastic-covered mattress, a couple of blankets and a pillow marked with sinister stains. An uncloseted toilet stood unashamed by a handbasin. The unwholesome reek of Jeyes Fluid was everywhere.

'Make yourself at home, Arthur. I'll look in on you in the morning.'

'Francine? Am I under arrest?'

'Not at all, you're just sleeping here for the night. You can have the door open if you like. It's not locked.' After she had gone, I shut the door. I needed the reassurance of confinement. I made up a rough bed, lay down and allowed the drug to pull me down into a troubled sleep.

16

There was a small canteen at the Garda station, where I enjoyed bacon and eggs and baked beans for breakfast. It seemed that Garda tea was served strong and bitter. It tasted wonderful.

Gardaí in plainclothes and uniform drifted in and out of the canteen, all going about their breakfast and each eyeing me with the interest of visitors at a zoo. I overheard a male officer remark to a colleague, 'There's Frankie Bluetit's fancy man at his breakfast.' I thought I'd keep that one to myself.

As I was finishing my last slice of toast there was a sudden kerfuffle with accompanying grunts and swearing in the passage outside the canteen. Two Garda officers were dragging a chap along to the cells. He didn't want to go there. It wasn't a game, not a staged wrestling match for the TV, it was real-time live violence. I caught just a sort of peepshow glimpse of it through the open doorway. A tidal wave of jitters arose in me, nearly bringing my breakfast up with it. I glanced around the canteen, where ordinary morning life continued, wholly unaffected by the hand-to-hand struggle in the passageway. An arm twisted, a kick swung, hair pulled, faces contorted with effort, spittle and snot. Shouting. All this soon passed out of view as the Guards overcame the frenzied resistance of their prisoner. I wondered why the man bothered resisting. Why did he bother calling the Guards all those names? He must have known that it was all for nothing. The only audience for the performance was the uncaring Garda presence in the canteen. Maybe the man wanted to maintain a reputation for being a hard man? But judging by the names that he was called by the two officers, they didn't think much of him, for all his hard-man efforts. And the buzz of easy conversation in the canteen never registered the passing violence. It didn't even qualify as a side-show. Every day, I told myself, every day, these people must witness aggression on a scale unknown to ordinary people. Their bland, seemingly inhuman indifference to it left me trembling with panic.

Francine, in mufti and looking lovelier than ever, joined me and sat sipping a mug of coffee. I had enjoyed torrid dreams of breakfasting with Francine but, as usual with my life story, the reality of the cramped canteen at Bray Garda station with the undertow of violence was very far from the dream.

'We got confirmation that the shotgun is Fenton's own gun,' she said. 'It's licensed in his name.' She was observing me over her coffee.

I made no response. I had assumed that it was his gun. I suppose the Gardaí just don't think in assumptions.

'D'you think Alan Fenton killed himself, though, Arthur?'

'I hardly know the man. I never liked him. He must have

had some sort of conscience about ripping off all those investors. He'd just lost his business and was facing prison. But when I last spoke to him, he seemed to be fine. No remorse, no sense of guilt. His only concern was to stay out of the way of the Quinlan gang and have a rare steak. I'm no psychiatrist, but he didn't seem suicidal to me.'

'Was he wearing his shoes?'

'What?' I couldn't see the point of this odd question.

Francine leaned over the table, holding her coffee mug in both hands as she repeated the question, 'When you saw him dead on the floor, was he wearing his shoes?'

I had to force myself to picture again the awful scene of the bloody remains of Fenton lying on the floor of my bathroom, most of his head missing and his feet out the door. I remembered his gigantic brogues protruding into the hallway.

'Actually, he was. He'd been in his socks when I left, but he had his shoes on again when I found him.'

'Thing is, it's very hard to commit suicide with a full-length shotgun,' she said in a matter-of-fact tone. 'We had to do a module on forensic pathology as part of our training. The barrel of the gun is so long that you have to pull the trigger with your toe. You can't do that with your shoes on.'

The horror of suicide was bad enough to contemplate, but the grisly cold blood needed to take off your shoes, or one shoe anyway, before pointing the business end of a shotgun at your face and carefully reaching for the trigger with your toe before … But it seemed that this was not what Fenton had done. He hadn't killed himself, someone else had done it for him. I reckoned he couldn't have put his shoes on afterwards. Then a chilling thought dawned on me.

'Jesus, Francine, you're spoiling my fry-up now. Don't tell me you think I did it?'

'I'm not saying that. I don't think you have a murder in you, Arthur. But someone did it, and it wasn't Alan Fenton.'

As I was leaving the station, the Garda at the desk bade me a cheery au revoir,

'All the best now, Arthur. See you later.'

This first-name thing and presumption that I'd be back worried me. I gave no reply, just waved my hand in a sort of noncommittal way and stepped out into the early spring sunshine to make my rendezvous with Tom Farrington.

———

Tom was waiting for me in the coffee shop by the aquarium on the esplanade in Bray. This was a bright, open place filled with chatter and the hissing noise of the steam heater in the jug of milk was a low-flying jet. There were mothers with young children and strollers. I feared for their safety when the violence erupted, when the Gardaí came to drag the man away. But there was no man, no violence, this wasn't a place of commonplace aggression. I was superimposing the Garda canteen on the tranquil, untroubled café with its view out along the esplanade to the serene bulk of Bray Head.

'So, a night in the cells, *eh*? How are you doing? You look like shite.'

143

My best-man manqué could always be relied upon to call it as he saw it.

I told him about my evening with Alan Fenton and its grisly ending, including the intelligence that he had probably not killed himself. I left out the bit involving my putting on the rubber gloves.

'It seems I'm suffering from PTSD. The police doctor gave me some tablets.' I showed him my tiny bottle of little calm-pills and told him of the events that led up to my night as a guest of the Gardaí.

'Jesus, pal, no wonder you're a bit shook.' He went off to get coffees and came back in due course with a double espresso for himself and a pale beige affair in a glass with a saucer and spoon for me. 'That's a decaffeinated soya dairy-free latte for you,' he explained, as he saw my lack of enthusiasm. 'You need to go easy on the stimulants, buddy.'

When we were seated outside in the bracing sea-front breeze so that Tom could smoke, I explained my financial situation, stopping short of the Gizzard Man.

'You see, Tom, I put all my money into a joint account in both our names as part of the whole '*With All My Worldly Goods I Thee Endow*' thing. That was dandy right up until Minotaur was busted. After that she told the bank that withdrawals must have both signatures, and she's managed to block my debit card, so I can't get money out of the cash machine either. Now, with Alan's death, I can't very well go to Hilary and say, "Sorry about your brother but could you let me back into my bank account?"'

'Do you have a credit card?'

'No.'

'Every fool has a credit card. Why don't you have one, you gom?'

'It seems like a way of spending money you don't have. I don't trust myself.'

Tom sighed. The eyebrows furrowed in mild exasperation. 'Do you need a loan? I can let you have a few grand until you get this sorted.'

'Where would you get that sort of money, Tom?'

'I have a job, you know, Arthur. There's good money in music production.'

'Is that what you're into now, music production?'

'No, I'm just saying there's money in that business.'

'What *are* you working at right now?'

'Oh, this and that. You know yourself.' The eyebrows took on an evasive tilt.

'But I *don't* know, Tom. I've never known what it is that you do. Are you into computer software or something?'

'Yeah, something like that.' The eyebrows were evasive.

'You're a good pal, Tom. I'll take you up on that loan, please. And I'll pay you back when this nonsense is over.'

Tom grinned at me and shrugged. 'Whenever, it's cool. Now, we need to recap on the investigation.' He took out his phone and poked at it until it produced a photograph of our original Elastoplast notes.

I didn't know that he'd taken the picture. 'When did you …?'

'Just a bit of back-up, that's all.' He tapped the side of his nose and grinned again, his eyebrows arching craftily.

We studied the notes for a moment. It was like catching up with an old friend. Everything on the screen seemed to point at Fenton being the killer, but this theory had been scuttled by his own murder. The old notes also suggested O'Grady as the thief. I mulled over this for a while but got nowhere.

'OK,' I said, sitting back in my seat, 'but surely O'Grady wouldn't be so stupid as to steal the parish money himself? He was parish treasurer, for God's sake – he'd be the obvious suspect. And even if O'Grady stole the money, why would anyone kill him for that?'

'Ah yes, but, you see, Reverend Karen had the pass codes for the accounts.' His tone was infuriatingly patient, as if he was reasoning with a demented parent.

'Are you telling me that the Reverend Karen stole the money?'

'No, I don't think so. But Jennifer told me that Karen keeps all her passwords in a notebook in her desk. If Jennifer knows that, then someone else might know it too. Someone in that inner circle, someone on the parish council or select vestry or mother's union or whatever.' Tom's knowledge of the corridors of power within a Church of Ireland parish was startling. His eyebrows looked wise.

'But, Tom, look at the list of people in our notes. We've ruled out Hilary. I only put her on the list out of spite because she ditched me. Alan Fenton is dead, and anyway he had other ways of stealing money. You seem to think that neither Karen nor Jennifer did it. I don't think Geoff Quayley did it. I didn't do it and neither did you.'

Tom was writing the names on a paper napkin and crossing

them off as we dismissed them. I looked sideways at Tom's list. He had added 'Quinlan Gang' and had not crossed it off. The eyebrows flicked an 'I told you so' at me.

'Why're you frowning like that?' I asked.

'Well, you wouldn't concede that the mafia might have had a hand in the hit on O'Grady, but who busted your nose for sniffing around Fenton's business?'

I let that go. Privately, a renegade stream of logic was suggesting to me that both killings might be the work of the Quinlan organisation. And it was, after all, the murders that Sergeant Bowring was trying to pin on me.

But I was still convinced that the theft of the parish money had to be at the heart of it all. I couldn't see why an organised crime gang would bother pilfering the parish pot. If we could find out who had actually stolen the money, we might possibly discover who had killed O'Grady and Fenton.

'Tom, can we concentrate on the theft of the parish money for a moment? Let me see our notes again.'

He showed me his phone and flicked the paper napkin my way.

I was beginning to get a headache. Despite the kindly drugs given to me by the Eric Clapton fan police doctor, I hadn't slept at all well, and my head was buzzing.

'OK,' I said, 'who needed money enough to steal it?'

The eyebrows considered this line of enquiry for a beat or two, then their proprietor said, 'According to the best TV crime dramas, ordinary honest citizens will steal money only if they need cash to pay a bribe or they're being blackmailed.'

I could think of another reason, but kept quiet.

I wondered if Tom's life experience had been viewed almost entirely through a television screen. I wrote on the napkin, 'BRIBE' and 'BLACKMAIL'.

The notion of a bribe brought us into completely virgin territory. For bribery to fit, there would have to have been at least three illegal acts: theft of the money, payment of the bribe and acceptance of the bribe. My jerky concentration refused to focus on the ramifications of this three-ring circus. I didn't cross bribe off the list, but I decided to look more closely at the possibility of blackmail. If it was the motive for the theft, who were the dancers in this tango?

The money had been stolen from the parish, but the theft hadn't been reported. Why was that? Reverend Karen should be able to answer that question; she was, after all, the boss of the parish.

'Tom, I think we should talk to Karen Quayley again.'

17

The funeral of Alan Fenton was a strange affair. The scattering of embarrassed mourners cowered towards the back of the church, shy of association with the dead man and his family, in case attendance at the funeral might contaminate. A no-man's zone of empty pews isolated his parents and sister from the rest. The normal funereal susurrus was reduced to the odd cough or the knock of a shoe on oakwood. Even the organ's doodling overture was more muted than normal.

The collapse of Fenton's business had attracted a lot of press coverage, so there was a large contingent from the media outside the church, including several news cameras, all ranged just beyond the churchyard wall. Some of the more eager photographers had brought their own stepladders. Every new mourner was greeted by a frenetic *clickety-clack* of camera shutters and the whirring noise of cameras spooling on, sounding like a swarm of man-eating insects preparing to dine. Perhaps the press wanted to observe the defrauded at the funeral of the fraudster to see if they could keep a straight face.

It seemed to me that many of his defrauded clients would be glad to see him dead, although they might have preferred to see him suffering in prison for a longish stretch. I didn't think that many of his victims would be numbered among the mourners. Again, the police were there, represented by Sergeant Bowring and Garda Francine Bluett, discreetly positioned at the back of the little church. Francine was dressed in a tailored black coat that suited her figure well. Hilary and her parents were in the front pews, looking haggard and spent. The coffin was unadorned.

Karen Quayley addressed the congregation.

'Good morning and welcome to Kilmurray parish church. This is another sad day for our parish. It is the second tragic funeral here in the space of a month. We are here today to lay to rest the mortal remains of Alan Fenton, a man who showed much generosity to this parish. Indeed, we have him to thank for the sound system that makes it easy for you to hear me now. We are not here to judge him as the press have recently done. We are here to commend him to his Maker and to offer whatever consolation we can to his parents, family and friends.'

A hollow sob came from the front of the church, and I saw Hilary put her arm around her mother's shoulders.

The choir sang 'Abide With Me'. I assumed that it was Geoff Quayley on the organ. The church, the Reverend Karen, the thought of Geoff in the loft, triggered a sort of double déjà vu which set my nerves on edge. Despite the baffling effect of my last Valium, I found myself trembling.

Tom, who had come with me to the funeral, put his hand on my arm. I jumped and almost stifled my startled cry of '*Jesus!*'

Someone in the congregation responded '*Amen!*'

'Sorry, man. Just checking to see if you're OK,' Tom whispered. 'Need to get out and walk.'

We stood. I heard Tom saying, 'Sorry, my friend isn't feeling well. Excuse me. Sorry. Thank you,' as we created a sort of Mexican wave along the line of the pew. I almost ran to the door, half stumbling, suppressing a whimpering sob of panic as I passed through the vestibule and dived out into the open air.

Tom stayed silent as we paced the gravel together. The crunch of the little pebbles was strangely reassuring. From the corner of my eye, I watched Tom perform his own meditative calming routine of fishing for his packet of cigarettes, flipping the top, pulling out a cigarette and lighting it. These practised movements, performed unselfconsciously, reflexively, automatically by my old friend, were soothing to me also. I could almost feel the satisfaction of his first drag on the smoke.

We continued our pacing until the service was over. The undertakers emerged from the church with the coffin on a trolley and placed it in the waiting hearse. Fenton's poor distraught mother, supported by Mr. Fenton and Hilary on either side, followed the coffin. The husband and daughter were virtually carrying the weeping woman as they turned to face the sympathies of the congregation. For a moment, Tom and I were the only other people outside the church, caught like schoolboys smoking in the yard.

My ex looked worn out and pale, with shadows under her

red-rimmed eyes. She was dressed in black and held a small handkerchief in her gloved hand. I thought she looked beautiful, and I immediately crushed the thought.

I drew a breath, as I imagined a first-time high diver might, stumbled forward and shuffled my way into the queue of condoling mourners, fighting back my desire to dodge away and leave them all to it. What on earth do you say to the parent of a man you didn't like, who has brought disgrace to his clan and has met with a violent and bloody death as a result of it?

'Ah, Arthur,' said the devastated mother of the dead man, as I reached the head of the queue and shook her hand.

There is no word for a mother who has lost a child; that is because the grief is too profound to label. I'm not sure that she really saw me as I looked into her tear-raw eyes set in a wax-pale face. She looked to be near death herself.

'I'm so sorry, Mrs. Fenton. Sorry for your loss.' Trite trash, but what else had I to offer? I couldn't very well say that I was sorry that Alan had lost all the family's savings in the black hole of his failed financial wizardry, or sorry that his sister had cancelled our wedding on the shortest of notice, or sorry that Alan had ended his days in my apartment with his brains spread like strawberry jam all over the ceiling of my bathroom. A mumbled 'sorry for your loss', was the very best I could manage. I was saved from further awkwardness by Tom, who gently eased me to one side and simply took the poor sorrowing lady's hand in both of his. He said nothing, just shook her hand and moved on, nudging me in front of him like a broom pushes dead leaves.

I shook Mr. Fenton's hand too. All the alpha-male strut that Alan had inherited had drained away. He looked spent and lost, just like all his retirement money had been at the hands of the late Alan.

'I'm sorry, Mr. Fenton. Sorry for your loss.'

And I still had to face Hilary.

Tom got there ahead of me. I found Hilary clinging to Tom as if to a lifebuoy, arms around his neck, head buried in his shoulder. The pair were swaying slightly from side to side, almost like dancers in a slow set. I was beset by an unruly and unbefitting pang of jealousy. I put my hand on Hilary's arm.

'My poor Hil,' I said.

Her embrace on Tom loosened for a moment, then her arm went around my shoulders to include me in a threesome huddle. I felt so sorry for the girl. She may have had the organisational skills of a fascist dictator, she may have jilted me rather publicly, but she didn't deserve this level of grief. But there was only so much I had to offer to her now. After a moment or two I began to feel suffocated and superfluous. I gently pulled free.

'Mind yourself, Hil. This has been a bad few days ...'

I allowed my good wishes to trail away unheard. Tom was talking to her now, offering earnest expressions of sympathy and support that I couldn't rise to under the very strained circumstances that existed between me and the stricken girl.

I decided to let my best man do his best and cast around to see if I could spot Karen Quayley. I saw her just as she emerged from the porch, looking handsome in her robe and floaty surplice, her hair cut in a gamine style that suited her bone structure.

'Good morning, Vicar. Another sad one, I'm afraid.'

'Ah, Arthur. Why am I tempted to think that you are the cause of all this sorrow and pain?'

'I'm sure, Reverend, that your Christian charity can still shine through the darkness. Look, I was wondering if I might come around for a chat later today. It's about the money missing from the parish funds.'

She looked startled for a moment, then outrage took over.

'That is none of your business and this is not the appropriate time for discussions about money.'

'Please, Karen. It won't take long.'

She stared at me and then said, 'Very well, six o'clock in the parish office. It's at the back of the … but you could find your way around here blindfold, couldn't you?'

The press were relentlessly scrounging for titbits of newsworthy copy, photographers poking lenses where they shouldn't and reporters with microphones importuning mourners to record their take on the disgrace and death of the once great Alan Fenton.

I saw one crew scrambling to get into the undertakers' black limousine to interview Fenton's parents. Some prick with a microphone and headphones over his hat was shouting, '*Tell us how you feel about your son's death, Mr. Fenton!*' This was too much for Reverend Karen. She launched herself at them.

'*Get away from there, you! Come away from that, you ghouls!*' The word '*ghouls*' was given an added magnificence by her

154

Northern Ireland accent. 'You have no right to disturb the solemnity of a funeral. Let these poor people grieve in private. Move away from the car and let them be!'

While this was going on, I saw Francine and her sergeant emerge from the church. I hurried over. 'Sergeant Bowring, can you do something to stop the press from hounding the family? Surely it's not right for them to hassle the poor parents like this?'

Bowring stared impassively at me for a moment or two, then smiled a particularly reptilian smile.

'And what do you think your presence here is doing for their peace of mind, Mr. Cummins? Do you not think it must be hard for them to see you here, with the blood of their son still fresh on your hands?'

As Bowring was delivering these lines of misguided small-minded prejudice, Francine moved directly to the paparazzi at the funeral car, holding her badge in front of her.

'These poor people have had enough trouble and sadness without you adding to it,' she announced in the non-negotiable tones of a landlady moving in to break up a fight in her bar. 'Now back off and let them be, or I'll charge you with assault and threatening behaviour. There's such a thing as common decency, fellas. Get your damned cameras out of their faces!'

My heart, already melted, now became molten with desire for my pretty police officer, so forceful, so in command (rather like Hilary when she was on top of her game, in a way that I wouldn't fully admit).

18

In the midst of all this tragedy and chaos, life went on as normal. For example, my car failed its NCT. The report said that the brake-linings were burnt out. In fact, they said that it wasn't safe to drive and refused to give me back the keys. 'That thing's a death trap,' was the verdict from the cocky man in dirty overalls whose manner was brusque to the point of aggression. He told me to make arrangements to have it taken safely to a garage to have it fixed, explaining that if I left it at the test centre for more than a heartbeat I'd be fined heavily. My insurance covered the tow truck, but I was kept on hold for most of the morning while I waited to speak to a human in the roadside assistance department of my insurer, and then had to wait for most of the afternoon for the tow truck. I imagined that it would have been easier to repatriate a dead body from Yemen. Or perhaps that was just my funereal frame of mind.

I had stashed the money that I'd found on Alan Fenton in a plastic bag underneath the spare wheel in the boot of my car on the night of his death. There was forty-thousand euro there, mainly in five hundreds. I remember reading somewhere that the EU had ceased printing these high-value notes, because they were only ever used by the criminal fraternity. God alone knows where Fenton had robbed this money, but I reasoned that nobody knew he'd had it on him, therefore nobody was likely to question what had happened to it or to notice that it was missing.

I phoned for a taxi from the NCT test centre and took myself and the plastic bag to the pub where I had met with the Gizzard Man. While in the back of the cab, I counted out twenty-thousand euro. I reckoned that the over-payment would silence all the usurious claims by my lender. I also thought that it was rather apt that I might have been completing a circle: repaying the Quinlans with their own dirty money. It had an appealing sort of symmetry. I asked the taxi to wait for me.

The dimly lit pub and its long-haul drinkers looked as if it and they had been preserved in a time-warp since my first visit, including the smell of stale beer, ghostly cigarette smoke, and the grey-muzzled dog under the same side table, which growled at me again as I passed. I already knew my way to where the pale-eyed man held court.

'Hi, there,' I said to him, 'I'm Arthur Cummins. I've come to pay what I owe you. How much is it?'

'Ah, yes, Mr. Cummins!' he pronounced the name as if he were expecting a laugh from an invisible audience. 'I see you have met with a bit of an accident. Did you walk into a door, was it?'

'Something like that, yes. How much do I owe you, please?'

'That will be fifteen-thousand euros, to you, my friend. And that includes late payment penalties, interest and the additional expenses of the gentlemen you met the other night. Financial services don't attract VAT.'

Part of me baulked strongly at the idea that I should have to pay for the services of the two thugs who had beaten me so savagely, but I was keen to get away from this deeply sinister man. I paid the full fifteen thousand, redeemed my hostage passport, lurched out into the fresh air, and made my getaway in my waiting cab.

I felt the elation I imagined a devout Catholic might feel on leaving the confessional. Shriven, I think the word is. The rolls of notes were, to me, still warm from the dead body of Fenton. I had picked over his remains like a scavenger on a battlefield. Now I was rid of my dirty debt, I felt a freedom of movement that I hadn't had for months.

Back at my apartment, I stowed the plastic bag with the remaining cash in the freezer compartment of my fridge, behind a half-full tub of ice cream that might have acquired antique status. Twenty-five thousand euro in five-hundred euro notes is depressingly compact.

Then I remembered my appointment with the rector. My car was still up on a ramp without its wheels in the garage down by the Maltings, so I travelled to meet Karen Quayley by another taxi. I arrived punctually and crunched around to the vestry door. Overhead an extended family of rooks were settling in for the night, sorting differences and claiming territory in a state of noisy restlessness as they landed and took off repeatedly in a nearby stand of pines. They seemed as jumpy as my own nerves as they fidgeted and fussed. This was my fourth visit to Kilmurray church in the space of less than a fortnight and each visit offered flashback images of horror. I shuddered as I passed the door to the crypt.

The parish office lights were on, and I found Reverend Quayley waiting for me, although I was a good ten minutes early. There was organ music playing; it sounded as if someone was practising, because it kept stopping and starting again, a bit like the rooks in the trees outside.

'Good evening, Mr. Cummins,' the rector said as she held out her hand to me.

I shook her hand and begged her to call me Arthur.

She waved me into a seat and took her own position behind her desk. 'And what is it that you want to talk to me about, Arthur?'

'Well, Karen, here's the thing. The Gardaí, particularly Sergeant Bowring, seem to believe that I killed William O'Grady and Alan Fenton. The fact that there was no reason why I would want to kill either man doesn't seem to bother him. If I'm charged, I'm likely to lose my job and my reputation, such as it is. If I'm wrongly convicted, I'd spend a long time in prison. So, I'm looking for anything that might point to the real killer.'

'And how on earth do you think I would be able to help you, Arthur?'

Maybe it was her Northern accent, but there seemed to me to be a self-contentedness nestling in her tone of voice that made me want to shake her.

'When did the money go missing from the parish accounts?' I asked, surprised that my voice sounded so calm.

'That's none of your business, Arthur.'

'I think it's very much my business, because I think that the missing money is at the heart of all of this. Please tell me. I can't see what harm it could do.'

'Well, if you must know, it was in the week before Christmas, twenty-first of December, the shortest day of the year. The parish accounts were audited for the end of the year, and the auditors brought it to my attention.'

'And what happened next? You reported it to the Gardaí?'

'Good heavens, no, Arthur. I spoke to Mr. O'Grady. He seemed to be as shocked as I was. He couldn't offer any explanation then and there, but said he'd look into it.'

'How much was missing?' I could feel her stalling at this question, so I softened the brashness of it by adding, 'This will go public in the investigation of the murder of William O'Grady anyway, so you may as well tell me, Karen.'

Karen Quayley paused for a moment, fiddling with a glass paperweight with a white dove within it suspended in eternal flight. She put the dove down with some emphasis, signalling, perhaps that she had made up her mind about something. It might have been to be straight with me, or it might have been not to throw the paperweight at me.

She cleared her throat and said, 'Just over five-hundred thousand euros,' and waited for the enormity of the figure to devastate me.

I thought of Tom's expression *'half a rock'* and kept a straight face.

'What was the money intended for in the parish?'

'Oh, that's easy to answer. It had been collected to reroof the church and to build a new parish hall. Parishioners had been extraordinarily generous. The work on the roof is badly needed – you can't hear yourself think in here with the rattling of the slates every time there's a bit of wind.'

The organ rehearsal stopped abruptly in mid-bar, then restarted after a few experimental chords.

'That's Geoffrey, my husband. We have an Easter festival coming up and he likes to practise. I hope you don't mind?' This was tossed in more by way of a challenge than an apology.

I waved my hand to indicate that it didn't matter to me. 'So, William O'Grady, the parish treasurer, said he'd 'look into' a deficit of half a million euro in his books? And what did he find?'

'Well, at the Parish Council meeting at the beginning of February, he told the Council that he had found out who had taken the money and that if he didn't get it all back, he was going to report the thief to the Gardaí.'

'But he didn't report the thief, did he? He wound up dead on the floor of the church on what was supposed to be my wedding day.'

'Oh, I'm sure that there was nothing personal against you in that.'

'I can tell you that it felt bloody personal when I tripped over the body in the dark of the church that morning. Tell me, Karen, who had access to the parish accounts?'

'The treasurer, of course, and myself, as ex-officio CEO of the parish. And let me be perfectly plain here, Arthur, I did not take that money. If you want my opinion, it was Willie O'Grady himself. I think he was just playing for time so that he could try to replace it.'

There was a tentative knock on the office door. Geoff Quayley's jowly face peeked in. 'I'm just finished here, dear,' he said, then with a gesture of apology he added, 'Oh, hello, Arthur. Nice to see you again.'

The organ practice had ended some minutes before. I had unconsciously registered the silence without recognising its significance.

Karen looked happy with the interruption. She stood and said, 'Actually, I think we're finished here too, Arthur. I've another meeting here in ten minutes and I need to prepare. You can see yourself out.'

So, I was dismissed. I made my way out into the vestry and was phoning for a cab when Geoff Quayley overheard me and offered me a lift.

'I can drop you off, Arthur. It would be a pleasure. No trouble at all. Sure, your place is only a wee step away. The car is just here.'

How could I have refused?

19

G eoff Quayley wasn't a good driver. He tended to speed up and slow down in an arbitrary way which made a passenger very nervous. He seemed to be oblivious of other traffic on the road and kept his headlights on full beam, causing oncoming vehicles to flash their lights at him and cars ahead to tap their brakes and flash their winkers in an effort to get him to dip. He drove with his right hand on the wheel with his elbow resting casually on the sill of his closed driver's window. He kept his left hand on his knee.

He was silent for the first few minutes, then suddenly turned to me and asked, 'What were you talking to Karen about, Arthur?' He was staring at me, ignoring the road ahead.

I saw no reason to lie, and decided to give him a straight answer, in the hope that he might turn to look at the road. 'Just about the money that's missing from the parish accounts. I think the missing money may be at the heart of the mystery.'

He refocused his attention on the road just in time to swerve out of the path of an oncoming white van that flashed its lights and blared its horn in remonstration. My right foot stamped uselessly on the floor of the passenger footwell, pressing a phantom brake.

'Mystery? What mystery would that be now, Arthur?'

'The mystery of who killed William O'Grady and Alan Fenton, of course.'

'And what did my lovely wife have to say?'

'I'd rather keep that between her and me, if you don't mind.' I wasn't sure that I liked the slant of his tone.

'You know that she stole that money, don't you? And tried to pin the blame on Willie O'Grady?'

'I'm not sure that that can be true, Geoff.'

'What, her stealing the money or her trying to get Willie blamed for it?' He was staring at me to the detriment of his driving and had chosen this moment to accelerate jerkily as we approached one of the tight roundabouts that punctuated the route from the church to my apartment.

'*Jesus, mind the road!*' I shouted, reaching for the wheel in an attempt to prevent the car from careering into the kerb on my side. The tyres clipped the kerb just as he corrected his steering and the car bounced into the middle of the road which, by a complete fluke, was empty of traffic, otherwise I think we would both be dead. 'Please, Geoff, mind how you drive. You're making me very nervous.'

'Her and that Roundstock woman – I never trusted her. They had the codes and passwords for the account. They took the money. It was too easy. Like taking candy from a wee babba, so it was.'

'And what do you think they did with the money? You know it still hasn't been reported to the Gardaí?'

He laughed, a series of rapid rasping sighs without any humour. 'Of course it wasn't reported. Sure, why would my loving spouse squeal on herself? Not at all. What she did was turn the suspicion onto poor Willie O'Grady, the manipulating bitch! God love him, he was terrible upset – he thought he'd end up in prison, poor lamb. He was in tears when he told me.'

'Were you close?' I asked quietly, not being anxious to cause him to take his eyes off the road again.

'Ah, sure God love you, you're that innocent you'd be likely to be caught up in King Herod's next sweep. Of course Willie and I were close. We'd been lovers for three years before he was killed. We shared a bed at his house, so we did.'

'I'm sorry, Geoff, I didn't know.' I felt foolish for not having twigged this relationship. It made sense, in the same way that Karen Quayley and Jennifer Roundstock made sense, all comfortably within the parish and interlocked like a Chinese puzzle. 'You must have been devastated by his death.'

He sighed and pulled on his ear with the hand that wasn't supposed to be steering. 'Our relationship had ended just before Willie was killed,' he said. 'He had betrayed a trust and I broke it off.'

I couldn't turn to see the expression on Geoff's face. I felt that if I took my attention off the road for a second there was going to be a calamitous accident; at least one of us had to watch where we were going. Geoff swung the car into a left-hand turn and drove on the wrong side of the road for ten hair-raising seconds before swerving over to the left with an apologetic sort of jerk.

'I still cried at his funeral, so I did. I think we all cry most bitterly over what might have been.'

I remembered our meeting by the faces sculpture in Cabinteely Park and the sense of melancholy that he imparted then. But I also remembered the lie he had told me about his presence in the organ loft and what he might have witnessed that morning.

He stopped the car at my apartment block. He didn't really park the car, he just stopped it in the middle of the road beside the building's entrance. He didn't turn to me as I got out of the car. He stared ahead of him as I thanked him for the lift, wished him goodnight and closed the passenger door. I had never been so glad to get out of a car.

I had finally been allowed to move back into my apartment. The Garda forensic team had taken four days to examine the place. They had dusted for fingerprints, prised shotgun pellets from the walls and ceiling of the bathroom, collected blood samples and had photographed every inch of my cramped little home. The place smelled strongly of cleaning agent after the professional cleaners had finished mopping up. Francine had given me the name of the specialist firm and had warned me that they were pricey. She hadn't exaggerated but I hadn't the stomach to do the job myself. I paid with my new credit card, provided by my bank with wolfish ease, and scant thought for my ability to pay.

And I still had to face the cost of the repairs and repainting of the bathroom. My dislike of the late Alan Fenton had grown exponentially since his death.

To whom, though, should I send the bill for the cleaning and repairs? I started to make a list of everyone I could think of who might want to see Fenton dead. It was a very long list. Then I started a list of people who he might have allowed into the apartment after I had been sent to do the shopping for his dinner. I struggled to think of anyone other than myself. Who else would he have trusted? I drew a blank.

The steak I had bought for Fenton's midnight feast was still in my fridge. I had a sniff of it and decided that it was probably edible, which was more than could be said for the oven chips, which sat soggily growing black mould cultures in their plastic bag where I had abandoned them. However, there was nothing wrong with the bottle of wine that stood untouched on the kitchen table.

I indulged in a quiet solo celebration of my return home. I found that steak, all by itself, was rather nice when washed down with a bottle of Pinot Noir and a couple of Valiums. Before I passed out, I sent a WhatsApp to Tom, requesting the pleasure of his company next day. We needed to start another chart.

20

Tom arrived at my place just after I should have had breakfast except that there was nothing to eat in the apartment and anyway I didn't have the stomach for food after the bottle of wine the night before. He took an appraising look at me.

'Jesus, man, you look like something the dog rolled in.'

'Tom, you have a real way with words, you know that?'

'It's a gift,' he said and suggested that we hit Starbucks.

I ordered this time, for fear of a repeat of the anaemic concoction that he had inflicted on me the last time we met. I had grabbed the original Elastoplast notes and the coffee shop napkin before leaving the apartment and was rather looking forward to brainstorming with my pal. I thought it might help drive my headache away. I wasn't sure that Valium and a lot of wine was something I would try again.

We sat side by side in Starbucks, huddled over the Elastoplast notes. I brought him up to speed with my meeting with Reverend Karen and my conversation with Geoff during the drive of terror.

He took the pen and, working from the napkin, we listed the suspects for the theft on the margin of the old notes:

William O'Grady [parish treasurer]

Karen Quayley [rector and parish CEO]

Jennifer Roundstock [Karen's partner and pillow-listener]

Geoff Quayley [William O'Grady's (ex?) lover and housemate]

The Quinlans

'Ah, no, Tom,' I said, 'do you really think we can take on the Quinlans? Whatever about the others on the list, we don't have enough firepower to tangle with them. You can leave them on the list and we can bear them in mind as we go on, but if it begins to look like they're serious contenders, I'm going to hand over to the Gardaí and take my chances.'

Tom considered this and nodded in agreement, putting a question mark beside the name.

I then suggested that we ought to reinsert Hilary into the mix and was robustly shot down by Tom.

'Don't be a fuckin' muppet, Arthur! You may not be fond of her at the moment, but she's a good person. And anyway, there's no way she could have got into the account.'

I backed off, smarting slightly at the heat of the dismissal. I scribbled down the date of the theft of the parish funds above the list of names, and the amount that had been stolen.

Tom said, 'OK, we know when and how much, but who did it and where did it go?' His eyebrows were focussed.

It was, of course, possible that another random person had done it, but we decided to restrict our thinking to the people we knew. Tom said that he didn't see why Karen and

Jennifer would steal the money, as suggested by Geoff.

'Look at it, buddy,' said Tom. 'There wasn't enough moolah in the pot. I've calculated that you'd need at least ten million to make it worthwhile. You'd have to drop everything and vanish. That's expensive. Then you'd have to perch somewhere outside the EU that doesn't extradite to the EU, or to Ireland at any rate. You'd have to get a false passport and change your identity. That's expensive too. Then you'd have to exist somehow in your new place of residence, and that existence would have to be on the luxurious side to make the whole thing worth the candle. I'm talking mansion, swimming pool, flash wheels, hot and cold running servants, and a happy-ever-after lifestyle. That's going to knock a big hole in your bundle of wonga, man. I've looked into it and worked it out. All is missing here is five hundred thou. Not worth getting out of bed for, I tell you.'

Tom surprised me with his in-depth calculations of the minimum amount needed to justify a rob-and-run heist. But then, Tom always surprised me.

I wrote, 'WHY WOULD THEY?' opposite Karen and Jennifer's names with an attempt at a curly bracket which was so poorly executed that it looked like a sagging pair of breasts lying on their side. As we talked, Tom took the pen from me and completed the image by the addition of two nipples. I then decided that that sort of vulgarity was to be deplored and crossed off the whole booby-bracket thing, leaving only a splodge.

If the stolen amount was too small to warrant the exertion and expense of decamping, what could it have been intended for, among our comfortable middle-class list of suspects? This line of thinking brought me back to the possibility that someone was being blackmailed and needed cash to bung the blackmailer. I wrote down BLACKMAIL? And opened my case with Tom to see if he agreed.

'See, the thing with blackmail is, there's no point setting your demand too high," I said, "or your victim simply won't be able to pay. The hush money has to be within reach, particularly since the blackmailer will want to come back for repeats. A tapeworm won't want to kill its host.'

'But half a million bucks would be way beyond what anyone on our list could be expected to pay to a blackmailer,' said Tom, but he didn't sound wholly convinced by his own dismissal of the idea.

'I think that the thief was being blackmailed for a much smaller amount, say ten grand,' I suggested. 'They stole the full half a million, paid the ransom and popped the rest somewhere that would allow the capital to increase and multiply, so that there would be a decent bucket of money to feed the leech.'

'You're turning my stomach with your leeches and your tapeworms, bud. *Gross!*'

'Yeah, but do you agree with the hypothesis, Tom?'

'If I knew what a hypotheosis was, I'd agree with it.' The eyebrows were guileless.

'We know that there was an account with Minotaur in the name of William O'Grady. And we know that Minotaur promised large capital gains. But it doesn't make sense for Willie to steal the money and put it into an account in his own name.'

Tom was doodling bubbles on the A4 pad. Bubbles. We

sipped our coffees for a moment, then he said, 'I wonder could you open an account with Minotaur online?'

'I'm sure that Fenton had all the gadgets, so I'd say yes. And all you'd need would be a scan of a passport and some sort of proof of address. Do you think they'd be able to trace the computer that was used to open the account?'

Tom sat up straight, the eyebrows at attention. 'There would be an IP address, yes. And that might lead us to the thief. Phone your girlfriend there, Arthur. I'm sure she's pining for you.'

I took out my phone and sent a WhatsApp to Francine. 'Need to talk soonest' and added an emoji of a magnifying glass.

Tom finished his coffee and put his mug down carefully. 'I'm worried about Hilary, buddy,' he said, looking straight ahead. 'I looked her up after Alan's funeral. She's very shook.'

'That was kind of you, old pal. I was thinking that she's been through a lot all right.' I wasn't quite prepared for the rush of jealousy-juice that suddenly flooded my brain. My voice may have carried a hint of green but Tom, as always, kept his cards close.

He cleared his throat and said, 'It might be good if you were to meet her somewhere neutral. You guys go back a long way. I can broker a meet if you want?'

I stood up, my nerves still jangling despite the blanket of Valium that muffled them. I gathered up the A4 pad and headed back to the apartment, leaving Tom sitting, inscrutable, on the Starbucks sofa. His offer of a brokered meeting with Hilary had set off many unbidden alarm bells in my emotional head. Was he now standing, as a buffer or otherwise, between Hilary and me? And why should I care?

I bought a breakfast roll in my local convenience store and brought it home. My phone did its goosey honking thing. It was Francine.

'Good morning, Arthur. How can I help you?' Her voice sounded a tad supercilious.

I could think of any number of ways in which the lovely law officer might help me, but said, 'Actually, Francine, I think I might have something to help you. Your place or mine?' I thought I heard her sigh.

'I'll come to your apartment. If you come into the station, it'll only set Sergeant Bowring off again. He's still bulling about me deploying the armed response team that night.'

As I waited for Francine to arrive, I washed the pan from last night's dinner-for-one and put the empty wine bottle with the recycling. The place was pristine after the cleaners had been in, except of course for the shotgun damage in the bathroom. The ragged, savage hole blasted in the ceiling where the shotgun pellets had hit after they had done with Alan Fenton. Some had made it all the way without deflection, but most had passed through his head and had carried bits of his brain and skull into the plasterboard above. There was still a residual chemical smell from the cleaning. This did something towards laying the ghost of my ex's late brother – for which I was grateful – but I rather missed the homely man-cave funk I was used to living with. I popped another little tablet and washed it down with a slurp from the cold tap. I combed my hair.

21

Alone in my apartment as I waited for Francine, without warning my mind started to replay the scene outside the church at Alan Fenton's funeral. Tom and Hilary in what my agitated senses told me was an embrace. My embittered heart told me that there was more than comfort for the bereaved going on there. Some weird instinct had drawn me to insinuate myself into that huddle and the same instinct had made me pull away from its claustrophobic fug. If there was something between them, how long had it been going on? Was that the reason that she had ducked out of the wedding?

I went into the battle-scarred bathroom and splashed some cold water on my face. I knew that my present nervous state was probably interfering with my reasoning, and I needed to bring myself to my senses. I stood, my face dripping, and looked in the mirror. Tom was right, I looked like shit. Bloodless, gaunt, haunted. I needed some fresh air and exercise, as my mother used to say. But I couldn't be arsed. Or was that the tranquilliser talking?

The front door buzzer sounded, delivering its usual

defibrillating shock to my system. I let Francine in. She was in uniform today. I made a mental note to ask her what the dress protocol was in her line of work. When did she wear uniform and when did she go mufti? I knew I'd never ask that question, partly because I'd forget and partly because I didn't really care. I thought she looked splendid any way. She came in the door of the apartment, and I saw her casting an eye around the place, aware that the last time she had been there, Alan Fenton had been sprawled dead on the floor of the bathroom, liberally basted with blood.

I made tea. There was no milk.

'You said you had something for me?' she asked, staring suspiciously at the chipped mug of tea the colour of bog-water. Like a court taster, I put my own mug to my lips and took a large sip, forgetting that the tea was untempered with milk. The boiling hot liquid scalded my lips and mouth. Rather than spit out the searing mouthful, I swallowed it. It felt like molten lava scorching its way down my oesophagus.

'Are you all right there, Arthur?'

Although I knew for certain that I had no lining left anywhere in my mouth or gullet, I assured her that I was fine. I put my mug down on the coffee table.

'I know you take a dim view of my amateur detective work, but you must see that if I don't discover the real perpetrator I'm quite likely to be put on trial myself. So, I'd ask you to bear with me, okay?'

'I know you mean well, Arthur. What do you want to say to me?'

'Can I ask you if you have looked at the opening of the William O'Grady account with MinotaurMaze Solutions? We think it may have been done online. Can you see if you can trace the IP address from which the opening transaction was done?'

'Who's 'we'?'

'Me and Tom Farrington. My fellow degenerate.'

Her face gave me nothing, but she did take out her notebook. She wrote something, then looked up at me. 'Anything else?'

'Have you looked at blackmail as a possible motive for William O'Grady's murder? He was a well-known campaigner for gay rights and had a track record of outing people in places of influence. I've looked at his online profile and it doesn't all make happy reading. He liked to dig around to see what could be found in people's backgrounds and use the threat of exposure as a lever for what he saw as right. It didn't make him popular.'

'So, you think he may have been leveraging someone?'

'Blackmailing is closer to the mark, I'd say.'

'I'm not your grandmother,' Francine said, deadpan, 'but you sure seem to know a lot about sucking eggs, Arthur.'

'Please don't take offence, Francine – it's just that I feel like I'm fighting for my life here and I need to know that every possible line is being followed.' I was sitting, trembling, on the armchair opposite her, on the verge of a panic attack. I felt my lower lip start to tremble and my chin pucker up. Pride took over, and I stood up and went to the window to cover my hysteria. I made myself breathe more evenly and stuffed my shaking hands into my pockets. When I thought I had a better grip on myself, I went back and told her about my conversation with Karen Quayley and the fact that shortly before he was murdered, O'Grady had told the parish council that he knew who the thief was.

Francine sipped her tea. She wrote some more notes, then snapped the band back onto her notebook and stood, straightening her tunic. 'Thank you, Arthur,' she said, 'That's actually been very helpful.'

'Is Sergeant Bowring still looking to give me a fair trial and hang me in the morning?'

'Well, you're all he's got. He wants to close the investigation and move on to trial. If you must know, I've defended you as best I can, but he keeps pointing out that you were on the scene of both murders. He has threatened to take me off both cases if I keep questioning his judgement. That's why I came here instead of getting you down to the station.'

'Francine, thank you for what you've done,' I said and reached out to touch her arm.

She recoiled. 'Don't you ever touch me, do you hear me? I'll have you for assaulting a Garda officer. Do I make myself plain?'

'Sorry! It was only a gesture of friendliness.'

'Now understand this: you and I are not friends. You are chief suspect in two murders and I am one of the investigating Gardaí. That is the only connection between us.' She stared at me with her maddeningly beautiful blue eyes. I must have looked as foolish as I felt. She rolled her eyes in exasperation and said, 'Just say "Yes, Garda" and we can move on, OK?'

Meekly I replied, 'Yes, Garda.' But I confess that I was quite aroused. It surprised me.

There are women who play hard to get, there are women who are hard to get, and there are those who just don't want to be got. Through all the shell-shock and the anti-shell-shock drugs, I tried to interpret Francine's message and fit her into one of the above categories. My romantic heart didn't want to conclude that she was in the last category; I wouldn't allow myself to be so unwanted – to tumble down that well of misery and rejection; I had to hold my ground and persist. To me it increased the romance of my situation. When one is struggling for survival, one will grasp at anything. I saw the romantic possibility of my plight and her part in it and clung hopelessly to that foggy possibility.

22

I went to my GP and tried to tell him what had happened to me. I'm not sure he believed me.

'It's my nerves, doctor,' I said, feeling like someone in a joke. 'I can't sleep and if I do drop off I have these dreadful dreams that wake me. I haven't slept properly for about a week.'

I told him that the doctor at the Garda station had given me some Valium but that I'd finished them.

'She prescribed Valium?'

'It was a 'he' and he gave me a little bottle of pills.'

'What was his name?'

'I've no idea. He liked Eric Clapton. So do I.'

I must have been mumbling, probably because of my exhaustion.

'What?'

'I like Clapton.'

'You, like, gave him a round of applause? Were you high on something?'

'No, no, no! Old "Slow Hand" Clapton, the guitarist.'

'A slow hand-clap? Why would you do that?'

It was only then that I spotted the tiny wire that made its way mysteriously into his ear, somehow to augment his impaired hearing. The man was deaf. I shouted, '*I don't know the doctor's name! Sorry!*'

'Why are you shouting, Arthur?'

The GP stared at me, clearly wondering at my mental state. I could see him deciding to move on with his examination of me. He asked me to sit on the examination couch and took my blood pressure. As he pumped up the BP cuff, its grip on my upper arm put me in mind of the firm hand of an arresting officer.

The doctor said, 'You see, when you're in shock, your blood pressure drops. Diazepam can lower your blood pressure still further, which isn't always a good thing.' He deflated the cuff and took it off.

For some reason the ripping sound of the velcro made me feel queasy as I sat on the edge of the examination couch with my feet dangling.

'Just as well he gave me some Valium, then,' I ventured.

He looked at me over his spectacles. 'Valium *is* diazepam.' His voice sounded weary, condescending and judgemental.

I felt as if I had told him I had been given a baggie of heroin by the police surgeon and was now asking for more.

'How did you get here?'

'I took the bus. My car failed its NCT and I'm getting it fixed.'

This was more information than he needed – he was getting impatient with me.

'It's not safe to drive with diazepam. How long have you been taking the Valium? When did you take the last one?'

'Only a couple of days. I took the last one yesterday. And I didn't sleep last night. I've been a bag of nerves all day.'

'You need some exercise. You'll find that it works better than any drug for your present state of nerves. Go for a long walk every day. Take a water bottle and sip on it regularly, even if you're not thirsty. Stay away from alcohol and coffee. Come and see me again in a month's time. This is what we call watchful waiting. I'm hoping your agitation will calm itself in time.'

At the surgery reception I was charged €60 for this prescription of cold turkey.

My honeymoon leave was nearly over. I dreaded the thought of going back to work. Really all I was doing in the office was clerking. It was undemanding and correspondingly unrewarding, both financially and spiritually. I had put my name down with a recruitment agency, which came up with this job. My employer was a subsidiary of the agency itself, which provided clerical services under contract to a big multinational aircraft leasing company. The wages were bitterly mean in contrast to the chunky salaries available within the leasing company itself. To the world, I presented myself as an employee of the leasing company, although my contract expressly stipulated that I was not to do this. But how the hell else was I to describe my menial work? I counted aircraft and noted their location. All day, every day. There was plenty of management-speak about the privilege of working with an aviation giant and the great opportunities that this offered, but in fact there was no real hope of promotion and little prospect of pay increase. The recruitment agency had simply identified me among other helpless fish, had put us in a barrel and was now shooting us. My boss kept changing; it seemed that every three months or so a new manager would be appointed and the old one would disappear into the corporate weeds of the agency. Among my own low-grade peers, the rate of attrition was startling. Only the obdurate and subservient survived more than a year; anyone with get-up-and-go, simply got up and left. I had been there for five full years. We weren't unionised, and I suspected that if an employee made any sort of nuisance of themselves, he or she would be erased from the workforce, so that the company always appeared to the world as a happy little band of hamsters uncomplainingly trundling around within their prescribed wheel for the greater good of the multinational giant.

I felt trapped. To change careers, I would have to undertake a massive retraining exercise which I couldn't afford in terms either of money or effort. I felt as if I was stuck at the Everest basecamp, shovelling frozen turds, and the only way out was to climb the bloody mountain without oxygen.

This is what I pondered as I waited at the bus stop. Signs of spring stirred all around me in the suburban gardens but did not lift my mood. It was raining and the wind had an edge to it.

I asked myself what I had done to deserve this misery, and

came up with the answer that the problem was that I hadn't done anything much at all.

By way of convincing myself that I was moving forward, I phoned Hilary. To my surprise, she picked up almost immediately.

'How are you doing, love?' I couldn't break the habit of the endearment so easily.

'I'm fine,' she said, but I could feel the stress and tension in her voice despite the filtering effect of the mobile airwaves.

'Would you fancy a walk? We could chat.'

Again, to my surprise, she accepted, suggesting a stroll on the Bray Esplanade.

'You know that Tom says that an esplanade is an explanation offered by a drunk person?'

'Ha, ha,' she said, mirthlessly. 'I don't want to talk about Tom. I'll meet you at the car park by Martello Terrace at twelve.'

We strolled along the semi-deserted esplanade, wrapped up against wind and rain. I have always rather liked to walk in the rain. I'm a believer in the maxim that there's no such thing as bad weather, just unsuitable clothing. Hilary was sporting her long waxed hooded coat and green wellies, looking for all the world like an advertisement for Barbour. She clutched her hood at her throat to stop it blowing off. The stronger squalls brought us to a standstill as we leaned into the wind, frowning at the rain as it spattered our faces. And I remembered when I had loved this strong, energetic woman of spirit.

'*Are you OK?*' I asked her, shouting over the din of the surf on the stony beach.

'*I'm fine!*' she shouted back. '*When we turn and walk back the wind will be behind us!*'

This wasn't an answer to the question I had actually asked, but conversation was too laborious as we walked to windward. We reached the Bray Head end of the esplanade where the bulk of the Head mitigated the full strength of the wind. We turned and leaned on the wall to look out on the sweep of the bay, with the clouds scudding overhead in ever-changing patterns of light, carried by the gale. Occasional rays of light pointed out features of the shore, then vanished as the clouds hurried by overhead.

'It's so beautiful,' she said. 'We forget to look at it sometimes.'

'I'm sorry about Alan,' I said.

'You know he swindled my stupid, greedy dad out of his life savings, don't you?' She was looking at the shadow of Howth Head behind a veil of rain. I had nothing to offer this line of discussion. She continued, 'Alan brought nothing but grief to my family, with his narcissism and unjustified self-belief. He was, as the Bible has it, an empty vessel, clanging his false promises of instant wealth. He brought his own destruction on himself. It's bad enough that he believed in his own lies, but he undid so much good work, wrecked so many carefully harvested algorithms that had the business virtually running itself. He overrode and second-guessed the system.

He made mistake after mistake until the whole system got a sort of cyber-septicaemia and my algorithms stopped working. He fooled himself and managed to fool so many other fools, including my dear old man. My dad has nothing left but his pension. I'm not sure he hasn't hocked the house into the bargain.'

There was so much bitterness in her voice that her mouth had turned up into a sort of a snarl. There was no trace of sadness or mourning in her words. I supposed that anger was one of the manifestations of grief and didn't question her, but I did note her reference to 'my algorithms' – what was that about?

'Have the Guards come up with any theories as to the killer?' I asked.

She paused, pulling a tissue from her pocket and blowing her nose. 'Yes, several. The Quinlan gang, many other angry clients, and you, actually, Arthur.'

'Do you have any theories yourself, Hil? I mean, surely you don't think I did it, do you?'

'I can't see why you would have done it, no.'

'Hil, that's not the same as saying you don't think it was me. You do see that, don't you?'

She remained quiet and didn't look me in the eye. I wondered if she had been so ambivalent when talking to the Gardaí.

'To be honest, Hil, I've been having the heebie-jeebies since I discovered his body. I'm getting flashbacks and panic attacks. The doctor says it's PTSD, like the Vietnam veterans.'

'You were always too sensitive, Arthur. You need to man up a bit. Get over yourself.'

'Thank you, Hilary, that makes me feel a lot better.'

I was staring at the derelict hulk of the Bray Head Hotel, looking forlorn in its shabby blue-and-white hoarding in the rain. I tried to remember if it was that or the Strand Hotel that had once belonged to Oscar Wilde's father. I hoped it wasn't the Bray Head. Oscar wouldn't have been thrilled to see the buddleia growing from the gutters and the pigeons roosting in the upper-floor bedrooms, whose windows had long-since succumbed to stone-throwing vandals. The walls had been daubed with angry, aggressive graffiti that was meaningless to me. I had heard that vandals had wrecked the inside too, including pushing a piano through the first-floor bannisters. It's never the fall that kills, it's the landing. I wondered what that must have sounded like. The last elongated chord of the Beatles *A Day in the Life*, maybe?

'This place is supposed to be haunted by the ghost of the wife of the original owner,' I told Hilary. 'He's said to have murdered her in a jealous rage over an affair she had with another man.'

The rainwater streamed from the choked gutters and splattered on the crumbling, weed-infested tarmac of what had once been the car park. I shuddered as I told this story, wondering if Alan Fenton was likely to haunt my one-bed apartment.

23

The day after my meeting with Hilary, I got a call from the garage to say that my car was ready. On the interminable bus journey back to Bray, I thought over what Hilary had said about her brother.

Was Hilary involved in Alan Fenton's business? She had mentioned 'my algorithms'; it may have been a slip, but the sense of proprietorial dominion was quite clear. Was it she who had set up the software that had, as she had put it, virtually run the business by itself? She was very angry that Alan had destroyed the business, running a successful venture into chaotic loss. She seemed to blame him for everything that had gone wrong. She certainly didn't react with grief when I offered sympathy on his death.

The garage mechanic peeled off his blue rubber gloves like a defeated surgeon emerging from the operating theatre.

His sombre look infected my mood and I found myself asking in hushed tones, 'What's the news with the car then?'

I know people, mainly women, who like to give their cars

names. It seems to be a sign of affection. For example, I have a cousin who calls her car Penelope. But that may not be the best example, because my cousin is as nutty as a health bar. My point is that I couldn't bring myself to name my poor heap of junk. The thing simply didn't encourage any sort of affectionate identity. It functioned, in a damp sort of way, and consumed petrol in inverse proportion to its usefulness. But it was still handy for getting me places that public transport didn't reach, like where I lived. But here I was, facing a grim-looking mechanic, who was tossing his rubber gloves in a wastebin and seemed unwilling to let me have news of my vehicle. I felt an emotional pang of concern.

'Are you the '06' Golf?' he asked in tones that spelt doom, jerking a thumb at a VW Golf up on the inspection ramp. 'Because that thing's totally fucked.' His bedside manner clearly required some restructuring.

'No,' I said with a sense of relief like a fishwife on the breakwater seeing her man's boat returning after a storm. 'I'm the little grey one there.' I pointed to my shabby machine mouldering in a dark corner of the crowded garage.

'Oh, right,' he said with apparent disappointment. 'That one's all ready to go.' Recognition was slowly dawning. 'Mr. Cummins, isn't it? Didn't we drill holes in the floor to let the rainwater out of your machine?'

I nodded.

'Well, it seems to be letting in more than it's letting out. The auld carpet is all rotten and there's mushrooms growing in the roof-cloth. You need to park it in out of the rain.'

I wondered if the Gardaí had removed Fenton's gargantuan Rover from my underground parking space.

The mechanic presented me with an invoice for a figure that, after VAT was added by way of a twist on the knife-blade, would have cleaned out my current account completely (Tom's loan included) and drawn me into the jaws of overdraft. I paid with my newly acquired credit card.

'Oh, by the way, pal, we found this in the pocket of the passenger door. It'll need drying out. There must be four inches of water lodged in there, it's like a fuckin' swimming pool. Try putting it in a bowl of rice in the hot press.' He handed me a mobile phone that I had never seen before.

'That's not mine,' I protested.

'Well, it was in your car, mate. Must be yours.' He handed me my car keys and left me standing bewildered, keys in one hand and someone else's phone in the other.

He turned and added by way of dismissal. 'If you wouldn't mind shifting your car, pal – it's in the way.'

I climbed into my soggy car and drove away, the mystery phone sitting on the passenger seat and the familiar, high-pitched, sweet smell of rot all around me.

Back in the apartment, I tried to turn on the phone without success. It was as inscrutable as the black monolith in *2001: A Space Odyssey*. I felt like one of the apes in the opening sequence of Kubrick's masterpiece, awed and angered by its reticence. I couldn't work out how to get at the insides. The slim instrument was impervious to my squeezings and pryings. It yielded me nothing.

I wondered how the hell this phone could have found its way into my car. Mentally, I rewound my life to before the awful wedding-day-that-never-was and tried to think who had been in the car. I had left the car at home on the day itself, because I had intended to test the theory that you can't get drunk on your wedding day. Now my brain was so fried that I was unable to come up with anything like a list of people who had been in my car in the recent past. Anyway, surely they would have contacted me if any of them had been missing their phone?

I took the phone to Tom, telling him that the mechanic had found it in the side-pocket of my car under four inches of water. 'Do you by any chance know whose this is?' I asked.

'Well, it's not mine anyhow,' Tom said, producing his own phone from his back pocket as if by way of proof. 'That phone's an android. I'm all Apple, me. Essential for my work, y'know what I'm saying?'

'I never know what you're saying, Tom – it's one of your charms.'

He was peering at the phone, turning it over in his hands. 'It's an android all right, but I won't know which make until I get the back off it.' He removed the back of the phone with the irritating deftness of a conjuror. 'A Samsung.' He was squinting at the inside of the cover. '*Jesus Christ almighty! It's got William O'Grady's signature on it!*'

He passed the cover to me and, sure enough, there was the signature, '*William O'Grady*', executed with an indelible pen. The phone had belonged to the dead parish treasurer. But how had it got into my car? Had someone planted it?

I produced the very crumpled Elastoplast notes that Tom

190

had taken to referring to as the 'Murder Map'. I drew an unsteady line from O'Grady's name to a badly drawn small rectangle, which I titled 'Phone,' and from this I drew another wobbly line to my best effort at a drawing of a car.

'What the fuck's that?' Tom asked, his brows knitted to decipher my rendition.

'That's my car.'

'How the fuck did that pass the NCT?'

For clarity, I wrote 'Arthur's Car' beside the drawing.

Pointing towards this, I drew four arrows, beside which I drew a question mark. I intended to insert the names of people who had been in my car when and if the fog ever cleared from my memory. At this moment it was as misty as the interior of the windscreen of the vehicle itself.

'We need to find out what's on the phone.' Tom reached over and grabbed the biro. He drew a short string of bubbles emanating from the phone and ending with a cloud, in which he drew another question mark.

'The man in the garage said to put the phone in a bowl of rice in the hot-press to dry it out. Should it be fried rice or boiled?'

Tom ignored this. He said, 'I know a guy who knows his way around phones. Good that it's not an iPhone, they're the very bugger to crack. It may be possible to image the phone without opening it. You can use a hacked USB driver. If the content isn't encrypted it should be easy enough and, even if it is, we can use the technique those Russian guys were selling, by doing the cryptography on the back-end server by overwriting the TEA protected areas. OK?'

'Tom, you lost me just after "I know a guy". How do you know people like that? How do you know all this stuff?'

'I'm a member of Nerds Anonymous. We share stuff at our online meetings.'

The eyebrows were flatlining and I couldn't tell if he was winding me up. He had shaken out the battery and prised the SIM card from its niche, like I'd seen people do in TV crime-dramas.

'You know that if you turn on that phone, it'll bring the cops down on you quicker than you can say "Daniel Kinahan"?' he said.

'Still the obsession with organised crime, Tom? You should get out more.'

'I've proved my point before, and I'll prove it again when you wake up with a horse in your bed.'

'It was just a head, Tom.'

'Ahead of whom?' Inscrutable eyebrows. 'By the way, any tracker software wouldn't have worked while the phone was under water in your car. Trackers use GPS, which bounces off the surface. Maybe that's why the cops haven't arrested you yet.'

'Just take the phone with you and see if your friend can do his magic on it, will you? And thanks, Tom, you're the only person I can trust.'

Was it my imagination, or did he look shifty at the mention of 'trust'?

I decided to go for a hike to clear my brain, which kept shorting out with the thought of Tom and his buddy in a basement room waterboarding the Samsung to reveal its backdoor. I pushed the image away.

As I trudged up towards the Lead Mines' chimney, past the centuries-old slagheaps following the mile-long flue leading to the chimney itself with its elegant cantilever spiral steps, I tried to reason out my predicament.

I was certain that the phone had not found its way into my car by accident. Someone was trying to incriminate me. But who? And had I blundered by not handing over the phone to the Gardaí straight away? I concluded that no matter whether I handed it over immediately or delayed while Tom interrogated it, the Gardaí would believe that I had stolen it from the dead man and had tried to hide it. I couldn't just throw it in the sea or into the mud of Bray harbour at low tide. If it was found, my disposal of it would be read as an admission of guilt of various crimes, up to and including the murder of O'Grady. And it probably would be found. I remembered with a shudder the case of the man convicted of murder on the evidence of his jettisoned cell phone found on the shores of Poulaphouca. Besides, the garage man knew I had the phone, and so did Tom. The garage man owed me no allegiance and Tom's relationship with Hilary made me worry about him. I was beginning to think that the ice on which I stood wasn't fit to bear my weight.

Tom's pal was quick. Tom returned the phone that evening with a memory stick which, he said, held its entire contents. The battery and SIM card were loose in a plastic bag with the phone.

'It didn't put up much of a struggle,' said Tom. 'Easy when you know how.'

24

Marked Garda cars and a familiar large white van arrived outside the entrance of my apartment block. Blue lights were flashing like a monochrome disco. There was no point running away. Where could I go?

I felt the censure of a hundred neighbourhood eyes peeping to watch my further disgrace in the apartment community. I was certain that my tenancy of my cramped dwelling was going to be terminated. I remembered that there was a clause in my lease that said something to the effect that I was not to carry on, or permit or allow to be carried on, any carry-on on the premises. Whatever I had done, it was certainly 'carry-on' and I had either done it myself or had permitted or allowed it to happen in my flat. I could expect to hear from my landlord and the management company with my marching orders pretty damned soon.

When I answered the buzzer, Detective Garda Francine Bluett introduced herself and asked to be let in. I knew by her formality that she meant business. When I opened the door of my apartment, she was there in full uniform, looking fabulously formidable.

'Are you going to put handcuffs on me, Francine?' An erotic frisson ran through me at the thought of restraint at the hands of my crush.

'I wouldn't waste good hardware on an eejit like you, Arthur. Where's the phone?'

'What phone?' I tried to look gormless. The image of Tom and his friend torturing the phone flashed back.

'We know you have William O'Grady's mobile phone. Where is it?'

Without further struggle, I handed her the plastic bag with the phone, its battery and SIM card.

'I only found it today. The man in the garage handed it to me. It was in the passenger door pocket of my car. I've no idea how it got there.'

'Don't be telling me fairy stories now, Arthur. I think you'd better come with me and we'll have a chat down at the station. And, by the way, I think you should get a solicitor.'

I didn't know any solicitors. I had never bought a house or made a will. I had never been in trouble with the Gardaí before. What would I be doing with a solicitor?

'Can I phone a friend?'

'Don't be a smart ass, Arthur, for God's sake.'

'I meant it. I need to let someone know where I am.' I had my own phone in my hand.

Francine nodded and I phoned Tom to tell him what had happened. I asked him to ask about a solicitor.

———

The Garda at the desk seemed delighted to see me again.

'Ah, Arthur, nice to have you with us again. Welcome! I understand that this is a more formal visit than the previous ones but, look, you're welcome any time.'

Detective Garda Bluett went through the formalities of charging me with suspicion of two murders, interference with evidence, withholding evidence and misleading the Gardaí in the course of their investigations. She cautioned me, took my fingerprints, then took me through to the familiar interview room with its smell of guilt. I almost felt at home.

'OK, I'll lay some cards on the table for you, Arthur. We found William O'Grady's laptop in his house, but it was locked with a fairly sophisticated password. We had to get our technical guys onto it to unlock it, which took until yesterday. On the laptop we found where O'Grady has stored the IMEI number of his phone. Then we found the phone-tracking App that he'd downloaded. It's linked with GoogleMaps and operates even when the phone is switched off, as long as the SIM card is still in it. It's very accurate. When we activated the system, it showed us that the last traceable location was your apartment block. It's gone dead now. What were you doing with the feckin' phone, Arthur?'

'I don't want to be formal, Francine, but would you mind waiting with your questions until I've got a solicitor present?'

At this point the bulk of Sergeant Bowring imposed itself on the meeting. He burst into the interview room, nodded to me but ignored Francine. She looked annoyed. I thought I saw the hint of a blush. She swept a lock of her lovely hair off her face and snared it behind her ear. I thought how beautiful she looked when she was angry.

Bowring was exultant. He liked the bully's high ground.

'What's this about hiding the dead man's phone, Arthur. That's a criminal offence, you know.'

'I want a solicitor, please.'

'I thought you were pure innocent, Arthur? What would you want with a solicitor?' Bowring was leering at me, his lower lip wet.

'I've done very little wrong, but you guys seem convinced that I'm a murderer, so I'm pleading the Fifth, OK?'

'You're not in America, you know, so you can't. But sure if you've done nothing, why would you not want to chat?'

I continued to exercise my right to silence, and soon both Francine and her sergeant left me alone.

Locked into the interview room with nothing but my thoughts to entertain me, I sat it out until the door was opened and Tom came in with a middle-aged, heavy-set woman in an ill-fitting charcoal-grey suit and a cream blouse, decorated at the throat with a floppy bow. Her hair was arranged in an untidy sort of chignon (if I correctly understand that style of coiffure), showing a white stripe at each temple. Her rather long nails were painted a vivid scarlet colour.

'Arthur, this is Drusilla Doyle, from Rourke and Ruane, Solicitors. Hilary suggested her.'

I eyed Tom sceptically. So, he and Hilary were on solicitor terms now, were they?

Meanwhile, Ms. Doyle was wiping down one of the tubular steel chairs with a tissue before sliding her rather over-upholstered seat onto it. She opened her briefcase and produced a notebook and a pen. She looked at me expectantly. There was a pause. I was so distracted by the idea that Tom and Hilary were cheating on me that I couldn't think what to say to this stranger.

Drusilla Doyle broke the ice. 'Tom's already filled me in on some of the history of your case, and I have seen your statement of what happened on your wedding day. I understand that there is a movie?'

'A movie?'

'Yes, you know, one of those MCCTV thingies?'

I began to wonder if this lady was the right lawyer for me. I steadied, and said, 'Yes, Ms. Doyle, there is closed circuit television footage of me moving the body, exactly like I describe in my statement. But I think you'll find that the MCC is a cricket club.'

'So, how do you propose to defend the charge of tampering with evidence? I have to say that it doesn't bode well for you that the cricket club recording picked you up *in flagrante*. The State is bound to argue that it suggests guilt of darker deeds. Placing the *corpus* in the crypt *absens haeres non erit,* out of sight, out of mind as it were, will be interpreted as an effort to hide a crime.' Then she added, by way of explanation, '*Res ipsa loquitur.*'

'But I can hardly withdraw my statement at this stage of the game, can I? I propose to plead guilty of moving the corpse and to plead extenuating circumstances.'

'And what circumstances do you think might excuse such an act?'

'Well, I mean, the wedding – my wedding – couldn't have gone ahead with the corpse in the middle of the church, could it? I made a split-second decision to move the body. I mean the poor man was already dead so I could hardly do him any further harm, could I?'

'So, you decided not to report a very serious crime and to conceal the evidence, so that your wedding could go ahead?'

'Well … yes.'

'And how was the big day? Have you photos?' She seemed suddenly enthusiastic.

'My bride called it off at the last minute. Did she not say?'

'*Numquam serius ad rectum,* as the saying goes,' said Drusilla Doyle, making a note on her pad.

I wondered if all her notes were in Latin. I stared at her blankly.

'*Numquam …*' She made gestures with her head as if to encourage me to remember my long-evaporated school Latin, then in tones of disappointment she translated, 'Never too late to get it right, *eh*? Sorry to hear that it was all in vain, then.'

'Will that go against me?'

'Well, you're going against yourself, in a way, by pleading guilty. By the way, did you kill the chap?'

I was so astonished by her question that I was unable to find suitable words to offer by way of an answer.

She decided to soften me up with some more lingo, 'Come, come, Mr. Cummins,' she made a face at the pun, took a breath and offered me '*Abbati, medico, patrono que intima pande.*' This time following up with a translation. 'Hide nothing from your doctor, minister or lawyer'.

I assured her that I had killed no-one. I retraced the facts of the discovery of the body in the church, then went on to outline the circumstances of Alan Fenton's presence in my apartment and his untimely, if not entirely unpopular death. I also covered my understanding of the anonymous planting of William O'Grady's phone in my car.

Ms. Doyle impaled her bun with her pen, steepled her fingers in a slightly irritating manner and said, '*Negare omnia*, is the best way forward, Mr. Cummins. Deny everything, and say as little as you can. There's nothing wrong with saying 'no comment' to any question the Gardaí put to you. And now, Mr. *Cummins,* I must be *going.*'

She stood without acknowledgement of my flinch at her wordplay.

'*Ave atque vale.* That's Catullus, you know. "Hail and Farewell". Oh, and by the way, because the case involves murder, we'll have to apply to the High Court for bail. That'll take a day or two and I don't know yet if the State is going to oppose the application. You should make yourself comfortable on remand in the meantime.'

Just before she left me, a thought occurred to me. I couldn't very well pay her using the hot notes I'd robbed from Fenton's dead body. As a solicitor and an officer of the court, she might have to report herself for money-laundering.

'Ms. Doyle?'

She stopped in the doorway.

'I'm not sure how I'm going to pay you for your services.'

She smiled for the first time and said, 'I bet you say that to all the girls, Mr. Cummins,' and left, leaving me very little wiser on any front.

25

I read somewhere that the ancient high kings of Ireland eventually outlawed druidism and the druidic language because the druids had gained too much power. They controlled the laws and did so through the medium of a special language that nobody else could understand. I wondered if Drusilla Doyle was a latter-day druid. Whether by the mystic exercise of the Latin language or other Tridentine occult powers, she managed to persuade the High Court to grant me bail at what she assured me was bargain-basement surety. This weighed in at €5,000 cash with a bond for the same amount, and I had to surrender my passport to the Gardaí.

I didn't dare pay for my bail with Fenton's money for fear that the notes might be marked and traceable to him, which wouldn't exactly assist my defence case. Tom, unflinchingly, put up the bail. I didn't ask where on earth he had laid hands on that sort of money. It was only when I walked out of court in exercise of my conditional freedom that my mind began to quibble at how cheaply the State had measured me as a flight risk. I also considered how tricky the condition of surrender of my passport might have been if I hadn't redeemed it from the Gizzard Man.

Instead of accepting Tom's generosity for what it appeared to be, I picked at it in my mind and questioned his intent. I made no objection to his stepping in in this way, and thanked him profusely for restoring my liberty, but internally I wondered if this was all part of a larger deception being practised on me by Hilary and Tom, a ruse to lull me into believing that nothing was happening between them.

Then I started to berate myself for being so stupidly paranoid and for allowing a useless jealousy to taint my thinking. The jealousy was useless because, if I were to be honest with myself, I was glad that Hilary had called off the wedding and that cancellation should have fully unchained both her and me from the bonds of our engagement. She and I should have no further obligation to each other. I also told myself that if I felt free to indulge my crush on Francine Bluett, Hilary should be free to do whatever with whoever she chose.

But Tom and Hilary ... please!

One of the many foibles of my leaky grey car was that the battery would go flat if the engine wasn't turned over every few days. When I made it back to my apartment and found my car stashed in the dusty corner of the underground carpark, of course the battery was as flat as a karaoke singer. My insurance didn't cover house-calls, so I called Tom, but he said he was in Sligo on (undisclosed) business. I was stuck. My last resort was Hilary.

She was very gracious on the phone and drove around to my place with a set of jump-leads. With typically efficient precision she attached the battery of her car to the battery of my car, started her engine and after an emphysemic cough or two, my car's engine was running in its own smoky way. I felt that I couldn't invite her for coffee in the scene of the death of her brother, particularly because the ceiling of the bathroom still bore the jagged scars of his demise. So, we manoeuvred our cars in the dim basement, until her car was in my space and my car was free to drive.

We drove to Kilruddery and sat in the lofty space of the Granary Café.

'Are you paying Drusilla Doyle's fees?'

'No, what made you think that?'

'Well, who's paying her? Is it Tom?'

'I don't know, Arthur. Tell me about the phone, will you?'

'What's to tell? Someone planted it in my car.'

'Or hid it? I believe the Gardaí tracked it to your flat.'

How had she known that? She could only have got it from Tom. The green gargoyle of jealousy with all its paranoia and twisted logic was sitting on my left shoulder, jeering in my ear. I told myself that of course Tom had told her – weren't we all on the same side? Gradually the goblin faded.

We walked around the ancient gardens of Kilruddery, which were beginning to awaken in these early days of spring. A swamp of purple crocus flooded a lawn and early daffodils bejewelled the fringes of the garden.

'Hil, you need to know that I was glad when you called off

the wedding. I'm fairly sure that we'd never have made a good Darby and Joan. Besides, all this drama has forced me to have a look at myself and take stock. I think I'm going to quit my job and start in a new direction. I'm stuck in a low mood and I need a fresh start.'

She said nothing, just kept pace with my walking in quiet companionship. The day seeped away and, after fish and chips from a place by Bray railway station, she suggested going back to her parents' house for a cup of coffee. She said that her parents had gone to their house in Spain. She said they needed a break.

The density of the thick pile Axminster in the hallway created a sort of soundproofing effect. Picture lights glowed reverentially over what I knew to be (because I had been told) originals by highly collectable Irish artists. Hilary brought me into the Aga shrine of the kitchen and put a kettle on. Then, leaning against the stainless-steel rail of the iconic cooker, she smiled at me and offered me a drink. I settled for a gin and tonic, although I was still nervous about what alcohol might do to me in my skittery nervous state.

I followed her into the drawing room and stood admiring a large painting that dominated the room. It looked rather primitive to me, the figures stiff and slightly unnatural. Hilary arrived with two cut-glass tumblers clinking and fizzing, bright lemon shining on the surface. She handed me my drink and raised her glass.

'To the bride and groom!' she said.

We drank the ironic toast. We both stared up at the big picture, vibrant under its shaded light.

'It's a MacGonigal. Daddy says it's worth a lot of money.'

She slipped her arm around me and gave me a sideways squeeze. I was trying not to tremble, but the plush room and the nearness of Hilary was beginning to trigger a panic attack. I took a gulp of my gin. She had her head on my shoulder.

'I haven't had a chance to say sorry for abandoning you at the altar,' she said. 'It was a horrible thing to do. But I think in the long run it was better than marrying you would have been. I still love you, Arthur. I love you too much to marry you.'

I started when I felt my crotch being fondled. I didn't know whether to surrender or put up a fight. Was I being led to heaven or to hell? In my confusion, my body started to respond and I must have let out a small groan.

'Are you OK, Arthur?' She was looking up at me, her face furrowed with innocent concern.

I glanced down to see the family Labradoodle nuzzling my groin.

'I'm fine, thanks,' I said in a voice that emerged several tones higher than normal. I patted the dog and took another swig of my drink. The gin was beginning to relax me, but I was still struggling to get to grips with the surrealism of the situation. I suddenly felt very tired.

'Hil, I need some sleep. I got very little while I was in the cells, and it's catching up with me like jet-lag. Could I spend the night here? Would it be OK?'

'Sure, no problem. I'm in the granny-flat. The sofa's a pull-out bed. It's quite comfortable. I'll show you.'

She led the way out the kitchen back door and into what looked like a garage, with a stack of firewood that gave off the rich incense smell of chopped oak. A nicely made flight of stairs led to an upper floor.

'Daddy didn't bother with planning permission for the flat. He says that if there's any trouble, the Minister will fix it for him.'

I tried to digest this superfluous information as we climbed the stairs. The kitchen/sitting room upstairs was stylish and well appointed. A wood-burning stove stood on the back wall with a large sofa sagging comfortably in front of it. With a typically deft tug at the bottom rail of the sofa, Hilary transformed it into a double bed. 'I'll just get you a duvet and some sheets,' she said, having vigorously plumped up the cushions and redistributed them in a bed-like manner.

I sat on the edge of my transformed bed. My mind started to race, keeping pace with my pulse, which was running at an unhealthy sprint.

What was I doing here? Was my own place so cursed and tainted after what had happened there that I couldn't bring myself to sleep there anymore? Was this place any better? Did some prehistoric urge within my subconscious desire to have sex again with Hilary?

On the mantle above the stove were some family photographs. Despite my agitation, my curiosity gave a quiver. I stepped closer to have a look. There was a picture of Hilary, dressed like a model from *Horse and Hound*, wielding a shotgun with the sort of casual ease that can only come from hours of practice. In the photograph, she was dispatching a clay pigeon with clinical accuracy. The next photo showed her holding a trophy and was captioned, '*Hilary Fenton, Ladies High Gun 2022 ICTSA 100 Shot, Glenealy Co. Wicklow*'.

This was a skill I didn't know that my ex had. I began to wonder how much more about her I didn't know, despite our long friendship and ill-fated romance.

When the bed was made up and Hilary had shut the bedroom door behind her, I began to undress. As a matter of habit, I emptied my pockets. Among the random pocket-trash, I found the Murder Map, much creased and dog-eared. I stared at it again, knowing that there was something on that sheet that would unlock all the secrets of the two deaths, if I could only read it. I remembered that I had originally been one of our possible suspects, as had Tom and Hilary, but all three names had been dismissed as being beyond reasonable suspicion. Looking at the three excised names on the original list, I tried to remember which of the three of us had pushed to have the names removed. I think Tom and I had agreed that Hilary's name be taken off the list. As I remembered it, we didn't want to upset her when we asked her to join the investigative team. But I didn't know then that she was a champion shot. This thought expanded like the plot of a nightmare and, before I lay down to sleep, I slipped down to the garage/woodshed below, picked up the hatchet that lay beside a pile of kindling and brought it upstairs. I slept with my axe beside me on the sofa-bed.

26

I slept relatively well that night, but woke well before first light. I drank some water from the tap in the kitchen and pulled on my clothes. I had a sense of plunging dread, which must have come from a dream, the storyline of which had vanished with my breath on the frigid air of the February morning. I put the axe back where I had found it, let myself out and drove out to Kilmacanogue and the little road that provides a muddy place to park at the foot of the Little Sugarloaf. The air was still and cold enough to sting the nostrils. An enchantment of frost enhanced the valley below me as I set off on the stony track. In the still air, the hiss and growl of the N11 still penetrated, but less as I ascended.

I found the business of walking soothing. The simple practicality of putting one foot in front of the other and moving forward distracted my conscious from the turmoil and incessant jabber of my inner voice, or were there voices now? Plural. Incessant.

Walking had become my way of sorting problems. On the

southern shoulder of the Little Sugarloaf, I had a flashback, vivid and gory. It was a fragment of a recurring nightmare, but it sometimes played on my inner cine-screen while I was awake.

The flashback resolved into a flash of inspiration, but it was a very scary inspiration, and one that I would have to keep to myself for the present.

Pushing the flashback aside, I concentrated on trying to knit together all the loose ends surrounding the murders into something resembling a whole.

I decided that it was time to call a meeting of what I had begun to think of as the Famous Three. Hilary had excused herself from this group after her brother's death, but I felt that peace had broken out between us, and her knowledge of the chief players was useful. She would be an informed sounding-board for my theories.

Back at the car, I called Tom. 'I think we should meet again at my place. And I think that Hilary should be there too.'

I think he said, 'Cool, I'll tell her.' But his voice was so squelchy on the line that it was nearly impossible to make out what he was saying. I wasn't asking him to contact Hilary, but his reaction implied that they were in close contact. The idea made me queasy.

Tom and Hilary arrived at my apartment together. Under normal circumstances I wouldn't have found this suspicious, but I found myself in circumstances that had strayed very far from normal. Hilary and I eyed each other warily, like two cats facing off on a garden fence. To stave off my incipient panic attack, I organised tea and supermarket digestive biscuits.

I decided to get to the point.

'I think I've sussed the riddle of the missing parish funds,' I said, sitting at the dining table with the Murder Map with the list of names and other hieroglyphics that Tom and I had developed spread before me.

Hilary viewed the dog-eared sheet with horror. 'Jesus, Arthur, don't ask me to touch that thing – it looks as if it's been twice through a recycling plant. What happened to the flip- chart?'

'Defenestrated, remember?' said Tom.

There was a silence, broken only by the crunching of Tom eating a biscuit. It sounded like a stone-crusher at work.

Hilary rummaged in her handbag and produced a Filofax and started making notes, while peering disgustedly at the Murder Map.

Through a mouthful of biscuit, Tom said, 'Is this guess-work or is it, like, based on facts? You're gone in the head, Arthur, you know that, don't you? It's this PTSB thingamybob. You're crazier than Tom Cruise, man.' The eyebrows suggested scepticism.

'What's crazy about Tom Cruise?' Hilary asked, creating a vacuum which took a little while to clear.

The other Tom shot me a glance.

Then Hilary decided to overlook the Hollywood reference and said to me, 'I hope you haven't dragged me down here to hear another conspiracy theory, Arthur.'

'Just bear with me a minute and hear this out. This is a list of the people who might have had access to the bank passwords and codes.' I pointed to the list, the Quinlans now having been redacted with a black marker.

William O'Grady [parish treasurer]

Karen Quayley [rector and parish CEO]

Jennifer Roundstock [Karen's partner and pillow-listener]

Geoff Quayley [William O'Grady's (ex?) lover and housemate]

I added the heading, '*PARISH ACCOUNT*' and under that the amount taken and the date on which this had happened: €500 k. 21.12.22.

'I think we agree that it's unlikely that Willie stole the money. As parish treasurer he would have been the obvious suspect. For the same reason, I don't think that Karen Quayley was the thief.'

'So, if you're right, we're left with Jennifer and Geoff,' said Tom, warming to my reasoning.

'You said that you had facts to back up your guesses, Arthur,' said Hilary. 'This is just a whole lot of guesses.'

Tom held up a digestive biscuit by way of protest, 'Hold on, hold on, let's just hear him out.'

'Guesses, yes, but not just wild speculation – informed guesses,' I said. 'Look again at the list of people.' I pushed the tattered Murder Map with the four names towards her. 'We know that there was an account with Minotaur in the name of William O'Grady. Now, we don't know that this was where the parish money was put, or if it was opened for that purpose but let's say it was.'

Hilary again started to object to all the guessing, but Tom again shushed her, putting his finger to his lips.

I went on, 'If the account was opened for the purpose of housing the money, it doesn't make sense for it to have been opened by Willie himself. So, it must have been opened by someone masquerading as Willie. And in order to achieve that, the account couldn't have been opened face to face. It had to be done online. Now, from the list, who, other than Willie himself, would have had access to Willie's identification documents – his passport, for instance, and his utility bills?'

'Not Jennifer Roundstock anyway,' said Tom, his eyebrows fully engaged in thought.

After a short pause, Hilary pounced. 'Geoff Quayley! He and Willie were lovers, they shared a bed in Willie's house. Geoff would have had access to the documents! He could have stolen O'Grady's identity. He could easily have scanned his passport and some utility bills. The way Alan was operating Minotaur, you could have opened an account with a dog licence. And if Geoffrey Quayley was being blackmailed by Willie, it makes sense to place the money somewhere that promised capital appreciation in case the blackmailer made another demand.' Hilary was now on the scent.

I sat back, satisfied that by guessing the shape of one piece of the jigsaw puzzle, I had identified where it would fit in the big picture. I was also pleased to have drawn Hilary into the guessing-game.

'It's a door painted bright yellow,' said Tom.

'What?' Hilary was lost.

'It's a lemon entry, my dear Watson.' Tom's eyebrows were supercilious.

The brutality of the Holmes and Watson pun on 'elementary' hit home.

'Jesus, if you can't take this seriously, I'll leave.' Hilary was in no mood for frivolity.

Tom flicked his eyebrows at Hilary in a manner that would have tried the patience of Buddha.

I went on, 'Look at it again. Geoff told me that he had parted from Willie because of a breach of trust. He also said that he and Karen came south because of some nastiness in the North. I'm guessing now, but I'd be willing to bet that Willie was putting the arm on Geoff over whatever had happened in the past, and this is the way Geoff found to stop the blackmail. Even if the Minotaur account was discovered, it painted Willie a very bright colour of guilty. Maybe not lemon, but awkward enough to keep him from dipping into the well again.'

'Your language has become very colourful since I broke it off with you, Arthur.' There was scorn enough in her tone to wither a rainforest.

'So, did he kill Willie?' Tom's eyebrows stretched into a vertical infinity.

'I don't think so,' I said. 'I believe that Geoff still loved Willie.'

'To coin a phrase,' said Tom.

The blowtorch of Hilary's glare was now focused on him. If there was any love being shared between this pair, clearly there was little to spare at that moment.

'I disagree,' she said, with some force. 'Quayley was hiding in the church when Arthur found the body. I don't believe his story that he was priming the organ for the wedding. And O'Grady had told the parish council the previous day that he knew the identity of the thief, *and ...*' She raised her voice and an imperious finger to emphasise the conjunction, in the manner of a prime minister at the dispatch box dominating an unruly house of commons, to clear the way for her final puzzle piece. '*And ...* he planted O'Grady's phone in Arthur's car when he gave him a lift after their meeting in Cabinteely Park. It was Geoffrey Quayley without a doubt. He's the thief and the murderer. No question.'

'*Quod erat demonstrandum*,' I muttered, and regretted it immediately. I felt that I had been spending too much time with Drusilla Doyle.

27

I called Francine.

'I need to meet.'

'Well, all you have to do is drop in here to the station any time – you're always welcome.'

I was unsure what level of irony was mixed in with this invitation. I decided to be cautious.

'Much as I enjoy the Garda station, Francine, I want this to be off the record. I'm not sure I would be able for much more of Sergeant Bowring. And I won't involve Drusilla Doyle this time. Just you and me.'

I heard a sigh. It wasn't a token of longing or desire, more of impatience.

'OK. I'll see you at eleven tomorrow morning in the Red Bird Café off the Southern Cross Road. And no nonsense, OK?'

'I look forward to a meeting without any nonsense,' I said, although I hadn't been aware of much nonsense prior to this. I resolved to invite her to dinner as soon as all the criminal proceedings had been put to bed.

I arrived slightly early. This had become a habit, which allowed me to acclimatise with my surroundings before getting down to any business. It also helped to fend off any panic attacks that might be lurking in the unfamiliar undergrowth. The little café was snug without being too full, and noisy to the extent that it was unlikely that anyone might overhear our conversation. The view to the west over the Scalp was really beautiful. So was Francine, when she turned up, wearing a jacket and jeans, her hair held back in a barrette, with one stray wisp floating by her left ear. It was all I could do to restrain myself from brushing it behind her ear.

She bought a coffee and sat opposite me at the plank table.

'I think that Geoffrey Quayley may be the person who stole the parish money,' I said.

Francine's rather severe countenance thawed by a degree or two. 'And what brings you to that conclusion?'

I brought her through all the reasoning of the Famous Three from the day before. I stopped short of showing her the Murder Map. She wasn't as enthusiastic as I had hoped she'd be.

'That's very interesting, Arthur. Do you have proof of any of that?'

'You're not being fair, Francine. I don't have the resources or authority to go looking for corroboration, and I'm not trying to prove anything beyond reasonable doubt, but I think my theory is pretty much waterproof.'

'OK, we'll look into it. But from what you say, William O'Grady was a habitual blackmailer. According to you, he did it as a hobby. But I can tell you there's no sign of any blackmail money coming into O'Grady's bank account. Nothing.'

'Can you tell me if you've traced the IP address of the computer from which the instruction to transfer the money from the parish account was made?'

She turned her wonderful blue eyes towards me. 'No. Anything else?'

Was there anything else? Oh, yes, there was. Other things. But not things I felt I could share with Detective Garda Francine Bluett.

I settled my features into what I hoped was a neutral expression and asked, 'Does Bowring still believe that I killed Alan Fenton? Even though I couldn't have?'

'Well, yes, he does. He claims that he was the one who spotted that Fenton died with his shoes on. He has drawn the conclusion that if it wasn't suicide, then you must have killed him. He says that you could have shot him and then come round to the Garda station to tell me that he was holed up in your flat.'

'Yeah, but I didn't do it, did I? And before you let Sergeant Bowring loose on me, can I again point out that he was twice my size – how could I have overpowered him and taken his gun? Can I also point out that I had no motive for the murder, unlike all his clients, including the Quinlans?'

In the background the espresso machine did its jet-engine impersonation as it heated some milk and the general clattery chatter of the café went on around us. I sipped my coffee while Francine digested the reasoning I had offered her.

'I'll see if any part of your theory checks out ... You seem a bit thoughtful, Arthur, is there more?'

'Well, yes, actually. Can you tell me about the CCTV footage at the door of my apartment block? Did it show anyone entering the building after I left to go to the station?'

'Not really.'

'Meaning?'

'There might have been, but a very powerful LED torch was shining into the camera, so the recording only shows shadows. Keep that to yourself. Bowring would have me transferred to Mullinahone if he thought I was disclosing any information to you.'

'Fenton must have let someone in. It must have been someone he trusted. I can't think of anyone other than myself who he might have trusted that night, and that points the finger at me again. But I was at the Garda station with you and the SWAT squad. That's a pretty solid alibi, don't you think?'

'Unless you killed him before you came to the station.'

'We're going round in circles, Francine. Can I ask you something?'

'What is it?'

'When can you have dinner with me?'

'Never. It's like doctors and their patients. I can't make a friend out of a suspect, but I can suspect a friend.'

'So, I'm off limits even if you did fancy me?'

'I'm not even going to answer that.'

'I'm thinking of changing my career. Do you think I'd make a good detective?'

'You're kidding me, right?'

'I'm going to hand in my notice in the aircraft-leasing thing. It's a nothing job with no prospects. I hate it. All this stuff has made me stand back and look at myself. I really enjoy investigating. I'd like to join the Gardaí. What do you think? I'm serious. Then we could have dinner, couldn't we?'

'You'd have to apply at headquarters. They'd assess you.'

'Seriously? I'd have to be assessed to take you out to dinner?'

'If you're as thick as you come across, I doubt if they'd pass you.' Francine stood. 'I think we're finished here. OK? Thank you for your thoughts.' She left, never once looking back.

Defeat beckoned me from a darkened corner, but I rejected the invitation.

———

It was Hilary that phoned me to tell me that the Gardaí had arrested Geoff Quayley. I turned on the TV news to receive a close-up of Sergeant Bowring's bloated face making a statement to the effect that Mr. Quayley was assisting the Gardaí with their enquiries. He smugly refused to answer any further questions. I wondered if he looked more revolting when he was snarling or when he looked self-satisfied. I switched off. I couldn't bear Bowring's ugly mug in my sitting room.

———

Drusilla Doyle's office was on the lower ground floor of a grand Victorian building on Northumberland Road. I had taken the train and walked from Lansdowne Road. The bare trees resembled diagrams of cardiovascular systems, reaching their grey capillaries up to a leaden sky. The neat streets of Dublin 4 looked rinsed and exhausted. Someone had planted some spring bulbs in what had been the front garden of the house. I wondered who had taken the trouble. The sad-looking little flowers merely added to the general feeling of exhausted anxiety that haunted these former residences.

An elderly lady (or so she seemed to me) courteously showed me into a reception room at the front of the house where a large table dominated. A bookcase stood at one end of the room, stocked with what looked like law books that hadn't been opened for many years, and an incomplete set of law reports. The wallpaper looked new, but soulless. The fireplace at the other end of the room was so clearly disused that it made the room feel cold. But a cleaner had given the place a wipe with a duster so that the obvious surfaces shone. My mood was fairly bleak, and I didn't risk making it any bleaker by investigating beyond the immediate. The mature lady receptionist told me that Ms. Drusilla would be with me shortly. I whiled away the moments by examining the spines of the books on the bookshelves in case any good might come out of them.

'Ah, Mr. Cummins! I believe we have some cause to rejoice, at the risk of being accused of epicaricasy. Not a word one encounters every day, is it? You might be more comfortable with *schadenfreude*, but I would always favour the ancients over the Barbarians when it comes to language. This time Latin, my *lingua franca*, has left a *lacuna*, but as usual the Greeks have a word.'

I must have looked unusually blank.

Drusilla paused to allow the semantic dust to settle a little before continuing, 'Of course we're talking here about rejoicing in the misfortunes of another. The DPP's office has been on to me to say that in the light of Geoffrey Quayley's arrest for, *inter alia*, the murder of William O'Grady, the case against you has been dropped.'

'What? So, I'm cleared of all the charges?'

'Sadly, no. The principle of *falsus in uno, falsus in omnibus*, doesn't apply in common law. So just because the Gardaí got it wrong in relation to the murder, it doesn't mean they got everything wrong, although many of the charges relating to the murder itself will fall away, *mutatis mutandis*. We need to make an application to the High Court, it being the court of appropriate jurisdiction or *forum conveniens*, to have the charges relating to the murder dropped. I can do this *ex parte*, that is to say, without your having to be in court, if the DPP doesn't object.'

'That's very good news, Ms. Doyle. Thank you.'

'Oh, please, call me Droosie, everyone else does. And, by way of *quid pro quo*, may I call you Arthur?'

'Of course,' I said, mentally rehearsing 'Droosie Doyle' and deciding that the full Drusilla had much more cachet.

'Of course, now that you are no longer accused of murder, the *forum conveniens* reverts to the District Court, which has jurisdiction over the more minor *acta rea* with which you have been charged.'

'Things like moving William O'Grady's body?'

222

'By the way, Arthur, if you didn't kill the poor man, remind me, please, why did you hide his body?'

'I know it looks crazy in hindsight, but at the time it seemed like I had no choice. If I didn't hide the body, the Gardaí would have sealed off the church and the wedding would have been cancelled. I thought that I couldn't let the whole thing collapse like that. Not after all the fuss and hoopla, all the expense. I probably wasn't thinking straight, but I felt I had to do something to keep the wedding on track.'

I stopped short of telling Droosie about the moneylender. If all of that was introduced into court, it might bring the law down on the Gizzard Man, which would bring his vengeance down on me. I'd already had a taste of that and I wasn't anxious to sample any more. Besides, she would want to know how I had repaid the loan, and I didn't want to shine any light on that. And, I didn't know who was paying Droosie's bill. It occurred to me that I didn't entirely trust my lawyer. A sad state of affairs in the middle of a very sorry tale.

Droosie seemed to be satisfied with my explanation.

'You had no choice? Oh, *bravo*, Arthur! You're beginning to warm to the language of the law, I can see it already! I think we might plead the *jus necessitates*, or *quod necessitas non habet legem*. Necessity, Arthur, knows no law. You found yourself *in extremis* and in deep shock, faced with a horrendous choice, between a veritable Scylla and Charybdis, a rock and a hard place. You had to choose between stopping your wedding by calling the police, and allowing the wedding to go ahead by hiding the body. I can argue that *actus non facit reum, nisi mens sit rea.* In your confused and shocked state you lacked the *mens rea* to commit the crime of which you were charged. The murder was clearly *non est factum*, not your doing, and the intent was not to cover up the murder, but merely to postpone its discovery so that your nuptials could continue. After your bride called it off, you confessed to the Gardaí immediately. No real harm done at all.'

I exercised my right to remain silent, my head spinning from the simultaneous translation from Latin to English and back again.

Droosie went on, 'Now the business with the dead man's phone is another matter, Arthur. What were you thinking? Those things can be tracked on the dark side of the moon, if you'll pardon my Floyd.'

'But, Ms. Doyle – Droosie – I didn't know I had it. And when I found it, I didn't know whose phone it was. I handed it over as soon as I found out whose it was.' Another very pale porky, if not entirely white.

'Then how did it find its way into your car?'

'I think it must have been planted. I think it stayed quiet because it was under water. It was hidden in the pocket of the passenger door. The car leaks badly and there is a pool of water there. As soon as the phone dried out, it started yelling for help. The Guards jumped to the wrong conclusion and charged me with concealing evidence. How could I conceal what I didn't know I had?'

'Very good, Arthur. You clearly have a good legal mind. You have gone to the heart of the thing, the very *cor rem*. Once again we have *non est factum* and an absence of *mens rea*. It wasn't your act and you didn't knowingly conceal the phone. You will defeat all charges *seriatim*, one by one, like shooting bottles on a fence. I'll make an application tomorrow to have all charges struck out and you should be in the clear. Keep your chin up, *nil desperandum*, Arthur, *omnibus bene erit*, all will be well.'

But Droosie hadn't met Sergeant Bowring.

28

I caught up with Tom later that afternoon and we enjoyed a pint together in the Harbour Bar. If my old friend was messing with my ex, I decided that my friendship with him was more important than my pride. Enjoyment of the pint was unblemished.

'Have you had a look at that memory stick I gave you? My guy gave the phone the full truth-serum treatment and it sang like a canary. It fessed up everything it knew onto that stick.'

'I'm not sure I should have all that information. It's a bit like eavesdropping. Doesn't feel right.'

'Ah, don't be getting the scruples on me now, Arthur. Someone bashed Willie O'Grady's head in, and the phone information may tell us who did it. That's what the poor man himself would have wanted, isn't it?'

'I suppose so.'

'Jesus, don't tell me you haven't checked out what's on the memory stick?'

'Well ...'

'Ah for the love of Mike! Have you your laptop with you?'

'No, of course not. It's back at the apartment.'

'Well, come on then, let's go back to yours and see what happens when we wind up the gramophone, shall we?'

We went into the off-licence on the way home and armed ourselves with some cans. There was nothing at home. I wondered why I still thought of it as home. Any domestic warmth that the place might have offered had long since dissipated with the tramp of forensic boots.

When we arrived at my door, I paused, key poised. The jamb was splintered and the door was slightly ajar. I listened carefully before pushing the door open. Tom took up station a cautious distance behind me.

'I'm watching your back, buddy.'

There was nobody there. The flat was empty. But it had been very efficiently turned over. All drawers had been emptied onto the floor, cupboards had been ransacked, the contents flung onto the floor as well, anything capable of being broken had been well and truly smashed. My bed had been stripped and the mattress ripped open. The intruder had taken the trouble to search in places that I didn't know existed. The kickboards under the cupboards in the kitchen had been pulled away. The lid of the toilet cistern had been smashed. My toothpaste tube had been slit open and the paste had been smeared all over the basin. The freezer compartment of my fridge was open, the glacier that had formed in it dripping on the floor, creating a puddle around the tub of antique ice cream. The bag with Fenton's money in it was gone.

This didn't look like a casual break-in. This was systematic and professionally thorough. And my laptop was missing.

'You can come in now, Tom. All clear, as they say in the American crime dramas,' I said, mentally pointing my imaginary sidearm safely at the ceiling.

Tom was keeping close to the wall and moving forward with caution. 'Wonder what they were looking for,' he said in a whisper.

'Why are you whispering?'

'You never know who might be listening,'

'Do you think they were after my laptop?' The theft of my computer was a welcome distraction from the fact that twenty-five thousand euro had also been pinched from my freezer.

'You're pulling my leg, buddy. They wouldn't break in just to steal that ancient hand-cranked thing.' Tom was admiring the thoroughness of the chaos. 'They've raked over this place with a nit-comb. Professional, like. They must have stolen the computer as a last resort. Desperation. They must think there's something on it. Did you download the memory stick?'

'No, I told you.' I held up the memory-stick, attached to my keyring.

There was nothing random about this break-in. It was connected with all of the crimes I'd had nothing to do with. I felt as if I was being picked on by some celestial bully. Or was it another warning from the Quinlans? But surely I was done with them?

I phoned Francine and told her what had happened. She said she'd arrange for a Garda team to come around.

Meanwhile we were to touch nothing. I didn't mention the memory stick. Or the deep-frozen money.

'Would it be OK if I waited somewhere else and your colleagues could call me when you get here. The state of this place is giving me the ab-dabs.'

'Fine.'

We went round to Tom's.

Tom had a bedsit of sorts, with no windows, only skylights. In one corner was a tiny stand-alone modular ensuite that looked as if it had been made from recycled plastic bags. Stepping into this windowless box was deeply claustrophobic, which added to the general penitentiary atmosphere of the place. His bed folded up against the wall when not in use. Beside his desk, which doubled as a dining table, complicated bits of electronic kit were stacked on a metal frame, standby lights twinkling and glowing, indicating that the machinery was ready for action and possibly thinking. I had never asked Tom what this machinery was for. In the centre of this array was a state-of-the-art Apple Mac laptop with every bell and whistle known to that giant corporation attached. He kick-started it and plugged the memory-stick into one of the USB ports. The computer screen came alive with neat little numbered boxes which Tom told me contained data. He told me that all Willie O'Grady's Apps, photos, videos, contact lists, emails and text messages, everything that had been stored on the phone's memory or on its SIM card, were all in that data.

'It'd make you think twice about what you do on your phone, wouldn't it?' said Tom, his eyebrows cocked in a knowing way. 'We need to take a few shortcuts, man. Otherwise, we'll be here for a week. We'll have to ask some leading questions so that we can get at what we want.' He looked at me, eyebrows poised like sprinters waiting for the start gun. 'What do we want?'

I shrugged, frowning. There was a sneaky-peepy element to this operation that I didn't enjoy. I felt that we had no right to intrude on the dead man's cyber-correspondence, beyond what was strictly necessary. I would have preferred, somehow, to confine our interrogation to things that were specifically relevant to Willie O'Grady's death. But we had no means of singling this data out from this end of the telescope, so to speak.

'This doesn't seem right,' I said.

'Coming over all squeamish again, are we?' said Tom. 'A bit late for scruples, buddy.' He swept aside my rather faint-hearted misgivings. 'OK, let's start with WhatsApp messages, they're the easy bit,' he said, his cursor flying round the screen like a wasp in a back-lit jam-jar. Obediently the computer brought up the dead man's WhatsApps. 'OK, and let's look at O'Grady's most recent messages.'

Then he did a vile thing, which I knew was his habit when warming to a computer task. He meshed his fingers and inverted the conglomerate, producing a stomach-turning crunching crackle of knuckles causing me to flinch and shudder. Then he froze. His head came up as he sat back from his desk and the screen, his hands off the keyboard, his mouse abandoned. For a ghastly moment I wondered if he had broken a finger.

'Well, fuck me sideways!' he said. '*Read that!*' He tilted the screen towards me.

It was a WhatsApp message to Geoff Quayley. It read: 'Meet in the loft at 7.30 tomorrow morning.'

The message was dated the day before the wedding. William O'Grady's last day on earth.

'So that's what Geoff was doing in the organ loft. He was waiting for his ex.'

'No wonder the Gardaí arrested him. Looks like they have him bang to rights.' Tom was clearly disappointed that the hunt's climax had arrived so early.

We sat for a while, the blue light of the computer screen glowing in front of us proclaiming Geoff Quayley's guilt. It looked like game, set and match for Sergeant Bowring. But there was something else troubling me.

'Someone did a very thorough number on my flat,' I said. 'I don't think they were after information about the murder. The phone wasn't in the flat, so I think they stole my laptop in the hopes that I had downloaded the phone's memory. They would only have gone to all that trouble if they thought that the phone had something very valuable on it. What do people store on phones, Tom?'

'Access codes, passwords?' The eyebrows were pricked.

I pulled out the Murder Map and smoothed its much-distressed surface on Tom's desk. There was no further space for ideas, so we stapled another sheet to one side of the original, Tom being without Elastoplast. Tom wrote down 'Access Codes and Passwords' beside my very bad drawing of the mobile phone, and stalled.

'What the hell was O'Grady hiding? Something he shouldn't have?' I found myself drumming my fingers on the computer desk. The eyebrows beckoned me on. After a little quality thinking time, I went on, 'When I told Francine about our theory that O'Grady was into blackmail, she said that there was no sign of hush-money coming into his bank accounts. I'm sure he was at it, but where did he put the money? Tom, hypothetically, if you had hot money, where would you keep it?' (Not in your deep freeze, I thought.)

'Somewhere pseudonymous,' said my friend, 'somewhere pseudonymous and fungible.'

'What on earth are you talking about, Tom?'

His face was a painting of innocence, but the brows gave him away.

'Cryptocurrency,' he said, the eyebrows doubly encrypted.

29

'Who is it?' I croaked. It was seven thirty in the morning. Who the hell pays visits at that hour?

I had been woken by the heathen shrieking of the door buzzer. It's a mistake to sleep with your mouth open. My tongue had shrivelled to a dried stick. I couldn't gather enough saliva to swallow. I'm not sure if I had slept at all that night, which had played out like the storyboard of a horror movie, one nightmare after another. I couldn't remember any of them. Now I was launched into another.

'*Gardaí. Open the door, Cummins.*'

I recognised the blunderbuss tones of Sergeant Bowring. All niceties had now been dispensed with, including first names. I was 'Cummins'. It was like being back at school, singled out for retribution for something I either didn't do or couldn't remember doing. I did as I was told. I let him in.

'You, me lad,' said Bowring breathing heavy from the exertion of the stairs, 'are under arrest on suspicion of murder, tampering with evidence, withholding evidence and misleading the Gardaí in their investigation of a crime.' There was a snarling glee in his voice.

———

I was behind bars again. The desk sergeant at Bray Garda Station had welcomed me like the manager of a fine hotel receiving a returning honoured guest and hoping for a good review on Tripadvisor. I had been put in my old cell and eventually brought into the defeated interview room again, where Drusilla had already taken up station, ready for an interview with Sergeant Bowring.

'How are you, Arthur?' she had asked in her hearty manner, all confidence and legal swagger.

It was easy for her, I thought, she could be certain of going home that evening to do whatever lawyers do in their time off. I was certain of nothing except at least one more night in the cells.

'I'm well, Droosie. Thank you. Do you have any news from the outside world?'

'Well, I've written to your landlord and to the Management Company of your apartment, reminding them that constitutionally you are innocent of all crimes that may have been alleged against you. They are all *factum probendum*, matters that have yet to be proved. I warned them that any prejudicial (and I used the word carefully and with its full meaning), any prejudicial action by either of them with a view to expelling you from your flat would bring a ton of writs down upon them before they could say Nick Robinson.'

'I'm not sure I care.' I was beginning to allow despondency to get the upper hand on my mood.

'Oh, but you mustn't buckle, Arthur. I've told you before, *nil desperandum*, and you don't want to lose your security deposit, do you?'

I didn't.

'Oh, and your friends Hilary and Tom have been cleaning up the mess left by the intruders. She asked me to tell you that they were keeping an eye on the place for you.'

'That's kind of them,' I said, summoning up all the sarcasm I could muster.

'Oh, and I understand that Garda Bluett has been taken off the case. I phoned the Station to let them know I was coming, and I got on to a very chatty Guard I know. Seems Francine had a lively disagreement with Sergeant Bowring about charging you with the murder of Alan Fenton. I'm told she's filed a complaint against the good sergeant. He, in turn, has reported her for insubordination and dereliction of duty. A nice mess.'

I was devastated at the thought of Francine being taken off the case, but very much heartened to hear that she had been defending me to Bowring. It meant that she was prepared to make serious sacrifices on my account. Could it mean that she was growing fond of me? I stilled my beating heart with a deep breath and told myself not to read too much into this turn of events.

'I don't suppose,' I ventured, 'that squad-room squabbles are of any help to my cause?'

'Not really,' she said as she produced a notepad and a pen. 'Now, would you like to tell me again all about the late lamented Alan Fenton, your relationship with him and the facts leading up to his death.'

When I had finished my account of events, Droosie steepled her fingers in her clichéd mannerism which wasn't helped by her chipped nail varnish, and said, '*Hmmm.* I see.' Her tone was that of a bridge player considering a singularly hopeless hand.

At this point Bowring burst into the room. I think that bursting was a habit with him, just as his belly was perpetually bursting out of his shirt. Having made his customary entrance, he was now in the process of taking his stomach back into custody and tucking his shirt into his waistband. Any thought that this was in an effort to present himself in the best light to my lady lawyer was quickly dispelled.

'Ah, Miss Doyle, I believe. I thought your practice was confined to defence of speeding tickets and parking fines. Murder is a new departure for you, is it not?'

'Be careful, sergeant. Any more disparagement in front of my client and I'll report you to your superintendent. Now, what do you have to ask my client?'

She angled her notebook so that I could see her written advice. '*Say nothing, or less.*'

Bowring flipped the switch on the recording device on the table and announced the names of those present, then gave the date and the time. The recording machine made an intermittent quiet squawking noise like a bilious bantam hen. Bowring allowed a long silence to expand into the room like a threat.

Droosie tapped her pen on her notepad, sliding her eyes at me to emphasise the right to silence.

After staring at me for longer than would be deemed polite in genteel society, Bowring broke his silence. 'I hear you owe some people money, Cummins. What's that about?'

'I thought that banking was a confidential business, Sergeant.' I decided to neither confirm nor deny. I didn't tell him that his intelligence was impaired, that he was behind the game.

'You wouldn't want to let those people down, Cummins. You've heard of the Quinlan gang, no doubt? Well, let me tell you that you don't want to get on the wrong side of those bucks. They're the boys that would teach you a lesson, oh yes!'

How the hell did Bowring know about the money I had borrowed? I had told nobody. Was he in cahoots with the Quinlans, for God's sake?

Droosie waded into the gathering tension, 'And where is the lovely Garda Bluett, today?' Her face was worthy of a Las Vegas poker queen.

'On other duties. Not with this case anymore.'

Droosie added another twist to the wind-up. 'That's a pity. You did rather a splendid 'good cop – bad cop' together. And do you really believe that you'll be able to persuade the DPP's office to have my client charged with this murder?'

'Your client, with all due respect, Miss Doyle, is a degenerate – a devious slippery hooer if ever I seen one. Full of smart-alecky wisecracks and disrespect for the Force. He may have slithered out of the killing of William O'Grady, but by Christ he'll not escape this one!'

'Well, I'm sure you're wrong, Sergeant. Just as I'm sure that you are unshakeable in your misconceptions on most things. Tell me, Sergeant, why have the pathology report and the ballistics report not been made available to me yet?' She was smiling in a crocodilian way.

'I have them right here, if you want them,' he said, but made no move to hand anything to her.

'And what do they tell us about the killing of Alan Fenton?'

'He was killed with the shotgun that was found at the scene. Single shot to the head.'

'Are my client's fingerprints on the gun?'

'Not exactly, no. There are only the dead man's prints but they're very smudged. We assume that Cummins wiped the weapon down after he killed Fenton. Also, there was a pair of rubber gloves on the premises. We think he may have worn them when he used the gun.'

'You are assuming a great deal, Sergeant.'

Droosie allowed another silence to blossom. She had made some notes on her pad and seemed content for the pause to continue eternally like the two minutes on Remembrance Day, climbing like ivy over the stagnant furniture and walls of the interview room.

Bowring made a snorting noise as he cleared his nasal

passages, and for a dreadful moment I thought he might hawk the bolus into his mouth to spit. Worse, however, he swallowed. I began to feel nauseous.

'My client,' said Droosie, 'has already made his position clear. He has been straightforward and truthful to the Gardaí *ab initio,* from the get-go you might say. He had no reason to kill Fenton. Many others did. He brought the Gardaí to the *locus delicti* and, although you seem to think that this was a bluff, it is quite clear that his actions were those of an innocent man.'

Bowring wasn't to be put off. 'That's what you would say, isn't it? But there is a clear *prime facie* case against Cummins. The dead man was a fugitive, he had a gun. He was found dead in Cummins' apartment, shot with his own gun. *Ipso facto,* Cummins has a case to answer.'

I now had my lawyer and a law enforcement officer batting Latin phrases between them like tennis players. I thought that this didn't bode well for my case. I would prefer to be tried, if I were to be on trial at all, in English (my Leaving Cert. Irish wasn't good enough to risk in open court).

Bowring ran his tongue over his lower lip, which now glistened in a sinister way. He stood, gathering his file to his belly, which had again escaped the constraints of his belt. 'We're done here, Miss Doyle,' he said and slammed out of the interview room.

30

Freshly released on continuing bail, I went immediately to my car, to see if by any chance the battery was still current. I had fully expected it to be as flat as a badger on a bypass, as Tom might say. However, in a totally unexpected gesture of co-operation on the part of my conveyance, the engine turned, fired and revved at the first attempt. Never being much one for signs and portents, I avoided reading too much into this surprise, but I couldn't help wondering if I hadn't turned a corner of some sort.

Back at my apartment block, I parked the car in a place where it was facing down a slight slope. I had sound reasons for this: first, it would be easier to start if the battery decided to give up the ghost again and, secondly, the holes in the floor were slightly forward of the centre-point, and the water had a better chance of finding its way out if I parked on a hill.

I phoned Tom to ask for his help in choosing a new laptop to replace the one that had been stolen. He arrived at mine armed with a six-pack of beer.

'Canned brain juice,' he said.

We had a beer together and I fought back the desire to ask my old friend straight out what the story was with him and Hilary.

'And tell us, how was chokey this time?' Comical eyebrows arched over a lazy smile.

'Fairly shit, since you ask. It's a bit like hospital, in that they always take you in just before a weekend, and you can't get sprung on bail until the Monday.'

I thought I detected a note of derision behind Tom's smile. I wondered if he was enjoying my jealous misery. My suspicion of betrayal by my two closest friends was undermining me like mica in a Donegal bungalow. I needed to concentrate on the replacement of my computer.

'What do you think I should get?' The question sounded phoney, a deliberate evasion of the pachyderm in the parlour.

Tom took the question on face value. 'Something lightweight would suit you, buddy. What system was the old one on? Abacus manual beads?'

I didn't reply in case Abacus Manual Beads was a computer software thing.

The visit to the computer shop was swift and decisive.

'Come on, man!' said Tom, at the checkout. 'Make with the fantastic plastic!'

I handed over my credit card and punched in my PIN with my head spinning with gigabytes and RAM. We took the new machine home and Tom spent an hour or so setting it up while I brooded.

Tom opened the last can of beer and plugged the little memory stick into the USB port to bring up again the page showing the neatly boxed contents of Willie O'Grady's phone. He went again to the box labelled 'WhatsApps' and brought up the seemingly endless list of messages.

But before he could go any further, I blurted out, 'Tom, you know you and Hilary?'

'What?'

'Are the two of you an item?'

I was blushing with jealous embarrassment, if such a cocktail emotion exists.

Tom slowly stood up from where he was crouched in front of the laptop. The glow from the screen made him look very pale.

'For fuck's sake, what sort of question is that?'

'Simple enough, from where I am: are you two an item?' I was trembling, almost in tears.

'Jesus, Arthur! I'm not going to answer that stupid-ass fuckin' question because it's none of your fuckin' business!'

'Well, I think it is my business. She would have been my wife only she decided not to. And you're my best pal. My best fuckin' man. And it's fuckin' hurtful if you're carrying on with her. And I'm not having it, d'you hear me?'

I was ready for Tom to swing a punch, or storm out of the flat, or smash the new computer on the floor. But he just sat again on the sofa with his hands on his knees.

'The truth is, I don't know, Arthur, my old buddy. I just don't know.'

'Don't start messing, now, Tom. What do you mean, you don't know?'

I exhaled and drew in another breath. Breathing had become a thing.

Tom said, conversationally, 'See, there I was testing my theory of irresistibility and she happened to be in the pub. You know yourself the way when you've had a few and all the edges get fuzzy. She's a lovely girl. But I haven't a clue if anything happened. The edges got so fuzzy that I can't remember how I got home that night.'

'So, you tried to chat her up?'

'Of course I tried to chat her up. I've been trying to chat her up ever since I first met her with you all those years ago. Been bangin' away at it like a poodle on the leg of a table. It's the habit of a lifetime. I don't think it means anything anymore. It's just a sign that I'm still healthy.'

'Don't try to make a joke of it now, Tom. I'm fuckin' serious. You haven't answered my question. Are you two an item?'

I stood there, fists clenched, ready to give my best pal a thick ear. But what he was saying had a ring of truth to it. I could see Tom, chatting and charming and drinking all at the same time. And I could see Hilary, still bruised from our virtual divorce, matching him drink for drink, but staying in control as she always does. I couldn't get my imagination to take the final leap.

Tom stood again and calmly left the apartment, shutting the door smartly behind him. Then he shouted back through the closed door, 'Don't be a fuckin' tool, Arthur!'

Was that a 'no'?

I brooded some more after Tom had left. He had neither confirmed or denied any serious liaison with Hilary, so the question remained open and infected in my mind.

The screen on my brand-new laptop had switched itself off. I nudged the mouse and the screen came alive again. I opened the list of Willie O'Grady's WhatsApp messages again and scrolled to the week before the wedding date. Apart from the message to Geoff Quayley, there was nothing there of any interest. I dug deeper, to the week before that. Still nothing. I scrolled to two weeks before the wedding date and found a message from O'Grady to Alan Fenton. The message contained nothing except repeated emojis of a skull, line by line, filling almost the entire screen. At the bottom right- hand corner of the screen was the single word '*Theseus*' like a signature. Whatever the message meant, it certainly had a strong degree of menace to it. I needed to share this bit of information with someone, but who? I was fairly certain that Tom had been carrying on with Hilary, which ruled out both of my investigative companions. I was the last man standing of the Famous Three. I was contemplating my lonely and miserable status when my flock-of-geese ringtone signalled an incoming call. It was Karen Quayley.

'I was wondering if you could possibly pop round for a wee chat,' she said.

Even on the phone her voice sounded righteous. She was asking me a favour, but she managed to make it sound like an imperative and as if she was helping me. I wondered if they teach those nuances of tone at vicar's training college – or was it something about the Northern Ireland accent?

I agreed to go around to the rectory right away.

After I had rung off, I realised that I was in a cul-de-sac of crap and very much in need of some means of propulsion. The Reverend Karen might have something to aid my paddling.

31

The Reverend Karen answered the door as if she had been waiting in the hallway. I was shown into a parlour that was decorated with studied simplicity. Everything was carefully neutral in style and colour. The only direct statement was the small wooden cross on a side table. I concluded that this was the room where Karen met with parishioners who had need of her ministry.

She offered me tea, which I declined. I asked for water instead, and spent a barren minute or two while she fetched it, contemplating the purposely bland room. I found it depressing.

'Please, Arthur, sit down. Make yourself comfortable.' She had re-entered with a single glass of water, which she placed on a coaster on the side-table.

I sat on an armchair that felt as if it had been chosen specially for its qualities of discomfort, so that visitors would not be tempted to dally.

'Actually, it's about something you have already raised with me, but it's also about Geoffrey,' Karen said, sitting opposite me on what looked like an equally unwelcoming chair. The table with the glass of water on its coaster was between us. She was wearing a pale-blue blouse with little purple silk-knot cufflinks, a clerical collar, and a well-cut blazer. She was tugging and fiddling with the button of her blazer, and I was afraid that it might at any minute go spinning. She was clearly distressed. 'He has withdrawn completely into himself since he was arrested. He's out on bail but he barely ever leaves his room, he's not eating and he hasn't spoken to anyone other than me.

'But there's something else. When we last met, you asked me about the money that had been taken from the parish account? Well, the Parish Council authorised me to engage a forensic accountant to investigate. The Council preferred to continue to keep the matter private and away from the Gardaí until we knew more about it. The forensic person came from our firm of auditors, a very pleasant young woman, smart and personable, glamorous, in an understated way, not at all like an accountant.' Karen shifted on her chair and drew a breath. I wondered what Reverend Quayley's vision of accountants was. She was blushing, possibly because she had been attracted to the forensic person, or maybe it was because of what she was about to reveal to me.

She continued. 'I authorised the bank to give her full access to the account for investigative purposes. She did some digging and turned up something astounding.' She paused again. She was looking down at her hands. Her fingers entwined and disentwined, then entwined again. She looked directly at me for the first time. 'Would you mind if I had a sip of the water?' I gestured for her to go ahead and she took a sip from the as yet untouched glass.

After she had somewhat composed herself, she continued, 'It seems that the electronic instruction to withdraw the money from the bank came from the IP address of my laptop.' Here she paused again, as if to allow this information to sink in. She took another sip of water and went on, 'The money was traced to another bank, but they refused to disclose the name of their customer. So, the accountant girl got a court order directing the receiving bank to disclose, on the grounds that there was a possible fraud behind the transfer. The receiving bank disclosed that it was for the account of MinotaurMaze Solutions – Alan Fenton's firm. Normally the firm wouldn't disclose their client, but my forensic girl had been thorough in her court application and the order of court obliged the firm to disclose the name of their client – it was William O'Grady. The account had been opened on the same day as the money was taken: the twenty-first of December last year. Midwinter's Day. And all from the IP address of my laptop.'

Reverend Karen paused again. I wondered if she thought I was slow of mind and needed time to catch up.

'Of course, the account is now frozen because of the collapse of the firm, so my girl was unable to go any further pending completion of the general investigation by the Gardaí and the Central Bank.'

Reverend Karen now stood and paced to the window to stare bleakly out at the leafless garden.

'I needn't tell you that wasn't me who transferred the money. I'd never do such a thing. And anyway, why on earth would I?' She was struggling to regain her familiar righteous smugness of tone. 'But we didn't want to report the missing money to the Gardaí until we had found out more about it. It wouldn't have looked good for me or for the parish. Of course we've told the Gardaí everything now, but I think they still suspect me for being so slow to come forward and because my IP address was used for the whole thing. Otherwise, it simply confirms my suspicion that the money had been taken by William O'Grady. We'll never know why, now, will we?'

She returned from the window and sat down again as if to punish herself with further torture from the chair. She remained agitated.

'Geoffrey asked me to contact you. He said you were kind?' She said this in the tone of a question, as if she had difficulty believing it. 'He needs someone else to talk to. I think he's afraid that his regular pals – they're mostly members of the parish –might have turned against him because of the murder investigation. He said that you were kind and sympathetic when you last spoke together.' She repeated the kindness piece as if this might make it true.

'Is he here now?'

She shrugged. 'He says he has nowhere else to go. He's upstairs in his room. Not exactly hiding, but not making himself obvious either. I think he told you about our unconventional marriage. But he may not have explained that it's not just a matter of convenience. It may surprise you, bearing in mind our very contrary predilections, but Geoff and I are a sort of queer love story. We have a very loving arrangement. And I'm concerned about the old boy. Will you have a word with him? See if it helps him. He's very down right now.'

Karen Quayley left the room to fetch Geoff. While I waited, I stared out the window to alleviate the merciless blandness of the room and tried to deal with the extraordinary information that had just been given me.

When Geoff came in, he avoided eye-contact and sat on an obscure chair by the wall, that looked like it had been divorced from the other furniture and had lost its purpose, like the chairs you find in hallways. He sat awkwardly, as if learning how to sit side-saddle.

'Good of you to come, Arthur. Thank you.'

'Not at all. I'm just wondering what I can do for you.'

He fidgeted a bit as if trying to make up his mind about something, then sat up straight, took a breath and said, 'D'you remember I told you that I broke it off with Willie because he betrayed a trust? Well, years ago, I'd been involved in a misunderstanding with a younger man in the North. The boy had lied to his parents, said I forced myself on him. All lies. The poor lad was trying to cover up that he was gay. The PSNI decided not to prosecute. But the parents got in touch with the UVF. It's why Karen and I came south. Willie had found out about all this and was trying to blackmail me. Now, you see, I'm in a bit of a fix. All the evidence points to me as the killer. I was in the church when the body was found, and

Sergeant Bowring declares that I had two motives to kill Willie – I was a spurned lover, and he was trying to blackmail me over that old business in the North – but, sure, how could I kill Willie? It was me ended our loving affair, and I still loved him, you know? And I miss him. It's still hard for two old buggers to team up nowadays, you know, no matter what the legislation says. There's a lot of prejudice. I must say that Karen has been wonderful. If I wasn't gay, and she wasn't gay, I think we'd have made a great couple.' He sighed and leaned forward in his chair. 'Listen to me, Arthur – you were there in the church that morning. Did you see anything at all that would help me prove that it wasn't me?'

I told him what I had seen and done that morning in the dim early light.

He sighed again. 'I didn't see the murder happen, but I saw whoever it was bringing poor Willie's body into the church. The body was on the trolley. I think it's usually used to move the stacks of chairs around. I couldn't see the person clearly. It was too dark, so it was. I could only see shadows and I was only peeping and squinting. The person had difficulties moving the body, as if it was too heavy. You seemed to manage without the trolley.'

'I wouldn't read anything into that, Geoff. But you say that whoever brought in Willie O'Grady's body used the trolley?'

'Yes – came in the main entrance. It has ramps for wheelchairs. When the trolley reached the transept, whoever it was just pulled poor Willie off the trolley like a sack of potatoes.' His voice tightened and his lower lip trembled. 'No respect for him at all. The person just dumped him, left him there and vanished. I didn't see where. Might have been out through the vestry, I don't know.'

'Have the Gardaí told you if they have found any of your fingerprints on the plastic sheeting that was wrapped around the body?'

'No. Because there aren't any. Because I never touched it. I never harmed Willie. I never could. And now all that stuff about the blackmail is going to come out. My life is over, Arthur. I can't see any way out. I'm doomed, so I am.'

He had produced a large red handkerchief, more like a bandana, and was mopping his tears and runny nose. I felt terribly sorry for him, but there was only so much I could offer him by way of comfort at that time. I was as sure as I could be that he had not murdered his ex-lover. I wasn't yet confident, but I thought I might be getting closer to the identity of the real killer.

32

I had only three days of holidays left, and I was sliding into a depression at the thought of having to return to the tedious drudgery of counting aircraft when I received a phone call.

'Is that Arthur Cummins?' a female voice said.

'This is he, yes.'

'Arthur, this is Sinéad Ní Neachtáin from Payroll and Performance Partners. Three Ps have a dynamic symbiotic relationship with your employer, Arthur, whereby we perform the interface function between your employer and your good self. Do you have any questions, Arthur?'

What earthly questions might I have? I answered no.

'Are you happy to continue with this discussion by telecom, Arthur, or would you prefer to go offline?'

'Sorry – Sinéad, is it?' I thought I heard her say '*Anseo*', but I could have been mistaken. 'I think you're telling me that you are my human resources person, is that right?'

'Well, Arthur, I'm not sure I would have put it quite like

that, but I can affirm that, yes, Three Ps have been tasked with all matters pertaining to your employment interface.'

There was an awkward silence. I was ready to receive the axe on the back of my neck. I wondered for a second if the guillotine made any sound when the cord or chain was pulled to drop the blade. I heard Sinéad sighing, or perhaps she was only breathing heavily. I decided to break the stalemate.

'*Um* … Sinéad? I think it was you who phoned me?'

There was a muffled sound suggesting that Sinéad was readjusting herself to her original role as the caller. Or maybe she was simply taking a moment to compose the next sentence in the strange language that she seemed to be obliged to speak in.

'Indeed, Arthur. We understand that you are OOO at this moment in time?'

'OOO? What is OOO?'

'It's shorthand for Out of the Office. We believe that you are on leave, Arthur?'

'I'm on holiday. I'm due to return next Monday.'

'Of course, Arthur. And we trust that your holiday is going well?'

'Wonderful, thank you. Now what is it that I can do for you all at Three Ps?'

'On a recent team diagnostic survey, Arthur, it has been noticed that you are currently a person of interest in more than one criminal investigation. You are under something of a cloud?' Sinéad liked to end every sentence on an up-note so that it sounded like a question. When I gave no answer, she garbled into another quasi-query, 'Let me sharpen the pencil a little for you, Arthur?'

'Sharpen away.'

'Sorry, Arthur?'

'You said something about me being under a cloud?' I had noticed that she constantly repeated my name, maybe to remind herself who she was talking to, or, perhaps, to remind me of who I was.

'Well, here's the thing, Arthur. Your employer is placing you on gardening leave until the various criminal issues can be clarified, one way or the other. You will be on full pay, but you are required not to attend at your office, going forward.'

'Oh, I see. Thanks, Sinéad. Thank you for the call. Goodbye.'

And before the person from the HR company I had never heard of could change her mind, I rang off. I neglected to tell her that I was thinking of quitting anyway, but there seemed to me to be no point in quitting a job that was paying me to stay away from the office, so I was just as glad that I had said nothing.

There followed an extraordinary feeling of wellbeing and satisfaction. I had woken that morning feeling oppressed, miserable and picked upon. I had examined my conscience to find any reason why the celestial puppeteers had chosen me as the patsy of the piece, to visit me with such an extraordinary array of bad luck and coincidental misery. I couldn't find anything in my past behaviour that might warrant the dumping of such a mountain of manure on my unsuspecting head. Was it worthy of punishment from heaven that I'd had such a casual approach to life? Certainly, I was perhaps over-endowed with optimism, I wasn't disposed to take anything very seriously and was constantly looking for the cheap joke in everything, but I had done nothing I could identify that could justify all this negative karma, this extraordinary run of misfortune. Now, perhaps the Great Puller of Strings was on his or her tea-break, but at last something had worked in my favour. I had become such an embarrassment that my employer was willing to pay me to stay away. At school I had been asked to mime in the choir for similar reasons.

I put a call through to Francine. I thought it was time to catch up with the progress of the powers of law enforcement. She was frosty with me on the phone, but agreed to meet again for coffee.

We met in a coffee shop on the Bray esplanade. There was a pleasant steamy coffee-scented fug in the busy little shop. I was feeling buoyant after the news of my paid suspension. Francine was not in a good mood. She certainly didn't seem pleased to see me.

'What's up, Francine? You look very gloomy.'

'I don't know why I've agreed to see you, Arthur. You know I've been taken off your case by Sergeant Bowring, don't you?'

'I had heard, yes.'

'And did you hear that it's your fault? Bowring found out that I had met you away from the station and had unrecorded interviews with you. If I had been my sergeant, I would have taken me off the case too.'

'Look, Francine, I'm sorry. But I don't know where else to turn.'

'If Bowring finds out that I've met you again he'll have me holding a speed gun out on the N11 for the rest of my career.' She sighed, casting a wary eye about the place in case of recognition. Then she turned her attention back to me and said in tones of resignation, 'Well, I'm in so deep now, there's no turning back. What can I do for you, Mr. Arthur Cummins?'

Our conversation was interrupted by an obstreperous toddler, who chose that moment to stage a full-blooded, shrieking melt-down because his mother wanted him to put on his shoes before leaving the café. The child was eventually dragged out the door, screaming and barefoot, by his overwrought mother, who then commenced a tempestuous second round of negotiations with him on the subject of getting into his buggy. The performance brought the coffee shop to a standstill as the patrons watched agog, all conversation, all business suspended pending the outcome.

Francine had twisted in her seat to get a better view of the proceedings. Then she turned back to me with an unreadable expression on her face, and muttered, 'In the name of Our Divine Saviour, why would anyone inflict children on the world?'

The finale was a disappointment – the infant fully deserved to be thrown to the bears, if any bears could be found in Bray – but in the end his mother just hunkered down in front of him on the pavement and talked gently to him. It was like watching a small insignificant miracle unfold as a favourite woolly toy got produced and offered to the red-faced incandescent child, who grabbed it and clutched it to his chest, still sobbing but now re-entering earth's atmosphere as his wonderfully patient mother talked soothingly to him, just beyond earshot of the coffee drinkers. The pair eventually strolled off, hand in hand, the mother pushing the empty buggy, the child, still without shoes, holding the toy lovingly in the other hand while wiping his nose on its head. There was a quiet round of applause from the patrons of the café.

'See that?' said Francine, with a smile. 'There are some battles that aren't worth the fight.'

'What do you mean?'

'I know you won't go away if I try to ignore you. I might as well work with you as against you. Between us we'll probably achieve more that way.'

I experienced a rush of affection for the lovely Garda, so pretty in her white hoodie, with her blond locks tied back in a ponytail.

It's little things like this – being put on unlimited paid leave, my car starting without tow-truck intervention, and now Francine agreeing to play detectives with me – things like these make life worthwhile for a simple soul like me.

I told Francine all of this. She was holding her coffee mug in both hands on the table as if warming herself. I reached forward, risking everything, and placed my hands over hers. Her lovely blue eyes darkened as she looked into mine. She leaned forward and murmured, in a tone that lovers might use to exchange intimacies, 'Take your fuckin' hands away, Arthur, or I'll break your thumb.'

The softness of her voice served to underline the real menace of her threat. I moved my hands apart and away from the table, raising them in an attitude of surrender.

'That's better,' she said. 'Now, what is it that I can do for you?'

I had to take a moment to regain my equilibrium. When my heartbeat slowed a little from panic mode, I managed to ask the question that was at the front of my mind.

'Did your forensic team find *where* William O'Grady was killed? I know you weren't able to tell me this before, but a lot of water has gone under the bridge since then.' I shrugged and offered a hopeful face.

She paused to consider, glanced around her in case of listeners, then again leaned forward and dropped her voice. 'Yes, but there wasn't much evidence. It was on the gravel path that goes round the church. The rain had washed most of the blood away. There were tiny traces of blood and brain matter matching his DNA on the wall of the church where it was sheltered from the rain by the overhang of the roof.'

'Is that where the murderer stood?'

'Not in the shelter of the roof, no. We don't think so. We think the assailant was standing on the flat tombstone just above the path. The victim was taking his morning jog along his usual track, which took him through the churchyard and along by the church. We think he was ambushed as he turned the corner of the church.'

'The murderer must have got very wet if he'd been waiting in the rain. Tell me, were there any waterproof clothes found in the church? A wet mackintosh or a parka?'

'No, only two umbrellas. One in the porch, belonging to

Geoffrey Quayley, and another in the vestry belonging to you.'

'Well, I saw Geoff Quayley coming down the stairs from the gallery, and he wasn't wearing any waterproofs, just warm indoor gear. It looked dry. I think he had originally come from the rectory with only the umbrella. It's just across the road, he wouldn't have needed anything more. If it had been him that killed O'Grady he would have been soaked. He couldn't have wielded a heavy blunt instrument in the rain while holding an umbrella. He'd have needed both hands.'

She nodded. 'By the way, forensics are sure now that the weapon was one of the brass candlesticks. You guessed that the particular candlestick was too clean. To be fair, Bollocky Bowring got that right first time too. The post-mortem examination confirmed that the head-wound was a match for a blow with something like a heavy candlestick. They re-examined the suspect weapon and found traces of bleach on it. Bleach wouldn't be used to clean church brassware. It must have been cleaned down after the murder and replaced on the altar. Bowring may be a misogynistic ape, but he spotted the damp patch on the altar cloth under the candlestick and the smell of bleach.'

'What about the timing? The murderer must have known when the flowers were to be put in the church. The body was dumped just after the florist had left. And whoever did it knew how to erase the security camera tape too. This was very carefully planned. The killer had hardly any time. The whole thing was very efficient and well executed. I can't see Geoff Quayley being that organised. Can you?'

'You're good at this, Arthur, I'll give you that!' Francine was sitting back in her chair, watching me assemble my reasoning.

I felt myself glowing under her praise. Endorphins popping all over the place.

'Do you mind if I share all of this with Geoff Quayley? I think he needs some help and I'm not sure he'll get it from Bowring.'

Francine shrugged and made innocent round eyes. 'It's not my case. And I gave you very little. You thought all this out without any help from me. So, by all means share it with Mr. Quayley. It would be a shame to see Sergeant Bowring's case collapsing, wouldn't it?'

I paid for the coffees. I was in a generous mood. When I reached my car, my phone made its noise to tell me that I had an incoming email. I pulled it out and planted my fingerprint. The mail was from Hilary.

'Hi Arthur. Tom and I would be delighted if you and your significant other could join us for a party to celebrate our engagement upstairs in the Martello Bar ...'

The date and time followed but I couldn't focus.

33

I felt as if someone had turned off the pump on my bouncy castle, like I had wandered into an empty lift shaft, like all the angels and saints of heaven had shat on my parade. The two people whose love I had valued most in the world had been canoodling behind my bicycle shed. Tom, who had been my stalwart rock, my steadfast go-to main-man, had lied to me about the canoodle. Hilary, who had been within an 'I Do' of marrying me, had deceived me cruelly about what had surely been a longstanding breach of faith. My two centre-forwards had been playing away from home – together.

I drove my reeking car recklessly to a salesroom on the Dublin Road and asked about scrappage deals. I wandered around the used car lot and kicked viciously at tyres, venting some of my anger on the defenceless pneumatics. I settled in the end for a six-year-old Korean tin box that came with an eighteen-month parts-and-labour warranty and a paint-job of a delicate shite colour that the salesman told me had reduced the price of the thing to something I could stretch my credit

card around, taking into account the generous funeral deal that
was offered in respect of my old car. It turned out that the poor
old leaky vehicle with the perforated floor was worth more to
me dead than alive.

The salesman encouraged me to search the old car carefully
for anything that I wanted to keep. I was flying on auto-pilot
at this time, but the advice seemed sensible, so I went over the
car with a fine comb. All I found was an eclectic collection of
copper coins, a perished rubber bungee, a golf tee (not a sport
I have ever played) and a loyalty card from a supermarket I
don't ever remember being in. But when I scanned the sodden
floor for forgotten treasures, I found a semi-disintegrated shred
of scarlet paper, which kicked off in my head a turmoil of
recollection that brought me up short. Trauma-induced brain-
fuzz had pushed these memories down below the surface of
my conscious mind, but now they came hurtling to the surface
like a pod of breaching whales.

That shred of paper was all that remained from a very angry
parting – that and the dent in the door where Hilary had
kicked it that night. She had been searching in the dark and
the wet with a frantic fervour. She never said what she'd been
looking for. But now, maybe because the process of searching
the fungal depths of the doomed car had brought to my mind
other finds that had been made in that same vehicle, an ugly
possibility was pulling itself from the primal ooze. My tangled,
emotionally jangled brain began to make connections. Was it
possible that she had been looking for Willie O'Grady's phone?
The phone that had so mysteriously turned up in my car and

had brought the full weight of Sergeant Bowring down on top of me? I had thought it had been planted. Was it possible that it had been lost? It might have hopped into the side pocket when the waterlogged Avoca bag had disembowelled itself into the car.

But what the hell had Hilary been doing with Willie O'Grady's phone?

I stood, leaning against my old jalopy, my mind scrambling to recall the sequence of events that followed that night. I was sure that after the incident of the Avoca bag, nobody other than myself had been in the car until I had brought the car to the NCT testing centre. The car had been declared unsafe and was taken directly to the garage in Bray to have its brakes seen to. It was there that the mechanic found the phone. So, the car and its surprising contents had been beyond Hilary's reach, more or less from the moment she lost the phone, right up until the moment I handed the phone to the Gardaí. Jesus, I thought, had Hilary orchestrated the ransacking of my flat and the theft of my laptop? Had she had my flat searched for the phone?

This brought my memory back further to the visit to my apartment of the thugs who had broken my nose after I had spoken to Alan Fenton about his connection with William O'Grady. Had these likely lads been sent by Hilary? No, of course not. I realised that was ludicrous.

I used to love her, and a bit of me still did, despite everything. She was to me like a pirate queen, although I've never met a pirate queen, so I can't be sure. There was so much of her that was magnificent and proud and beautiful and – ah, Jesus – sexy. I'd always be grateful to her for calling off our wedding. But I couldn't find any forgiveness in my heart for her skulduggery with Tom Farrington. That hole-in-the-corner stuff was beneath my image of her as the swashbuckling, skull-and-crossbones-waving heroine. I didn't mind that she'd lopped off my manhood rather publicly with her cutlass – that was well in keeping with her pirate status – but sneaky cheating with my best pal? You can go off people, you know. My mind offered me the image of a toppled statue of a former stateswoman lying in a city square, hand still raised in blessing of her now estranged people. And Hilary had jumped off her pedestal – nobody pushed her.

Wrestling my mind back to the present, I successfully completed the negotiations for the humane destruction of my old car and the acquisition of my new Korean shite-coloured biscuit tin. I sat into the driver's seat and pulled the door to with a very satisfactory clang. It felt snug and dry, like a cocoon against the world. And in this tiny tinny cockpit I allowed myself a scream. I actually frightened my own self with the force of this shriek. It came up from the depths of my soul, it seemed. A howl of anger, misery, woe, sorrow and betrayal. I beat my fists on the leatherette steering wheel, making the little car's horn squeak and attracting the attention of the bewildered salesman who had just sold it to me.

You might think that a distressed state like the one that I found myself in was perhaps not the best time to go about conducting business such as the trade-in and purchase of a car, but actually my new wheels turned out to be a good acquisition, and the dispatching of the old car to the knacker's yard proved to have a pleasingly cathartic cleansing effect on my psyche. I felt somehow reborn. The only stain on my soul was the debit balance in my credit card account. The new Korean car came with an original sin.

Of course, I'd have to accept the invitation and go to the party. It would appear small-minded not to. I brought my phone to life and tapped out a formal 'Arthur Cummins has great pleasure ...' The Martello Bar. More action on the seafront. It was supposed to be where Katie Taylor went for pints, but I'm not sure if that was true. The business of acceptance of the invitation was, I felt, like my first step towards acknowledgement that my longstanding thing with Hilary was finally over. I told myself that she no more belonged to me, any more than I belonged to her. What did I expect? For my permission to be sought before every future tryst?

And the caveman within me said yes, actually, even though my reasoning scrap of brain said no.

I realised very quickly that this sort of inner dialogue was unhealthy, and that what I needed was fresh air and exercise. I parked by the superfluous roundabout at the top of the Vevay Road (pronounced *Vivvy* on the local tongue, in the same way that '*curry*' is pronounced locally with two 'd's) and set off up Bray Head. Pausing for breath on the ascent, I put a call through to Francine to let her know that she had been nominated as my significant other for the engagement party.

'No, Arthur. Just get a fuckin' grip, will you? Not interested.

Unprofessional. Nonsense. What fuckin' planet do you live on, man?'

'I take it you're not keen, then?'

'Jesus Christ, you're like a fly in the kitchen. Will you not give up?'

'Will you hear me out before you hang up?'

'Go on then, sell it to me.'

And I sat on the broken masonry of an ancient wall, looking out over Killiney Bay and began to weave together for Francine the many threads that formed the tangled skein of raw material for the case of two murders. Only fragments comprised direct evidence, much of it relied on circumstantial stuff and shadowy conjecture.

To be fair to my fair cop, she listened patiently, and I imagined her even taking notes as I spun my yarn. I think the clincher was the WhatsApp message to Alan Fenton that I had found on O'Grady's phone, and my understanding of what it might mean. By her silence, I gathered that Sergeant Bowring and his team hadn't found that message or hadn't deciphered its meaning. Or maybe Francine had been left out of the loop following her removal from the case and had not been told about the message. When I had finished talking, she remained silent.

'Francine … are you still there?'

'Yes, I'm afraid I am, Arthur.'

'So, will you come to the party with me? Oh, by the way, it's fancy dress.'

'Ah, God almighty, Arthur, no.'

'Ah, go on, Francine. It means that you can go incognito. I see you in a black leotard with black tights, a cute little cat mask and a tail.'

'I'm not sure that I want to know how you see me, Arthur. You sound like one of those heavy-breathing phone callers.'

'Do I detect a softening?'

And the lunatic gods that had been put in charge of my existence made a decision in my favour.

'Yeah, OK then. But no monkey business, do you hear? This is not a date.'

I brought my phone to my lips and kissed it, then felt foolish and stuffed it back in my pocket and continued my walk with a spring to my stride that I can only put down to romance.

When I regained my little dung beetle after another hour of healthy exercise, I began to wonder if I had not been rather harsh in my scatological condemnation of its colour. The registration details described it as 'bronze', but then I wouldn't have thought that describing it as 'shite-brown' was going to sell too many of that or any model. Before driving home, I took a photo of the car and sent it to Francine with a message 'My new bronze bomber. What do you think?'

'Shite,' came the reply. Maybe I had pushed a little too far. But I was already getting fond of my khaki runabout and wasn't prepared to accept any gratuitous slurs lightly.

I needed a more immediate medium through which to defend the honour of my new wheels, so I switched to phone-call and my heart did a little Riverdance solo when she picked up straight away.

'You're being unfair to the car, Francine!'

'No, I'm not. Look at the thing, for God's sake, Arthur!'

'But it doesn't leak, and everything works! It's got a rear-view camera for driving backwards and the wing mirrors are electric. You can make it wiggle its ears! The colour may not be very attractive, but you don't notice that when you're driving.'

'Yeah, but everyone else does.'

'Anyway, that's how Cinderella will be travelling to the ball next Friday.'

'I'd have preferred a pumpkin, to be honest. I'm just glad that nobody knows me.'

34

The main painting man was a heavy-set, dark-haired guy with a pencil-line moustache that I thought he must have grown for a bet. He had a powerful eastern European accent and a lounge-lizard look to him that was strangely complemented by his preference for wearing shorts, which allowed his clients to see the dark tan on his legs beneath the dense hair and paint splashes. For some reason it pleased me when he told me his name was Narcis. He spent most of the time standing, smoking king-sized cigarettes on the little balcony while he supervised, I supposed, the work of his assistants.

Narcis introduced me. 'This is Nico, this Mica. They twins.' His tone was disparaging as if it was annoying to have indistinguishable workers on his force. He left me with no clue as to which was who. The twin helpers were identical.

I didn't ask if any of them knew the history of the holes and pockmarks in the bathroom ceiling.

The insurance company had at first assessed the damage as

'wear and tear', and therefore outside the cover of the policy. Their assessors must have been trained in some very savage places if the décor damage caused by indoor shootings was regarded as normal knocks and scuffs. I had to ask the Gardaí to weigh in with an outline of the forensic report. This didn't seem to move the computer either, so I phoned Droosie.

'Ah, Arthur, how are you enjoying the qualified freedoms of bail?'

'It's bird-like, thank you, Droosie. Look, I'm having a bit of a barney with the insurance people over the repairs to the flat. Between the shotgun blast, the blood-spatter and the breakage and loss from the break-in, a lot of damage was done. The insurers say it can be put down to wear and tear and that it's not covered.'

'Damn those people! They seem to think it's their mission in life to refuse to do what they have been paid to do. *Uberima fides* my arse, if you'll pardon my Latin. They quibble for the sake of quibbling. I think they have a dedicated team that specializes in obtuseness and unreason. Leave it with me.'

Later that day, I was copied with her email to the insurance company, in which she told them to pay up or face a Civil Bill for breach of contract. 'Your denial of this claim isn't even pettifogging, it is dishonest,' she concluded. The good Droosie was handy with the pen. Her straight shooting was up there with Annie Oakley, and not a trace of a dead language.

The insurers didn't give in immediately. They wanted to know who had been responsible for the damage to the flat. Well, now . . . I thought I knew, but I couldn't share my conclusions with the underwriters just yet. Droosie told them to go to hell, and a reasonably generous offer followed.

'Is finish,' said Narcis, standing on the balcony with a cigarette gripped in his teeth.

'Do I pay you, or does the insurance company look after that?'

'You pay me if you want,' he grinned a wolfish grin that was wasted on my desert air, 'but insurance, she pay anyway. Is good job. You happy.' This wasn't a question, it was a statement, and the smoke-filled grin defied me to argue. I didn't.

Grimy, paint-laden dust sheets were lifted, last scraps of masking tape were peeled, and a final going-over with what I was told by Nico/Mica was a caulking gun (this caused me a stupid shudder), left the flat looking as good as new. Except that my memory constantly offered overlays of gory horror to the now pristine décor.

I phoned Droosie to thank her.

'Are you invited to the party this Friday?' she asked.

I was cautious with my reply. I was still uncertain who was covering Droosie's bill.

'Are you?' I countered, and then gave the game away by asking, 'What are you going as?'

'Judge Judy. And my partner is going as Mr. Punch.'

This reminded me that I hadn't yet settled on my own costume. The hassle of this both annoyed and distracted me. I could never think of a witty or a practical costume for fancy dress. Most costumes were unwearable after five minutes. For example, the spaceman will either spend the whole evening taking the goldfish bowl on and off his head, or he'll put it down somewhere and lose it, leaving his goldfish homeless. I needed something that was plausible as a costume but would be tolerable to wear for a period of time. This ruled out Darth Vader, or anything that involved a rubber mask.

I had allowed time to trickle, so buying a costume online was both against my grain and too late. I was watching Niko/Mika doing some final cleaning when I had a brainwave. After they had left in their enormous van, I headed for the décor store and made some purchases.

Some two hours of cursing, glue-gun burns and much duct tape later, I surveyed the finished costume in the bathroom mirror. I'd have to lose my head in the car but, I joked with myself, that wouldn't be the first time. I was fairly sure that I'd be able to keep it at the party, and that *would* be a first (*ha, ha*). Pleased with my costume and my clever joke, I phoned Francine to check on progress.

'Leave me alone, Arthur. I'm not in the mood.'

'How's the costume going?'

'Still with the obscene-caller script, eh?'

'Do you want me to pick you up, or do you want to come here first?'

'If I give you my address, you'll only be hangin' round here like a bloody poltergeist. If I agree to meet at the Garda station, everyone will know that we're going to the party, and I couldn't be seen in this gear anyway. I can't meet you at the Martello – I might have to say who I'm with. I'd better go to yours.'

'See you here at eight thirty, then.'

Francine buzzed the apartment intercom at eight twenty-five. I should have asked Narcis to jam something in the buzzer, or give it a smack with a hammer, or anything to soften its shriek. Actually, I think he, or one of his helpers, had removed the baffling bit of pizza box that I had stuffed into the works, so that, newly unmuffled, it now sounded like the warning klaxon on a diving U-Boat. I was unprepared for the raw bark of this, and my hand slipped as I was applying a final dab of glue-gun to my costume. I packed myself into my outfit and bounded down the stairs with my keys in my hand.

Francine was wearing the same overcoat she had worn to the funerals; for a utilitarian garment, it must be said that it was nicely cut and followed the curvature of her body with loving attention.

'What the fuck, Arthur?' she said, staring at my get-up. 'No, seriously, Arthur. What the fuck?'

'Good, isn't it?' I turned to model the costume and show her what it looked like in 3D. I was very pleased with the effect of the cardboard box over my head. OK, I'd broken all my own rules with this one, but I was out to impress, and I was convinced that the assemblage of gear from the décor store was a winner.

'No, Arthur, it's mingin'. What the fuck are your supposed to be? And what's that on the front of your shorts?'

I tried to look down to see what she was pointing out, but the box kept getting in the way. Squinting through the gaps in my costume, I saw that a long string of glue-gun glue, semitransparent and suggestive of intimate body fluids had looped around the front of my shorts.

'It must have spurted from my gun when you pressed the buzzer,' was the best I could offer. I tried to brush it off, but it refused to yield to any of my efforts to remove it. We walked in silence to where the dung beetle was parked.

My lovely date was unimpressed by my new vehicle. 'For fuck's sake, Arthur. Are you serious?'

The little car still retained something of its showroom smell. I think the showrooms have a special aerosol that they spray around the interior. A mix of old leather, new plastic and solvent. I'm not sure that I didn't sniff some of that aerosol with Tom back in the day. The silly memory brought my mood crashing. Losing Hilary was one thing, but the thought of losing Tom left me bereft. And that was why I had accepted the invitation, that was why I persisted with the brave front of not caring about the nefarious pairing of the two people closest to me. My self-esteem felt hacked about, like a lone tree on a battle-front. The distraction and challenge of making the costume had helped, but the wounds were still very raw. I hoped that the triumph of my disguise and the thrill of being with Francine would restore me. But Francine's sour mood of disenchantment wasn't helping.

I popped my cardboard-box head in the boot and scooted round to open the passenger door for Francine.

'I think I can manage a car door, Galahad!' she said as she folded herself into the front seat. I closed the door and retreated to the driver's side. As I swung into my seat, I rejected the temptation to remind Francine that Arthur was the king, and Sir Galahad was just a horny knight.

'You still haven't answered my question, Arthur. What the fuck are you supposed to be?'

'SquareBob SpongePants, of course!' As soon as I had uttered the inverted title, I realised that making the costume from memory had been a mistake. A little research might have put my character the right way up. It had been a while since I last visited Bikini Bottom. My memory may have taken a wobble or two in the interim. As I drove, I could feel the oblongs of yellow sponge that I had so carefully glued together to make my sponge-pants begin to separate like the tiles on a disintegrating space shuttle. I hoped we wouldn't be stopped by the Guards.

35

A hailstorm engulfed us as we arrived on the Bray Esplanade. It was like travelling in a badly tuned TV. I could see hardly anything and the roaring drumroll on the roof drowned out all other sound. I drove cautiously along the sea-front, searching for a parking space. There were lights everywhere but it was hard to make anything out through the dense white veil, despite the heroic swishing swipes of the windscreen wipers. Everything was glare and reflection. People were dashing in every direction holding umbrellas, newspapers, plastic bags and coats over their heads as protection against the hail. The people seemed to have a death wish, or at least a desire to get injured under my wheels. From the road, it looked like there was a sort of jolly riot happening at the Martello and the other pubs on the strip. I picked my way along but couldn't find anywhere to park. The hail shower was losing its enthusiasm as we reached the big car park at the Bray Head end of the seafront. I pulled in between two camper vans and turned to Francine.

'Do you have an umbrella?' I asked, thinking that my cardboard headgear wasn't going to last as far as the pub if the heavens went on shot-blasting us with hail. She didn't answer me, but opened her door and let out a screech that made me jump.

'*Agh! For fuck's sake!*'

'What's up, Francine? Are you OK?'

'No, I'm not OK! Look at me! How could I be OK! I'm goin' to a fuckin' fancy fuckin' dress with the biggest eejit in Ireland in the ugliest car in the world and now my fuckin' costume's destroyed.' She waved the soggy end of what might have been a black velvet belt in my face. I had caught whatever it was in the passenger door when I had closed it, and it had trailed in the mud and wet all the way to Bray.

I was out of the car to fetch my cardboard cube from the boot. I admired her lithesome slither from the passenger seat, still holding the end of the black belt. I needed her to know how much I appreciated her support.

'Hey, Francine, I just want to say that you're a good sport, OK? Thanks for doing this. For coming with me tonight. It means a lot.'

'Now lookit, Arthur, you're a lovely guy and all that, but you and me's never going to happen. OK? This is business. Besides, I'm not going to catch you on the rebound. You're only here because that other one dumped you. I'm only here to get my own back on Bollocky Bowring for taking me off the case. I'm almost certain sure it'll all end in tears, so you'd just better pray that something goes right tonight!'

I was praying, all right, but not necessarily for the same things as Francine.

We scampered from the car, all the way back up the Esplanade and ducked under the tent-like awning of the Martello just as the next pulse of hail came through. I took my headgear from under my arm and put it on.

Francine shrugged off her overcoat and, as she crossed the foyer to check it into the cloakroom, I caught the full voltage of what she was wearing, radiating enough raw sex-appeal to fuel the nation's pornography channels for a month. I stood there dumbstruck, jaw swinging open like a broken cat-flap. She had taken me up on my Catwoman idea. A black vinyl Basque with spray-on black plastic leggings and a long tail (with a soggy end). There were zips everywhere, as if to invite unzipping and rummaging in random places, defying imagination. She wore very high black stiletto boots that laced to mid-calf and she had a cruel-looking whip looped onto her belt – straight from a recently raided dungeon, I imagined. She pulled on an entrancing vinyl half-mask hood with cat-ears on top. She had taken trouble with her make-up, so that what could be seen of her eyes was heavily accented with eyeliner.

'Are you goin' to stand there staring like a gobshite all night?' said Catwoman.

'May I just say that I think you look utterly wonderful, Francine?' I countered.

'No, Arthur, you can't.'

We asked at the main bar and were directed up the stairs to the party. There were other revellers drifting in the same

direction. A pirate, a sheikh, what might have been an octopus
– which made me feel at home – and a cowgirl, looking good
in little boots, a big hat and an extremely short cowhide skirt.
Catwoman gave me a very unmannerly dig between cardboard
and sponge.

'Mind your manners, Arthur! Get your eyes off that
cowpoke!'

I had my head in a cardboard box. How could she have
known what I was looking at? Did Catwoman have super-
powers? I couldn't remember. Then I realised I was confusing
fantasy with reality and dismissed the thought. Anyway, her
resentment of my distraction filled me with joy. I pretended
that the jab in the ribs, delivered with considerable venom,
hadn't hurt quite as much as it had.

There were two huge bouncers at the door. They had a
Tweedledum and Tweedledee look to them, brought on by
their matching baseball caps and the fact that someone had
left a large umbrella with them for safekeeping. They were
dressed in black tie outfits, which made them look entirely
villainous. The jackets were stretched to the extremity of
tolerance over over-developed musculature, so that the men
looked as if they had been poured into the jackets and had
then expanded. Massive necks bulged from the collars of their
shirts, clearly resisting all efforts to close at the throat, so that
they looked as if they had been tied together by the black bow-
ties that bound them. A big paw was placed on my chest to
halt my progress.

'*Name?*'

I told them my name and showed my invitation on my phone. A clipboard was consulted and a mark was made beside my name. The hand that held the pen had a small tattoo of a swallow, or was it a fly?

SquareBob and Catwoman made their way to the bar. I decided that I'd allow myself a taxi home, so I ordered a gin and tonic for myself and, on her advice, a vodka tonic with lime for my companion. As we waited at the bar for the drinks, I spotted Hilary. She was at the far end of the room, looking not just radiant, but radioactive. I think it must have been my hyper-emotional state that attributed this look to my ex, but she seemed to draw all eyes to her – she magnetised the attention of the room to focus solely on her.

'There's Hilary,' I said.

'Who? Oh, her,' said Francine, reducing the Geiger-count somewhat.

Hilary was dressed as Bo Peep, complete with bonnet, ringlets and shepherd's crook.

'She looks like she's ready to compete in a Feis,' said Francine.

Then Tom sidled over. He was dressed, so I was told later, as Lurch, the butler from the Addams Family. It was a shock to see him. I was so used to his sleeves and cuffs being too long, it took me aback to see so much wrist and ankle on display. He didn't recognise Francine, but that might have been because he wasn't paying much attention to her face, concentrating instead on the ins and outs of her magnificent costume.

'What's new, pussycat?' The eyebrows took a hop. 'What's

your name? Or is it on your collar?' Not in the least bit disappointed at his failure to get any rise out of my lovely companion, he decided on a change of tack. 'What are you doin' with this loser, Kitty?' The brows flicked at me in utter disparagement.

I had my full costume in place, cardboard box and all. Tom hadn't recognised me, if he'd even seen me. Now he turned his foggy vision onto me and snorted, 'Jesus, he looks like a bag of chips upside down!'

I took the hint from another encouraging dig from Catwoman and said nothing. I kept my incognito rolling, sucking my gin through a straw, led through a carefully crafted hole in my cardboard.

Tom was in full flight. 'What's that you're drinking there, Ms. Galore? Tell me all about yourself.'

'It's a vodka tonic,' said Francine, straight-faced. 'I find it helps me to mind my own business. Would you like one yourself?'

Tom went to the bar in search of vodka. Bo Peep was making her way in our direction, the sea of partygoers parting before her crinoline and panniers. I was dreading this, but I couldn't put it off.

'Hi, Hilary. You're looking fabulous.'

She stalled in her progress, confounded by my disembodied voice, muffled, amplified and ventriloquised by the cardboard box, so that it remained mysterious as to where I, as the owner of the voice that had delivered the fabulous compliment, actually was. Because of the quirky acoustics, my identity as the cubic owner of the sponge-pants also remained a secret.

Hilary turned towards me and surveyed my costume. I felt like I was hiding in a cupboard, quaking and wanting to pee, while my pursuer's shadow could be seen peering through the cracks.

'I don't know who you are, but welcome to the party. I'm not sure I get your costume – are you some sort of scouring-pad?'

Before I could answer, Francine chipped in with, 'Hi, I'm here as a Significant Other,' in a voice full of otherly significance. 'Like your drag, Bo Peep!'

Through the impaired vision of my box, I watched as Hilary struggled to place the outrageously sexy feline person who had addressed her. She was lost for words. Maybe it was the surreal admixture of my disembodied voice and the cartoon-dominatrix apparition that caused her to dry, but dry she did.

At this point, Tom lurched back from the bar with a pint of Guinness in one hand and a vodka tonic in the other. He seemed only slightly put off his stride by the arrival of his fiancée into the mix of his continuing experiment with irresistibility. I think he may have considered that the proof offered by the surrender of Hilary needed empiric confirmation. He ploughed on unabashed with his gruesome chat-up of Francine.

'I got you your vodka, Mrs. Whiskers.' He handed her the drink, raised his glass and said by way of a toast, 'Here's to nine out of ten cats!' and took a substantial pull from his pint.

This was too much for me. I burst out with, 'You are some bollox, Tom! Do you know that?'

Again, the SquareBob effect was wonderful to behold. No

doubt Tom was already a little troubled with ale, but my voice, offering him insults without any suggestion as to the source of the voice, seemed to plunge him into total bewilderment.

'Arthur? What the fuck? Where are you, buddy? Where are you talkin' from? Speak to me, bud!'

I couldn't take any more. Besides, it was getting very hot inside my square head. I doffed my box, feeling at once the colder air around my sweaty head.

Tom, pokerfaced as always, took bleary stock of me. 'That's a fuckin' horrible costume, Arthur. Only sayin'! He held his spare hand up in appeasement then raised his glass to mine. 'Hey, no hard feelings, buddy, eh? But full marks for your girlfriend. It has to be said. Fair fucks, man!'

My old pal didn't blush or shrink in any way as he met the full ferocity of Hilary's glare, a glare that would have burned a hole in a welder's helmet. I remembered that he had once told me that the word 'insouciant' was a descriptive noun for a person eating Japanese food. That was, more or less, how he looked.

He leaned forward and murmured, 'Hey, buddy, need to talk to you. I think I've found something.' And before I could tell him to get lost, he added, 'It'll blow your mind.'

Whatever Tom had found, I didn't think it could have been the Theseus message. His brain was tuned in a nerdy way, but the classical reference of the message would probably have passed him by.

Hilary was ignoring Tom. She was staring at me. 'Arthur! I didn't recognise you in your paraphernalia! What are you, do you mind me asking?'

I suppose I could have told her that I was Squarebob Spongepants, but I had lost faith in my costume. In fact, I was beginning to lose heart altogether. Even if I had got the wretched character's name right, the gear didn't work. I wanted to put my cubic head back in place and slide anonymously away. In a vain attempt to boost my flagging morale, I gave her what I thought was an exceptionally witty riposte.

'I'm a cardboard box, but I could have been a container.'

Hilary blanked me. She either didn't get it or didn't find it funny. Always in command, she caught the attention of a barman, then she indicated my glass. 'Another? Since we can't smoke a pipe of peace in here, we should at least have a drink together, don't you think?'

She gave me her old smile. It wasn't worn-out, it was just familiar to the point that its significance had blunted. It was still a lovely smile but, although it was aimed at me, it wasn't for me anymore.

'You should introduce me to your plus-one, Arthur,' she said, turning the beam of that same smile towards Francine who held out her hand, gloved to the shoulder in shiny black acrylic and adorned with scarlet talons that looked as if they could disembowel an armoured personnel carrier.

'Hi, I'm Frankie. Thanks for havin' me.'

The need to pee had become real in the stress of the moment, and I sidled off to the gents, leaving the other three to chat among themselves. At the urinals, I had a little difficulty sorting out the best way of gaining access to my pertinent parts between the layers of sponge, and the process of relieving myself took a little longer than it might otherwise have done.

On my way back to where I had left the others, I caught sight of Tweedledum and Tweedledee near the entrance in animated conversation with the Phantom of the Opera. I couldn't hear what they were saying, but it seemed friendly and jocose. The mood seemed out of place for those two. It was like watching elephants dancing. The Phantom was giggling and slapping away a stray hand.

When I got back to the table, I found Hilary sitting by herself with two drinks, and my head on the table beside her.

As I sat to join her, an announcement came over the pub's PA system to the effect that a car alarm had gone off. I paid no attention. I'd never had a car with an alarm.

'So, how are you doing, Arthur?'

'I'm not too good, to be honest, Hil. You and Tom as an item came as a fair old slap in the face, you know.'

'I didn't see that I could do you much more damage after bolting at the altar. Sorry if you've been hurt again. I meant you no harm.'

I could discern no genuine contrition in her voice.

'Yeah, but Jesus, Hilary.'

She changed the subject. 'Have you seen the Reverend Karen? She's come wearing a mitre and a ballet dress. Bishop Tutu, I understand.'

'Where's her husband?'

'Oh, he's here somewhere. I'm not sure he wanted to come.'

'I'm not surprised, Hil. Geoff Quayley is on Sergeant

Bowring's list for special treatment and, no matter how that goes, it's bound to have a nasty outcome for the Quayley family. It's not very fair really.'

'Haven't they arrested him for murdering William O'Grady? I thought they had him more or less bang to rights? Motive, opportunity, forensics: a complete wrap. And aren't they doing him for stealing the parish funds as well? Proper order.'

'You are too quick to condemn, Hil. Very righteous.'

The announcement about the car came again, this time with more detail. A meaningless registration number was read out.

'You've gone all solemn on me, Arthur. Come on, this is a party, for God's sake. Drink up and be merry!'

She raised her glass to me and I drank her toast.

I caught a glimpse of a full-bottomed woman wearing a full-bottomed wig over a mob cap, her cheeks and nose livid with bright red make-up: Judge Judy. A meek-looking man in similar make-up trailed after her wearing a red velvet tunic and a hat that came to a point over his forehead. He held some sort of baton: Mr. Punch. I waved at Droosie and wondered who her brave partner was.

Two gins is about my limit before I start getting maudlin. I was on my third at this stage, and already I wasn't certain if I wanted to laugh or cry. I pulled my cardboard head towards me in a protective way, the better to ensure that it wouldn't get left behind anywhere.

'Did you see Droosie?' I asked Hilary. But she had already left the table and had gone over to talk to the bouncers about something.

I didn't know where Francine had gone – she had probably abandoned me. I wondered where Tom was on his path to irresistibility. And my mood took a massive dive, loosened by the third gin, the lemon of which had by now gone aground.

How, I wondered, could I be sitting here drinking at a party to celebrate my own betrayal? Did Jesus feel like this after a few wines at the Last Supper? All the stresses and pressures of the past weeks began to crowd in on me like a howling mob. A surge of self-pity took hold of me, bringing with it big, salty tears of misery. I saw Hilary glancing back at me and saying something to the bouncers. I wiped away the tears and went in search of Guinness – always a good steadying influence in times of stress, as Tom would say.

By the bar I found Geoff Quayley dressed as the Phantom of the Opera, complete with half-mask and silver cloak. He looked very sinister. In fact, I didn't recognise him, it was he who hailed me.

''Bout ye, Arthur!' He was standing with his back against the wall. I wondered if he would be able to stand without its support.

'How are you, Geoff?'

'I'm rightly steamed, so I am. I can't hold my drink the way I used. Shouldn't really be here. Only came to support Karen. And to tell the absolute, I'm a bit scundered as well, so I am. The polis have me charged with murder, and it looks like I'm going down. Serve me right.'

'What do you mean, Geoff? You told me you didn't do it.'

'Do you know Oscar Wilde's "The Ballad of Reading Jail"? Poor wee Oscar. He wrote:

Yet each man kills the thing he loves
By each let this be heard.
Some do it with a bitter look,
Some with a flattering word.
The coward does it with a kiss,
The brave man with a sword!

The man I loved is dead, Arthur. I killed him.' His lip puckered and he drew in a ragged breath.

'I don't know why you think that, Geoff. By the way, did I see you chatting to the bouncers just now? Are they friends of yours?'

'*Ach*, they're part of the gay scene here in Bray. If you fancy a bit of rough.' He swayed. 'I think I'm goin' to boke. 'Scuse me.' And he staggered off to the toilets.

It was a jigsaw puzzle assembled on time-lapse footage. Bits of information fell into place. I remembered the two huge pall-bearers at William O'Grady's funeral. He had been part of the Bray gay scene too. They had been there to mourn the death of a friend. Nothing more.

I heard the third announcement about the car. The word '*bronze*' struck a chord. Jesus! My dung beetle? I gathered my pint and made for the reception desk. The receptionist confirmed the make, model and colour, preferring the sanitised '*bronze*' over the more pejorative 'shit-brown'. I swallowed what remained of the pint, turned and launched myself into the outdoors to check on the wellbeing of my new wheels.

The air was formidably bracing, but the hail showers were taking a break as I made my way along the glittering nightscape of the esplanade. I began to feel the effects of the fresh air on my equilibrium. In my experience, a cold blast after the fug of a snug pub will either clear your head or make things a lot worse. And I was feeling very strange.

I heard footsteps coming up behind me. I'm very fond of Bray, but rapid footsteps approaching from behind is not usually a good sign in that urban district. My instinct was to turn to face the owners of the footsteps, and as I did so I felt my knees give way as my peripherals became cloudy and dark, leaving only a vague tunnel of visibility, as if I was looking at the world from within a deep anorak hood. Strong hands grasped me by my arms as I sank towards the pavement.

'There you go, pal!' said a voice. '*Oops-a-daisy!*'

And now my feet were dragging along behind me as I was propelled along by my assistants. Whether they were good guys or not was beyond my powers of discernment. I turned my tunnelled focus to the hands that held me upright and saw a familiar tattoo – was it a fly?

36

We were suddenly indoors, somewhere very dark and cold with an over-arching reek of decay and freshly turned rubble. An unloved, neglected place of draughts and drips. There was a huge staircase. A sole work-lamp threw a frigid glare over whatever was within range and exaggerated all the shadows. I had been carried up two flights and now I was seated on a chair, one that had been left out in the rain, judging by the wetness of the seat. I was on a landing, facing the banisters. In front of me was a jagged, broken hole in the rail. Far below me on the floor of the hallway lay the shattered remains of the piano that had met its vandal-propelled fate there, its keys grinning like a skull from a tomb. *Yes, it's never the fall that kills, it's the landing.*

I tried to speak, but my mouth wouldn't co-operate with my brain. Oh Jesus, I thought, I shouldn't have had that last pint. I retched and instinctively leaned forward to save my clothes. I found myself balanced on the edge of a void with my head between my knees. I vomited all that I had over the edge and down into the black hole of the hallway below. As the echo of the awful sounds of my retching and the splash and splatter of my spew died away, I heard a voice that at first gave me the feeling of rescue.

'Thanks, lads. You can get back to the Martello now. OK?'

Two bulky shadows lumbered away, leaving me alone with the voice.

'Are you feeling better now, Arthur?'

I was shivering and I had no co-ordination or control. I was only barely aware of what was happening, but all of it was beyond any influence from me. Something had been put around my neck. I sat slumped in the chair with my feet almost dangling in the void of the stairwell which yawned below me.

The voice, so reassuring for its familiarity but for contradictory reasons so very frightening, continued, 'Sorry about all this, dear Arthur, but you were getting too close. I popped a little roofie in your gin, I hope you don't mind. You seem so sad, dear Arthur. Sad and mixed up. Over-extended. I suppose me and Tom getting engaged was just too much for you. Too much to bear. Enough to push you over?'

Hilary walked around me to a spot where she was more clearly in my line of vision. She contrived, somehow, to look prim, in her shepherdess outfit, prim and impossibly proper. This nursery-rhyme look heightened the grimness of her calm.

I wondered if I was hallucinating. I was having difficulty concentrating, but for some reason I wasn't feeling nervous. Everything about my surroundings should have sounded alarm bells. But even if all the very bells of hell were ringing, there was nothing I could do about it. My arms and legs felt as if they belonged to a stranger, and an uncooperative one at that.

'What the fuck, Hilary?' was what I meant to say, but it seems that I had also borrowed the tongue that now flapped senselessly in my mouth and reduced my intended speech to a jibber.

'Oh, Arthur! Always interfering, always in the way. Too clever for your own stupidity. And now, so sad. They say that drink is a depressant, and you've been on the Valium too. Nobody will be surprised when you're found swinging here. Dangling in the stairwell of the old Bray Head Hotel. Maybe you'll meet that ghost. Have a little party?'

I summoned up my rubberised features. 'Hilary, what are you doing?' But the sounds that came out didn't sound remotely like the words I had intended. I felt like a badly manipulated ventriloquist's dummy with Hilary as my operator supplying both lines of dialogue.

'What was that? Did I kill Willie O'Grady? Of course I did. Me and my fuck-brained brother. O'Grady was going to blow the whistle on the investment business. He had been blackmailing Alan, sending him threatening messages, signing as Theseus, the Greek hero who killed the Minotaur.'

Oh Christ, I thought, *I was right!*

Hilary went on, 'I couldn't let O'Grady bring down Minotaur. If he did that, my involvement in the firm would have been exposed and I would go down with it. I couldn't let that happen – not when I was about to break through the glass ceiling like a dancing girl from a birthday cake. My useless fool of a brother was supposed to deliver the blow but, entirely predictably, he funked it at the last minute. Didn't want to get his hands dirty. So, I had to take charge of everything, as usual, while Alan kept nix. That was just about all he was capable of.' She swung her crinoline a little and waved her crook. 'Poor Willie, I was waiting for him as he came trotting round the corner of the church and caught him smack between the eyes with the candlestick. Never knew what hit him. I regret that, in a way. I would have preferred if he knew, like you will, Arthur. It's much more satisfactory, if you're going to go to the trouble of killing someone, that they know that it's you. My idea was to leave the body as a warning to anyone else who might feel inclined to blow a whistle. The corpse was also to serve as a stopper for our wedding – but then you had to interfere, didn't you, Arthur? I had got home in time for the hairdresser when I saw what was happening on the CCTV. I'd tuned my phone in to watch online. I saw you dragging Willie's body out of the church. What were you thinking, you idiot? That's why I had to send my cretin brother to tell you that the wedding was off.'

I tried to say, 'And Alan?' It came out something like 'Ananan?', but she got my drift.

'Alan? I shot the stupid bastard. He had it coming. I knew that if the Gardaí got him, he'd tell them everything. He let me into your flat that night. He even put the shotgun down to open the door. You should've seen the look on his face when he saw it pointed at him. Nothing quite like looking down the barrel of a loaded shotgun for concentrating the mind. It was meant to look like suicide. But you had to interfere again, didn't you, Arthur? Telling the Guards that he couldn't have pulled the trigger with his shoes on! But you, Arthur, you are going to hang for that, and the verdict on your death *will* be suicide.' She shook her head at me so that her ringlets bobbed and bounced.

I tried to tell her that it was Francine, not me, who had come up with the shoes thing, but she ignored my mumblings.

I saw that the thing around my neck was a blue plastic rope. It was chafing and prickling. It was annoying me, but I couldn't be bothered to move it and my hands wouldn't do as I told them. Hilary had said that I was going to hang. 'Fuck,' was all I could say.

'Oh, and I meant to tell you that it was me who planted Willie O'Grady's phone in your car. It was the night you drove me home and the bag burst. That was a nice bit of accidental diversion, wasn't it? I pretended to hurt my hand and kicked your door. I was quite proud of that little performance. I slipped the phone into the door pocket. I assumed that the police would track it to you straight away, but I didn't bank on them taking quite so long.'

She continued her solo duologue, turning again to my supposed state of mind. 'It's sad enough, when you think about it, Arthur, my dear. Jilted at the altar, witnessing the blood and guts of two murders then betrayed by your best man and your bride. Enough to destabilise the best of us, wouldn't you think? And let's face it, Arthur, you're not really up there with the best, are you? And why am I telling you all this? Because, like

I say, it's not as much fun if the person you are about to kill doesn't know what's happening, why it's happening or who's doing it. I'm going to tilt your chair forward until I tip you into eternity with your suicide noose around your neck. I've tied the other end of the rope to some good banisters, and I've left enough slack for a nice drop. I'll be there to watch you twitch and kick. They say you get a hard-on – I don't know about a happy ending. Still, it's something for you to look forward to, isn't it?'

I felt hypnotised. I was weirdly anxiety-free, although what Hilary was saying was very clearly deranged. She intended to kill me. I knew I had to move, but my body wouldn't respond. Hilary had her dainty foot poised on my soggy chair, tilting it forwards as I sat slumped, my neck in a noose and awaiting that final push. I was starting to slip on the seat as the angle increased and neared the point of tipping me out into the empty hallway to my end. But I couldn't get myself to do anything about it.

I'm uncertain as to exactly what happened next. My vision was peculiarly fragmented and I was struggling to stay awake.

I heard a voice. Tom's voice. Saying something like, 'What are you at, Hilary? For fuck's sake, you'll kill him!'

In my peripheral vision I saw Tom putting his arms around Hilary from behind her, or I think I did. I certainly remember feeling annoyed and jealous that he saw fit to embrace her in my presence. Some sort of tussle ensued. Maybe she wasn't in the mood? She said something like, '*Fuck off, Tom! Get off me, you idiot!*' except that it was delivered in an angry scream as he pulled her away from me.

Then something like a Marvel Comic character arrived into the middle of my confusion, '*Stop! Gardaí!*'

I had one last strobe of unbelievable erotic intensity as Francine in her wonderful outfit stepped out from the shadows of the doomed hotel. Surely, I thought, I must be dreaming.

Tom and Hilary looked like they were doing a clumsy sort of dance. He was still holding her from behind, but he let go when she stamped, hard, on his foot. She whirled around and he tried to grab her again, this time face to face, but she broke free. Her own momentum made her stagger. She took a step backwards. Her arms flew up and her hooped skirts ballooned like an ineffective parachute as she fell backwards through the broken banister into the dark.

37

My legal representative told me that the DPP had entered a *nolle prosequi* against me for the murder of Alan Fenton. I think that meant that I hadn't done it.

The murder charge had also been dropped against Geoff Quayley for the killing of William O'Grady and there seemed no appetite to prosecute Geoff for the theft of the parish funds. Bowring was lazy. It was easier to lay the blame on the murdered parish treasurer. After all, most of the stolen money had ended up in an account in his name, swallowed up in the black hole that was Minotaur.

I was glad. Geoff and Karen Quayley had already suffered a lot, and they didn't deserve to lose everything, which was what would have happened if the theft had been laid at his doorstep. Instead, Geoff had another skeleton to squeeze into his closet. I hoped it wouldn't undo him.

A quick visit to the District Court disposed of the charge against me for moving the body. The judge kept referring to my offence as 'tampering with evidence', which I found ghoulish and vaguely indecent. However, I was given the Probation Act and left the courtroom with an unsullied record and a warning not to indulge in any more body-snatching.

Droosie eventually disclosed that Tom had agreed to pay her fees. That explained why Judge Judy and Mr. Punch had been at the party. It seemed that Tom had been a good friend as well as a disloyal bastard behind my back. To say nothing of saving my life.

Tom had seen Hilary leaving the party and had gone after her, wondering where she was off to. He followed her into the derelict hotel but quickly got lost in the dark. It was the sound of her voice that brought him to us in the end. Meanwhile, Francine had called for back-up when she saw the bouncers follow me out of the Martello. She had tailed them, slipping unnoticed, a black cat in a dark place, up the staircase, and had paused on the turn of the stairs to witness the whole of Hilary's taunting confession. She had recorded it on her phone to make sure of the job.

I summoned up all my forgiveness and phoned Tom. We needed to talk. Anyway, he had said that he'd found something, and I wanted to know what it was. He agreed to come round to mine, which was brave enough, considering everything. He arrived half an hour late with an apology and a six-pack. We circled each other like boxers in a ring, each one waiting for the other to commit the first blow.

'That was some do,' was Tom's opener.

'I don't want to know what you were up to with Hilary, OK? I'm not interested.'

'I told you I'd always fancied her.'

'There's 'fancied' and 'fiancée' – they're not the same. Anyway. I told you I don't want to know.'

'I've been to the hospital. She's under police guard. She refused to talk to me, except to say it's off. I don't know what I'm supposed to have done. She's all wrapped up in bandages.'

'Good, I hope it hurts like hell. Anyway, you told me you'd found something?'

Tom sighed. He went rooting in my kitchen drawer for a bottle opener. I don't think he had registered the depth of my hurt at his treason – if I was entitled to call it that. But I couldn't see the point in trying to convince him that he had wronged me if he couldn't see it himself. He flicked off the caps of two bottles and put one on the counter in front of me, his eyebrows poised in question, as if my acceptance of the bottle might signal a truce.

'Look, man,' he said, 'it was all a big mistake. Hilary came at me like a bull at a gate – or should that be "like a cow"? – but that sounds like baby food.' He scratched the back of his neck in thought. 'Anyway, there was no refusing her. She said that you and she were all done, "a thing of the past," – she said – "history". What was I supposed to do? Refuse her offer? Tell her thanks, but a ride was out of the question? Refusal was never going to happen, I'm afraid. So, there you are. Never underestimate the power of the mickey.'

I knew very well what Hilary was like when she had set her sights on something. But that still didn't excuse my best pal for his betrayal, even if he didn't see it like that.

Tom went on, in a lower voice, 'I think she only picked up with me to get at you, Arthur, old pal. She used me as a tool.'

'A tool. That's you all right, Tom. A tool. Anyway, let's change the subject, what's this thing you've found?'

'Ah. Yes. Well, I copied the memory stick onto my computer before I gave it to you. I assumed that you'd assume that I'd do that. Then one quiet evening I had a shufti at it, and I found a list of numbers. Long numbers. I thought it might be a code, so I put it through some filters and things, but I couldn't get anything. But I know a lad who's part of a team that specialises in unlocking lost cryptocurrency wallets. If you've lost your private key, he can help you get your money back. There's billions locked away in cyberspace because people have lost their computers or have written down their private key codes and have lost the piece of paper.'

'Hang on a minute, Tom.'

The eyebrows looked worried. 'What?'

'You lost me at 'shufti'. And how is it that you know 'lads' like your friend? Is what he does even legal?'

'Oh, perfectly legal and legit. Honest to God. The money may be hot as hell, but my lad works on a retainer and a percentage finder's fee for anyone who comes to him. Makes a good living out of it, too.'

'I thought it was impossible.'

'Ah, yes, but that's why it costs what it does.'

I tried to figure that out and gave up. It felt good to hear Tom's nonsense again. 'Was your lad able to help with the numbers?'

'He said they sounded like they might be private keys for bitcoins.'

I pretended that I understood what a private key was. There's a certain art to remaining perfectly still when surrounded by stuff you don't understand. If you can remain motionless for long enough, it either goes away or someone with patience and lots of time might explain it. It's like when you're surrounded by velociraptors, or is that just in the movies? Being with Tom can be confusing. I didn't blink. I offered him a frown of concentration to encourage him to go on.

'There are a lot of these numbers. I think Willie O'Grady liked to stash the proceeds of his blackmailing hobby in cryptocurrency. It's a wonderfully anonymous way of hiding money. The real owner is whoever has the private key. There's no other identification needed. If you have the key, the currency is yours. The other thing is that there's no record of who paid what into Willie O'Grady's hush fund. The sources are as anonymous as the cryptocurrency itself.'

'But –'

'No, hang on,' he said, quieting me, 'Willie O'Grady's estate has no legitimate claim on the money. It's what-do-you-call-it?' His hand described spirals in the air as he searched for the words. 'Wronga Wonga, immoral earnings. But nobody knows it's there. And there it is, shouting "finders-keepers"!'

This was one of the longest speeches I had ever heard Tom make. Maybe he was feeling guilty about Hilary and was inclined to babble. Hilary may have guessed too late that these magic numbers were on Willie's phone after she had planted it in my car. That would explain her urgency to recover the phone. But I had underestimated her in so many other respects, I decided not to be surprised. It was no surprise that the significance of the numbers had been overlooked by Bowring.

'But, Tom, if you're right, that money was gouged from people through blackmail. It's dirty. If you're suggesting what I think you're suggesting, I don't want to play. It should go to a charity, into the poor box.'

And that's where it went, all five million euro of it, less the five percent finder's fee that found its way into Tom's bank account.

I'm a lightweight, I like to live life on the surface, like one of those little bugs that rely on the surface tension of water to scoot over ponds on their tiny hairy feet. Not that my feet are particularly hairy. I wonder if there's any real depth to me at all. If I turned sideways, would anyone see me? I like to think that they would. I like to think that people like me. The choices I have made have tended to be driven by lunatic optimism and my desire to be liked, my desire to please.

Sergeant Bowring wasn't pleased at all. He was displeased that Francine had gone to the party in the Martello, displeased that she had dressed as Catwoman, displeased that she had gone with me, and extremely unhappy that she had followed me from the Martello to the Bray Head Hotel and, standing in the shadows, had witnessed Hilary's explanation of events and her attempt to murder me.

Bowring was angry that Francine had made the bust that solved the double-murder case that he had driven into a dead-end doldrum – he may indeed have been disappointed that my life had been saved – but he was most deeply upset when Francine's complaint against him for bullying and harassment was upheld and he was transferred to the Fixed Charge Processing Office in Thurles, to fill out the days until his retirement checking paperwork for road-traffic offences.

Francine told me all this over a drink in the Harbour Bar. She had asked me to join her for a quiet celebration. 'Don't be getting any ideas, now, Arthur,' she said, 'This isn't a date. Do you hear me? It's to say goodbye.'

And there I was thinking that the night at the Martello was the start of something beautiful.

'We're all done, Arthur, you and me. I'm going on a training course in Templemore. You're no longer wanted by the police (and that includes me). Your days as an outlaw are over. My career in the force is on the up. I tell you, I'll be Garda Commissioner one day. Watch this space, boy.'

———

I've quit counting aircraft for a living. I've installed a glass screen in the middle of a rented room above the tattoo parlour just off Bray Main Street, and fixed a sign by the front door, '*Cummins and Farrington, Inquiry Agents.*'

THE END